BLUE
DOORS

JOHN A. ROGERS

Note for Librarians: A cataloguing record for this book is available from Library and Archives Canada at www.collectionscanada.ca/amicus/index-e.html
ISBN 1-4120-9337-6

Printed in Victoria, BC, Canada. Printed on paper with minimum 30% recycled fibre. Trafford's print shop runs on "green energy" from solar, wind and other environmentally-friendly power sources.

Offices in Canada, USA, Ireland and UK

Book sales for North America and international:
Trafford Publishing, 6E–2333 Government St.,
Victoria, BC V8T 4P4 CANADA
phone 250 383 6864 (toll-free 1 888 232 4444)
fax 250 383 6804; email to orders@trafford.com
Book sales in Europe:
Trafford Publishing (UK) Limited, 9 Park End Street, 2nd Floor
Oxford, UK OX1 1HH UNITED KINGDOM
phone +44 (0)1865 722 113 (local rate 0845 230 9601)
facsimile +44 (0)1865 722 868; info.uk@trafford.com
Order online at:
trafford.com/06-1091

10 9 8 7 6 5 4 3

Dedication

DEDICATED TO THOSE EXECUTIVES in Commerce and Industry who have lost their jobs and livelihoods, not through any lack of skill or devotion to duty, but purely through the greed of high finance, mergers and acquisitions.

About the author

John Rogers was born in 1929 in County Down. He went to Rockport prepschool, then to Charterhouse in England. At eighteen he started work with a National Billboard Company, and worked in Belfast, Liverpool and Glasgow. In the late fifties he returned to Ireland to take charge of the company's affairs there. Ten years later he became the loser in a fierce take over battle with a conglomerate company and lost his job. For a time he worked for the Canadian Poster Industry, then returned to the UK to work once again in the Poster Industry. In the mid seventies he returned home to Ireland and set up his own Financial Services Company in which he still works.

Blue Doors is John's second novel and is based on his many business experiences. He is happily married with four children and eight grandchildren, Marcus, Thomas, Geoffrey, Amy, Molly, Michael, Oliver and Jack. He is lucky enough for the extended family to live all within a ten mile radius.

BOOK ONE – 1950

"So, you want to be Office Boy, is that it?" Mr Meadows asked.

CHAPTER ONE

IT WAS FIVE TO nine by the clock above 'The George' public house at the corner of the street, when Everton turned off Hope Street to enter his employer's office. The Head Office of 'Meadows & Son' was as much of a mess as the whole of the City of Liverpool in 1955. Un-spared by the Nazis' raids in the early forties, most rebuilding had been postponed; all that had been done was to clear the derelict sites and tart them up a bit, a garden here and there and masses of car parks. The Corporation had put many plots out to tender for advertisement hoardings on short let and many of these hoardings proudly displayed 'Meadows' nameplates.

Meadows' premises were like Liverpool on a small scale. The centre of the building had been burnt in the blitz and had been cleared. It had been turned into a car park for employees lucky enough to have company cars. The two halves of the building had been repaired and the long suffering staff had doubled up and had put up with great discomfort; but they didn't complain. Why should they? They knew that they had come through a war and survived. They had employment and now, at long last, business was beginning to pick up.

Twenty-two year old Everton, baby faced and with a mop-like head of hair, came through the main door into the reception area. Meadows' had done their best with the ramshackle building with its narrow corridors and pokey windows. The reception desk had been gently curved and built into a corner of the room to make it resemble a plush city office. The walls were brightly painted and tired looking pots of ever-green plants sat in the other corners doing their best to grow; if anyone remembered to water them. Meadows' policy was that first impressions must be excellent, so behind the reception desk they placed glamorous receptionists. They lasted just as long as young Mr Colin Meadows had succeeded in bedding them, before they fell out and a new receptionist would be installed. Gillian had been there for some time, probably because she was less glamorous than the others and had kept her virginity. What she lacked in looks, she made up for by a broad grin and a non-Liverpudlian telephone voice; Colin Meadows' wife had chosen her.

"Good morning, Everton," Gillian greeted him.

"Morning, Gillian. Mr Smiley in yet?"

"Beaten you to it again, Everton."

The nickname, 'Everton', irritated John Smyth, though it did perhaps hide his very common name. He mused about how he had got it. Five years earlier he had gone for an interview as an 'Office Boy', attracted by Meadows' extravagant advertisement which claimed bright prospects for a smart boy. John had not cared much whether he got the job or not; in a matter of months he would be joining the Army for his National Service. However, Meadows had given him a promise that they would find a place for him when he re-joined civilian life again. John was a meticulous boy who did everything in logical order; to safeguard his employment for so long in advance was a plus point, and, who knows, he might end up by running the company one day? One thing he did know was that he would advance one step at a time.

When John had gone for his interview he'd had to wait for a long time. The Receptionist had reported his arrival several times to a number of people. Nobody had seemed interested in him. He'd sat in his short trousers, embarrassed by his dress, but his Mum had not been able to afford long trousers.

Eventually the Receptionist spoke to him, "Mr Smiley was to have interviewed you," she said, "but he's off sick today. Mr Davidson, the Chief Clerk, is on an extended lunch break but young Mr Colin Meadows will see you. It's for the Office Boy situation, isn't it?" and she stared at his short trousers.

"Yes."

"Ok, follow me."

They'd gone out into the street to enter the other part of the building, on the other side of the car park, and together they climbed the narrow and steep steps to the top office where he was handed over to Mr Meadows' Secretary; in turn, she took him in to see the great man. He was huge, lying back in his swivel chair and his feet were on the desk.

"So, you want to be Office Boy, is that it?" Mr Meadows asked.

"Yes Sir."

There then followed a deathly silence, the longest John had ever experienced; it wasn't his turn to speak, so he waited. Clearly Mr Meadows was at a loss to know what to ask him, never having interviewed an Office Boy before. Suddenly he stirred and asked, "What football team do you support?"

"Everton, Sir," John had quickly replied.

"Right then, you're in; start on Monday, and, ah, get yourself a pair of long trousers."

The story of his interview had been folk lore, and after he'd started on the Monday, with long trousers, he was nicknamed 'Everton'. Mr Colin Meadows supported Liverpool, but the boy had given a positive reply and that was good enough.

"Where's Mr Smiley?" Everton asked the female Clerk in the Planning Department, "Gillian said he'd come in."

"Mr Colin Meadows wanted to see him," the girl replied.

"This early?"

"Mr Colin came in real early. He had a man with him."

"A man?"

"Tall bloke, smart suit, 'Purvis' I think Gillian said his name was."

"Purvis?"

"Yes, I think so."

"Who is Mr Purvis?"

"Honestly, I don't know, I only work here."

Everton realised that he'd been too demanding. It was just that he didn't like his routine broken. Mr Smiley should be at his desk at this time of morning. He was his immediate boss and they should be discussing the work for the day and who would do what, over a nice cup of tea. Mr Smiley's cup was still sitting there, untouched and going cold.

Sighing, Everton took a sip from his cup and skimmed through the papers on his desk. There was that big order from 'Army Recruitment' to be posted by the end of the month and it was nearly that now. He'd get on with booking it in and giving instructions to the billposters.

Everton struggled on and time flew. When he looked at his watch it was past ten o'clock. Twenty minutes later Mr Smiley returned, his characteristic broad grin had gone. His face was drained of blood and he looked ill. "Are you all right, Mr Smiley?" Everton asked anxiously.

"No," Mr Smiley replied. Everton had always called him by his surname; he didn't even know his Christian name.

"Why don't you go home; we can manage here."

"I'm not ill, I'm furious. I may have to resign," Mr Smiley shouted.

Everton had never heard him raise his voice before. There must have been some crisis next door, in that upstairs office, and now the days work would be disrupted and he'd feel obliged to work late, but his immediate concern was for Mr Smiley.

"Whatever is it?" he asked.

"I half expected to get the Sales Manager job when Mr Stokes retires at the end of the year, but now...It's outrageous."

1

Everton had fully expected that Mr Smiley would be promoted and in turn he would take over from him and he only had five years to retirement; then he would have been Sales Manager. It was all that you slaved away for, uncomplaining. It was how companies progressed, it was what made the world tick, it was justice. "Are you not getting it?" Everton asked. "Is it something to do with that Mr Purvis who came from nowhere this morning?"

"Dead right you are; typical. I've given forty years of loyal service. But Mr Purvis is a Meadows crony; they went to school together, they're chums. He's been something or other in the City; now Mr Stokes has been retired early and Mr flipping Jack Purvis gets the job, becomes Sales Director and a seat on the board to boot. What does he know about poster advertising, I'd like to know; we shall have to teach him everything?"

"That's terrible, Mr Smiley. Is there anything we can do about it?"

"Absolutely nothing. I just have to see out my time and preserve my pension – and you needn't think you'll automatically get my job. The Meadows' will produce another crony from somewhere. Take my advice, Everton, stop being so bloody good at your job, it'll finish you. When I remonstrated, Mr Colin had the nerve to say that I couldn't be spared from the job I was doing because I did it so well and nobody else could do it. Well, at least he admits that."

Suddenly Everton's world seemed to fall apart – the world of honest work, capability and loyalty, resulting in a steady progress up the ladder until in turn, he would be running the company and retire on a fat pension. But he wasn't a Meadows' crony from the City and he didn't go to the right school. Should he move out now before it was too late? He noticed that Mr Smiley had fallen silent and sat still at his desk, looking blankly at the wall in front of him, his cuppa untouched. "Your tea's gone cold, Mr Smiley, shall I get a fresh cup?"

"No thanks, Everton; I'm going home now, take the day off."

"You never take a day off. What shall I tell Mr Meadows if he asks?"

A smile at long last lit up Mr Smiley's round face. "Tell him I've gone to the City," he said.

CHAPTER TWO

GILLIAN BEGAN TO RING round the department heads, repeating, "Mr Meadows is here." New members of staff couldn't understand this routine and so it was explained that the call was required in the main office block; the building creaked as Mr Meadows manoeuvred his big frame up the narrow stairway and round the bends, grasping the handrail which somehow remained intact. His office was on the first floor. If you were immediately above or below him you could hear him walk across the room. While junior clerks crammed into small offices, Mr Meadows Senior had a whole floor to himself, and then only occupied it for a few hours each day. The injustice of it all never entered his head. Why should it? He had created the company out of nothing, and had learnt early on to spot a bright young lad and got them to do the work. If they did well, they got paid well. If not, they were fired. It was a policy which had worked and the company had grown as a result.

In a slightly less plush office in the other block, Colin Meadows pondered his future, the company, and more importantly his father; all of them connected. The call that Mr Meadows was in had been relayed to his Secretary and in less harsh tones, she had come into Mr Colin's office and said, "Your father is in now, Mr Colin." Sighing, he picked up his papers from the desk, ready to do battle once again.

Colin fully appreciated his father's past skills. He'd had the courage to found the company, single handed and with little capital, and then to have grown it so successfully and so rapidly. In Victorian style he had ensured that Colin had got suitable training in every department, and then at his natural retirement age, had partly handed over the reins to his son. But 'Father' couldn't keep away. He interfered in every big decision and schemes which Colin had tried to drive through were frequently blocked. With a great deal of patience he hung on, feeling like an overpaid Office Boy. His father was eighty. He couldn't last forever, and then everything would be his. "What have you got for me today?" Father asked.

"We'll have to decide what to do about Mr Stokes and find a replacement."

"I like Mr Stokes. Could he not work on for a few years yet?"

"I don't know that he'd want to, but in any case we badly need new blood; someone who would introduce new techniques. Mr Stokes is a Salesman, not a Marketing Director."

"What's marketing?"

"Well, it's…, it's selling in a more…"

"Why not call it selling then?"

"I was going to say…"

"Have you asked him?"

"Asked him what?"

"If he would like to stay on?"

"It doesn't arise, and in any case I've found a fantastic replacement; if we delay we'll miss out."

"What's wrong with Mr Smiley?"

"Father, have sense. Mr Smiley is not long from retirement, and in any case he can't be spared from what he's doing."

"Mr Smiley has given loyal service for forty years."

"Old Joe in the yard has been with us for fifty years but you're not suggesting him."

"That reminds me, last time he cleaned the Rolls he left…"

"Father, can we talk about Mr Stokes' replacement?"

"He's not going, is he?"

"Yes, he is," Colin lied, "and we have an opportunity of hiring Jack Purvis. I've known him for many years, we were in the Guards together and went to the same school. I've talked to him and he really understands marketing, and that's what we need."

"Purvis?"

"Yes."

"Jack Purvis?"

"The very same."

"Went to Radley?"

"Yes."

"The boy who spent two weeks with us in our cottage in North Wales?"

"That's right."

"Such a nice boy, polite and could charm the back end off a donkey. Your Mum took a great fancy to him. Is he going to join the company?"

"Yes, that's just it. He's agreed to fill the role of Sales Director."

"Where does that leave Everton?"

"Everton?"

"Yes. Mr Smiley was expected to take over from Mr Stokes, and

Everton from Mr Smiley. I don't suppose Everton will like these moves above him, blocking his path. We need to hang on to these bright young lads; I was one once and so were you. Let's give Everton a rise."

"It wouldn't be appropriate to consider that now; we'll mark his card for the salary review at the end of the year."

"We need to deal with Everton now."

Colin relented and went along with it. He had got what he wanted and Everton's rise was cheap at the price. Father would think that he had won, and forget that he'd agreed to hire Jack Purvis who would have to start tomorrow, before Father changed his mind.

Colin Meadows met 'that nice Jack Purvis' in the Adelphi Hotel cocktail bar at eight that same evening, as previously arranged. Both men were punctual and Colin found Jack sitting in an easy chair with a pink gin and puffing at a large cigar.

"Well?" Jack asked.

"All agreed," Colin replied.

"And the salary?"

"A matter of detail; you can't rush Father too much, just leave it to me. You must have made a good impression on him all those years ago in North Wales."

"I can't believe that your Dad is still sticking in there. Why doesn't he retire and enjoy life?"

"His idea of enjoying life is to come in most afternoons and have the staff jumping through windows. He can't see the overall global picture; he'll spend about an hour on some small detail, like why aren't we getting more for a poster site which he'd noticed coming in to the office."

"I plan a marketing shake up, Colin. I hope that your dad doesn't obstruct that."

"You leave that to me, too. Presentation is the key. If he doesn't understand something he'll think that someone is taking him for a ride. Any plan you might have must be in plain language. And there's another thing, we have a bright young lad in there called 'Everton'. Father says that Everton could be upset by appointments above him, so we're going to give him a rise. Try not to upset him because that would upset Father."

"What does Everton do?"

"He assists Mr Smiley in the planning department. He's good promotional material for the future. I suggest that at the first opportunity you push him out of that crowded office and try him on selling – cold calls, that sort of thing."

"Would he be any good?"

"Try him. If he's not Father will be disappointed, then it'll be easier for you to control him and keep him in his place – he's very good at the job he's doing, but then any monkey can do that."

"Colin, I don't like the sound of all this political stuff. I want to do a great job for Meadows. Do I have to be considering other people's feelings all the time? Do I have your full backing on all occasions?"

"Of course."

Later in the morning Mr Stokes crept into Mr Smiley's office, red in the face and appearing very excited. "Heard the news?" he gasped.

Mr Stokes was a rumour spreader and did it very well. Every now and again he would make the most outrageous statement and wait for it to be denied, which it usually was. Just now and again he'd strike lucky and his statement would not be denied; then he knew that it was true. "Well, have you?" Mr Stokes repeated.

"You're resigning?" Everton suggested.

There was a long pause and Mr Stokes looked taken aback. "How did you know?" he asked.

"And Jack Purvis is taking over."

"How do you know? Why do I always hear everything last?"

Everton laughed at such a naïve remark. Ignoring the question he asked, "Do you want to retire?"

"Can't wait."

"But what will you do all day?"

"Pursue my hobby."

"Which is?"

"Visiting graves."

Everton laughed. "A bit morbid," he said, "but what about the living? How are you going to manage?"

"Easily now that I've been given a generous golden handshake."

"That was a bit quick," Everton commented. "Is Wonder Boy going to do all our jobs so that we can all get compensation and go and look at graves?"

"Oh, I don't know about you, and frankly, I don't care now that all this worry and strife is out of my hair."

"When exactly are you going?" asked Everton.

"Right now."

"No party tonight? No drinks at The George? No presentation? You don't give us much time."

"I don't want any of that. I just want to go."

Mr Stokes short appearance was followed by Colin Meadows and Jack Purvis. Jack was wearing a smart light grey suit, a blue shirt and what Everton took as either a regimental or old school tie. Come to think of it he was sure that Mr Colin wore the same sometimes. He didn't know much about such things and didn't care. He noticed Jack's tall height and slimness, his dark hair rapidly receding from his forehead; he would soon be bald. He was irritated by the sight of a silly little short beard, as if to compensate for the lack of hair; it was well groomed and he probably took ages each morning grooming it. In fact the aroma of aftershave or scent, the well pressed trousers and freshly polished shoes gave Everton a London toff impression, and someone unused to work in the dirt and grime of Northern industrial England. This man would not fit in here. Everton was unhappy.

Mr Colin said, "I want you to meet Mr Jack Purvis; he's our new Sales Director, with immediate effect. I expect both of you will be working very closely with him. Everton held out his hand and was immediately repelled by Jack's wet, clammy palm.

"What are you doing right now?" Jack asked, in his London accent.

"Writing billposting instructions for The Army Campaign."

"Surely that's a clerk's job?"

Everton felt flustered. What was wrong with this man, throwing his weight around already? "Well…I don't know – its part of my job and it has to be done."

Everton noticed that Colin Meadows made no effort to intervene in the conversation. "What else do you do?" asked Jack.

Everton knew full well what he did. It was a long and complicated routine, demanding strict accuracy and keeping to deadlines, but how was he going to explain that to this man who was determined that he was wasting his time and talents? "I assist Mr Smiley," he said.

"Where IS Mr Smiley?"

"He's not well; he's gone home."

"What sort of 'unwell'?" Jack persisted.

"He's had a shock."

"What sort of a shock?"

Everton was getting angry. Who did this Jack Purvis think he was? He decided to be less defensive and go on the attack. "About your appointment, above us, and yet you know nothing about the work here, and I suppose I shall have to support you on a salary considerably less than yours? Mr Smiley and I need to consider our position."

"Now that's enough, Everton," Colin Meadows cut in for the first time. "We work as a team here and those remarks are unhelpful. I expect you and Mr Smiley to help Mr Purvis to settle in."

"I have nothing more to say at the moment, Mr Colin, and I expect Mr Smiley will speak for himself when he returns to the office."

Colin faced Jack and said, "I'm sorry about that but I can understand the staff's first reaction. When Mr Smiley comes back in again I'll sort it out with him. In the meantime I'm sure Everton will tell you all you want to know about this department."

Ignoring the drama Jack Purvis asked Everton, "Why Everton? Is it your real name?"

"No Sir, my real name is John Smyth, with a 'y'."

"So why do we call you Everton?"

"It's a long story," began Everton.

"Then it'll have to wait."

"What should I call you?" Everton asked bravely.

"You've called me 'Sir', that will do."

"Is it a long story, too, Sir?" Everton boldly asked.

Ignoring the last remark 'Sir' said, "Would you like to do some real selling, Everton?"

"Yes Sir," Everton replied, surprised. There was nothing he would like to do more, and to get out of that cramped over-heated office.

"We'll have to arrange it," 'Sir' continued, "then you'll be more than just a clerk. Mr Meadows has confirmed that you are to receive a rise of two hundred pounds per annum, with immediate effect. See that you earn it."

Everton was puzzled but pleasantly surprised. He had been about to hand in his resignation and if Mr Smiley went too, then 'smarty pants' would have to do all of it himself; then he and Colin Meadows would be begging them to come back. He couldn't stand this prig, but he'd have to give it a go; and another two hundred would help! "Thank you, Sir," Everton gasped.

"Anything else?" 'Sir' asked.

"I don't think so, Sir."

"Good," and 'Sir' and Mr Colin turned to leave.

As they closed the door behind them Everton heard Mr Colin say, "You handled that very well, Jack." Everton did not hear the reply, "That young man is too full of himself. I'll soon knock the stuffing out of him."

CHAPTER THREE

THE NEXT DAY MR Smiley came back to the office in a better frame of mind. "Are you feeling happier?" Everton asked.

"My wife let off at me. She doesn't like it when I'm at home and she's doing the housework. She said that I worry enough doing my job and I'd probably worry even more doing a better job, so I'll just have to stick it and see what happens. I doubt if Purvis will last long anyway."

"You mean, 'Sir'."

"What?"

"We must call him 'Sir' – he said so."

"Bugger that! I'll call him Mr Purvis and if he calls me 'Smiley' I'll drop the 'Mr' in front of his name. I'm rather looking forward to this."

Jack Purvis soon got into the habit of being available at about four o'clock each day, in case Father wanted to see him, or if he wanted to see Father. Jack's first task which he set himself was to appraise the poster sites which had been unsold for more than three months. He was aghast. Some of the sites were so bad he wanted to give them up immediately. He reckoned that they might have sold 'in the old days' when advertisers and their agents bought blind, but things had changed and quite rightly. Poster agents inspected poster stocks on a regular basis and knew what they were buying. Jack raised the matter with Colin. "There are at least a hundred sites in Liverpool alone which should be given up - save the company on rent and rates."

"I know."

"What's stopping us?"

"Have patience, Jack, its Father you see. He once had a cow called Daisy. Daisy was old and was no longer capable of yielding milk. His farm manager said that Daisy should be slaughtered. 'Oh no,' Father said, 'you never know, Daisy might well yield milk again.' Father doesn't like giving anything up; he considers it a defeatist ploy."

Not to be diverted, Jack continued, "Well I can't sell these sites, and won't. It would be dishonest of me to try and it would deceive customers."

"I said, have patience. Father goes on holiday to Spain for three weeks at the end of the month. When he's gone we'll have a cull."

Jack looked amazed. "But what happens when he comes back? Won't there be a row?"

"Not a just a row; a bloody big row - but it'll all blow over, eventually."

Jack was unable to take all this in. He was sure that it was not the way to run a business, but he had another problem. "This new Bus Station concession at Horley Cross - I've seen the panels and they're ok, but Horley Cross! Clients won't even buy road sites there, so what hope is there for the Bus Station?"

"Why don't you go out and sell locally? It's not something we do enough of and that's why we hired you."

"Me?"

"You could get help, take Everton with you."

Everton, thought Jack. The very one. Pass this to him and if he fails he's doomed. If he succeeds we'll all be pleased, and just in case that happens, I'd better have an input myself so that I can take credit, if there's any of that being handed out.

"Perhaps we can discuss all this with Father this afternoon, if he's coming in?" Jack said.

"He is, but don't mention the question of poor sites, only the Bus Station."

Colin and Jack found Father in a good mood. At first he talked about his horse which had been entered for the Grand National, and then he fiddled about in the drinks cupboard to make sure everyone had their tipple; he helped himself to a weak gin and tonic, mostly drowned in tonic.

"Can we discuss Horley Cross Bus Station?" Colin asked.

"What about it?"

"Sales are non-existent. National advertisers won't take it."

"I warned you, didn't I?" Father said, his voice reaching a high pitched note.

"You did," Colin replied, "but you also said that you didn't want anyone else to get the concession."

For a moment Father appeared speechless, and then he took a small sip of his drink. "Have you a proposal?" he asked.

"I think we should try to sell it locally," Jack continued.

"Of course we should, and now that we've got you, you can get on with it".

"I thought we should put Everton onto it – I'll give him all the support and guidance he'll need."

"Fine fellow, Everton. Problem solved then. What's next?"

"I'm concerned," Jack started, "about the quality of some of the unsold – ." He stopped suddenly in response to a sharp kick he received from under the table.

Jack burst into Mr Smiley's office, for once with a broad grin on his face and appearing to be in a good mood. "I've got a job for you, Everton," he said.

"Yes Sir?"

"Horley Cross Bus Station. Why haven't we got a sale?"

"Nobody wants it."

"Exactly. I've been ringing your praises up there," and he pointed to the ceiling, "and we've decided to put you to the test. Go out there and sell it. Mr Smiley can spare you for a bit."

"I would have liked to have been consulted," Mr Smiley said, rather pompously, "and actually I can't spare him right now."

"You'll have to manage," Jack replied dismissively.

"How do I get there?" Everton asked, warming to the task.

"To begin with we'll go out together, and then you can work it in with your other duties. Mr Smiley will have to be patient."

Everton sat watching the end of the news on television, followed by the weather forecast. They managed to put bold lines very close together, the whole forming a large circle with Lancashire in the middle. The forecaster said, "There'll be heavy rain and strong wind all day in all areas but the worst of the weather will be in the North West of England. Structural damage can be expected." Everton and his mother could already hear the wind increasing outside, and the first drops of rain were starting to beat on the window.

"You going out to Horley Cross in that tomorrow?" Everton's Mum asked.

"Yes Mum."

"Give it a miss, we don't want you catching pneumonia."

"I can't, I have to do what I'm told, and Mr Purvis is coming with me."

"I'll ring tomorrow morning and tell him you're sick."

"I'm not sick, Mum, and in any case this is an opportunity for me to prove myself."

"Well, take your big trench coat, umbrella, waterproof trousers and your Wellington boots then."

"Mum!"

"You'll do as I say too, just as you do for flipping Mr Purvis."

Everton discarded all his heavy weather clothing except for his trench coat, before departing for Horley Cross with Mr Purvis. The latter was less well dressed than Everton, just a light plastic mac and an umbrella which Everton knew would be torn to shreds if used, but it looked good neatly rolled up. They travelled to their destination in 'Sir's' up-market Ford car. They said little on the way and Everton was happy to be driven in luxury and listen to the gentle purr of the big engine, where he was dry and warm out of the storm. One day he would have a car like this, but first he would have to prove himself, starting from today.

On arrival at Horley Cross they visited the Bus Station and Mr Purvis took Polaroid photographs of the unsold panels. They retreated to the sordid atmosphere of the run-down café in the Bus Station. Over lukewarm coffee in dirty mugs, they arranged the photographs, together with leaflets from the Bus Company giving circulation figures, in brightly coloured folders.

"Remember this," Jack said, "No discount. The prices have already been discounted – remember that one. Mr Meadows won't allow discounts for this or anything else. He regards it as a sign of defeat."

In the pouring rain they went to the top of the High Street and looked down the long and now wet shopping street towards The Roxy Cinema at the extreme end. The left side of the street seemed to contain the more prosperous shops, while on the right the businesses appeared to be mostly 'trade'. "I'll take the left side, you take the right," Mr Purvis said.

He would, thought Everton. Everton had only once sold something in his uneventful life. He once owned a battered second-hand motor scooter. On his way home one summer evening it broke down yet again, and hard as he tried he couldn't get any life out of it. Standing on the pavement he shouted out to passers by, "I'm auctioning this scooter, any bids?" Somebody offered a pound, another three pounds, and finally there was a bid of a fiver which he accepted, then he walked home.

Everton went into the first business, a wool shop. He hung about on one leg and then another until a young girl was able to attend to him. "Can I help you Sir?" she asked.

"I'd like to speak to the owner," Everton replied.

"I'm sorry, Mrs Woodstaff is only here on Mondays. Can you call back?"

His other calls were also negative for one reason or another and his early zest rapidly diminished, until, drenched to the skin despite his trench coat, he entered a record shop. A polite elderly gentleman listened to his pitch with great care and attention. He made no immediate decision but promised to look at the panels and took full details.

With a lighter heart, Everton joined the storm and went to the next door down. He started his patter all over again but was cut short. "I do admire your enthusiasm," the gentleman said, "but you've already told me all that, this is the same business as the one above, it's a double frontage."

Everton had nearly given up when he entered a D.I.Y. store with the name of 'Cartwright' above the door. Dripping onto the wooden floor he waited for a Mr Cartwright to see him, and eventually was shown into a small glass box office at the back of the store where he stated his business. Mr Cartwright had a hard looking face as if business had been a struggle and he wasn't going to be messed about by anyone, and would drive a hard bargain. He lent back in his chair to listen to Everton, and stuck his well chewed pencil into the niche above his ear. When Everton had finished Mr Cartwright told him that he had recently started up business on his own, facing up to the multiples, and was hoping to give a personalised and speciality service. They had a number of agencies for specialised products, all of which required a separate advertisement panel at Horley Cross Bus Station. It was not long before Everton had talked him into taking eight of the ten spaces, then the bargaining began. Mr Cartwright said, "Nothing wrong with the price, but we'll need something off because we're taking so much. Let's say twenty per cent volume discount?"

"The price is already discounted," Everton said, "and I have instructions not to allow any discount at all."

"Come on now, you haven't sold any spaces yet; you need my business."

"I appreciate that, Mr Cartwright. My boss is somewhere over the road; I need to consult him."

Everton looked out of the window into the dark wet afternoon but he was nowhere to be seen. He tried again, "I could provisionally let you have ten per cent, if I can get my superiors to agree."

"Fifteen per cent," countered Mr Cartwright.

"Only fifteen per cent if you pay for three months display in advance," Everton suggested, talking off the top of his head.

"Done."

Mr Cartwright picked up his cheque book, adding, "You're a bright lad who'll go far."

Everton had no idea what Mr Meadows would say, certainly Jack Purvis would kill the order if he could. He spent a further hour discussing artwork with Mr Cartwright. Armed with an order, a cheque and rough artwork drafts, he stumbled into the street, apprehensive but also elated. He knew that he'd done well. It was still raining and the strong wind had freshened. Huddled into his coat he made for The Roxy and the café there, but there was no sight of Jack Purvis. He gave him an hour, then left to see if the car was still in the car park, but it had gone too. He made his weary way to the railway station, his shoes squelching, wet about his neck and the bottoms of his trousers soaked through. He was most uncomfortable.

Everton went back to the office and locked the order and the artwork safely in a drawer in his desk. Then to satisfy his Mum he put his waterproof trousers over his wet trousers, removed his shoes and put on his wellies. Looking as if he'd obeyed his dress instructions he made his way home. "Sensible boy," his Mum said. It wasn't the first person he'd trick within the next twenty-four hours.

The next morning, Everton saw Jack Purvis. He deliberately did not tell him about the cheque which he kept in his pocket for plan B. He kept a copy of the order and artwork in his desk. He had ignored 'Sir's' rude behaviour in leaving him stranded in Horley Cross and asked, "Did you have any luck yesterday, Sir?"

"Where did you get to? There was no sign of you in the café. What do you think you were playing at?"

Everton dismissed that remark and repeated the question. "Did you get any orders, Sir?"

"No, of course I didn't. There were a few enquiries, and I have some letters to write, but nothing definite. I shall advise Mr Meadows to cut and run."

"I don't think we can do that, Sir, I sold eight panels yesterday."

'Sir's' nervous blinking went into overdrive. Everton had floored him.

"You what?"

"I have an order for eight panels from Cartwright DIY."

Everton produced the order and copy of the artwork. 'Sir' quickly spied the bit about fifteen percent discount. "That won't do," he said, and with great theatre tore the order into small pieces and dropped them in the waste bin. It was down to plan B then.

That evening Everton heard Jack Purvis go into Mr Meadow's room. He knew that he would be discussing Horley Bus Station. In a few minutes there were angry words and 'Sir' stormed out. Everton heard him gather his stuff together, before clattering down the narrow stairs and leave. This was his moment. Everton knocked on the Holy door and entered. Father pointedly said, "We don't see junior staff on their own."

"I thought it important, Sir."

"What is it?" Mr Colin asked.

Uninvited, Everton sat down, facing Father and son and half drunk gin and tonics.

"I have an order for Horley Cross Bus Station, eight units, and a cheque for the first three months display."

You could have heard a pin drop. Father went very red in the face and was speechless. It was young Mr Colin who came round first. "Are you sure?" he asked.

"Quite sure," and he held up the copy order.

Father studied it with undisguised glee, but Mr Colin noticed the discount bit first. "It says fifteen percent discount," he said.

"I know, but I got it down from twenty percent. I have a cheque for the first three months display."

Father sprang to life. "Well done lad, wait till I tell Jack about this. Where's the original order?"

"Mr Purvis tore it up, Sir."

"He what?"

"Tore it up, Sir. That's a copy; I retrieved the original and stuck it together with sellotape."

Father became very agitated. "What did he do with the cheque? He didn't tear that up too, did he?"

"I took the precaution of not giving it to him, Sir," and he held it up.

Father snatched at it and the two Meadows' studied it in great detail, as if their lives depended upon it.

Father beamed and said, "Can you send Mr Purvis in?"

"He's gone home, Sir."

"Has he, indeed, well he's in trouble."

"Does that mean I can accept the order, Sir?"

"You can indeed; look after all of this on your own, without interference from Mr Purvis. Now, if at any time you have any bright ideas, don't hesitate to come to us. My door is open."

"Even if I'm junior staff?" Everton dared to ask.

Father smiled. "You're a cheeky monkey as well," he said, " and I like that."

CHAPTER FOUR

IN A FOUL MOOD, Jack Purvis retired to his temporary digs, in the up-market locality of Hoylake in The Wirral. The only thing he'd liked since coming up North was his digs, his Landlady, Mrs Biggs, and his evening meal. The same could not be said about his co-lodgers. But he would not stay here long. He needed his own flat and his own space, then he'd also get away from the uncultured Dick, from Bolton, whose only interest was football, which he couldn't stand, and Jamie from Scotland who spoke a strange language which wasn't English. He was surprised that Mrs Biggs had taken these two in. The rent was definitely up-market and they were decidedly not.

On his way upstairs to wash and brush up, he spied Dick and Jamie in the front sitting room, beside an inviting coal fire. Dick was recalling the game between Man City and Liverpool over the weekend, ball by ball, his active hands moving this way and that to demonstrate the mounting drama. Jamie wasn't listening and was pouring himself a 'wee dram' from his private bottle which he didn't share. Later, he'd become more communicative and even less comprehensible. Jack made a quick retreat; he would go out for his meal, and then maybe do a movie. He needed time on his own to consider his future, and he didn't want to make small talk with these morons. Mrs Biggs appeared from her quarters and Jack said to her, "I've a late business dinner appointment, Mrs Biggs, and I won't be here for your excellent meal."

"But it's your favourite, lamb chops and corn on the cob for starters."

Jack's mouth watered. "I really am very sorry," he said.

"And he shot, and the ball hit the cross bar – would you believe it!" he heard Dick's high pitched voice while a disinterested Jamie looked at his bottle.

"Has anyone helped themselves?" he asked. Jack knew that he'd made the right decision.

By the end of the evening Jack had wound down; he'd conveniently dismissed the matter of Horley Cross Bus Station as a white elephant, not of his making, and he'd have nothing more to do with it. It was Everton's job to sell it, without discounts. Any monkey could sell anything at a discount. He reckoned that he'd put Everton totally in his place. He slept well, in the secure knowledge that he was beginning to impose his authority over everyone at work, including Everton and the two Meadows'. He'd been brilliant the night before, demonstrating his firm grip on sales policy, and the need to rid the company of its unprofitable parts, starting with Horley. The company badly needed new blood, in particular the type of analytical foresight he could bring. The rest of them had been standing too close to the problem. He'd been able to stand well back and see clearly the overall picture. On the morrow he'd begin his presentation of site classification and value, and make out the first listing of sites to be ditched.

The next morning, Jack was therefore surprised to find a note on his desk, reading, "Your behaviour last night was unacceptable. I'll be in late. Come to my office at three," and it was signed by Colin.

Unfriendly that, Jack thought. Colin wanders in here about eleven, swans about the place for about an hour, then takes an early lunch. If he had a problem he might have suggested lunch together. Difficult issues could be sorted out so easily in congenial surroundings, over a Port. Well, he had a lot of things to do anyway, and he'd start by sorting out that young Everton. He pushed Mr Smiley's button and asked for Everton.

"Yes Sir," Everton said.

"Come up here now."

"What shall I bring?"

"Bring yourself," Jack replied and rammed down the receiver.

Everton was beginning to irritate Jack, and the sight of his cheerful face round the door annoyed him even more. He would really wipe that grin off his face. "You better get back to Horley Cross, on your own; you didn't do too well there," he said to Everton.

"No point."

"No point. When I say 'Go', you go, not 'no point' me."

"What to do?"

"Sell it lad, sell it – and not at discount prices."

"It's already sold, Sir."

"You haven't sold anything. I tore up the Cartwright order because the terms were unacceptable; there are ten panels to sell, do you hear? Ten?"

"I sold two this morning, to the wool shop lady I missed when I was there. I told her that there were only two panels left. She booked them at once – she didn't want to miss the boat."

Jack felt slightly sick. It was dishonest to sell something by saying there were only two left when in fact they were all left; a bit like Estate Agents selling apartments. All the same, he was impressed and he'd have to show some kind of appreciation. After a long pause he said, "That's a start, anyway. But get out there and sell the rest, and tell no more lies. I'll give you my notes on follow ups."

"The other eight panels have been sold to Cartwright."

"Do you ever listen, Everton? The Cartwright order is dead."

"No, it's not, it's alive, A, L, I, V, E, alive. Father and Mr Colin are delighted, even at the reduced price. The cashier is already on the way to the bank to lodge Mr Cartwright's cheque."

This news hit Jack like a thunderbolt. He couldn't stand this Everton, his long, untidy hair, his permanent grin, his boyish expression and little turned up nose. He couldn't have him running off to the Meadows' behind his back. He would have to get to the bottom of it all. "When did you see the Meadows'?" he asked in a more composed tone.

"Last night, after you'd gone."

"Did they send for you?"

"No."

"So you just went up there, on your own and uninvited, and without any word to me?" Jack asked in a raised voice.

"Yes."

"Why?"

"I wanted to seek their advice about the Cartwright order."

"Ah, so they don't know about the discount?"

"Yes, they do."

"Did you tell them?"

"Mr Colin spotted it at once."

"And?"

"And the cheque swung it. They were delighted."

Jack became extremely nervous, and he couldn't stop his nervous rapid blinking rate as he tried to come to terms with this rebel. His world was falling apart all around him, and it was all due to this upstart. At that moment he was reminded of his father's advice, 'Never dwell on defeats, move on.' Well, he'd move on but first he had to try and retrieve the situation. Leaning forward he wagged his pointed finger at Everton and said, "You've shown considerable initiative, and you've done well, but there's one lesson you haven't learnt. Mr Smiley and you have me as your superior, and in future you come to me about everything. It is up to me to decide whether we should take the matter further and go to Father or Mr Colin, or both. Don't ever go to them on your own, and without consulting me, ever again! Do I make myself clear?"

"Perfectly."

Jack did not think that Everton meant it.

At three o'clock Jack entered Colin's office. "You wanted to see me, Colin?" he said in as cheerful and relaxed a mood as he could manage.

"Yes," Colin said, "first of all I expect an apology about your attitude last night. It won't do." The bloody man, thought Jack, his old mate was really taking the huff. He would try contrition first, and then try to muscle into some of Everton's glory.

"I was depressed," Jack said, "about Horley Cross, and lacked confidence in Everton's ability of closing on the various deals I had set up for him. I had discussed the Cartwright job with him and suggested that I would try to persuade you and Father to accept the discounts, but he seems to have forestalled me. I was keeping the news from you as I had hoped that Everton and I might yet get Mr Cartwright to agree to a more reasonable price. Besides, it's not healthy that one advertiser should take eighty percent of the space – it leaves us too exposed. We have got another order this morning, from a lady in a Wool Shop, at the full price, so it's all sold now."

"Jack, I've said my peace, and now I want to move on, but you'll have to learn to agree everything with me, and keep me fully informed. I have to do this with Father, and I expect Mr Smiley and Everton do it with you."

"Fine fellow that Everton," Jack said, sensing that praising him at this moment might please Colin, but he didn't mean it, and then added, "I'm glad that I'm giving him new opportunities and seeking his potential."

"I'm glad we're all agreed about that," Colin replied, "but now we're faced with the more important problem of the cull of sites. You see the problem you've created, don't you? You tell Father that Horley Cross must go because it's not sellable, and then it's sold, so how are we to convince him that this list of poor sites is not sellable?"

"But I thought we were going to cull the sites when Father went off on holiday?"

"He's changed his mind, he's not going."

Jack gasped. The silly old man, why couldn't he make up his mind; what's the matter with him? "Why?" Jack asked.

"He has that sixth sense - always has done. He starts to imagine that others are plotting against him and his gut wishes, so he decides to stay put to find out for himself."

"But you haven't said anything?"

"No, not at all."

"So what do we do?"

"Confront him with hard facts, make it out that our profits will increase. Get your list out, showing the savings, and for God's sake make it simple so that he can understand it. In the meantime I'll create a diversion to make him think that that is what we were plotting."

"What kind of diversion?"

"I'll tell him that I'm buying the Isle of Man business for myself. He'll explode and say he knew that I was up to something, and if anyone is going to buy that business it should be the Meadows' Company."

"Do we want the Isle of Man business?"

"Good God no."

"Is it for sale?"

"Shouldn't think so."

Everton wasted no time in telling Mr Smiley about his success and 'Sir's' defeat. Mr Smiley chuckled but warned Everton, "Don't make an enemy of him. We all have to live with him and we don't always want to be daggers drawn. Butter him up a bit, get him on our side, even if we don't like him."

It had suited Everton to have such an ass of a boss, with opportunities to knock him off his pedestal every now and again. He was about to reply when the door flew open and the man himself appeared.

"I've got a job for you both," Sir said. They waited as Sir settled into a chair, then lay back with his feet on the desk and started to light a cigar. He's come to stay for some time, Everton thought.

"What was our selling capacity last month?" he asked.

"Seventy-six percent," Mr Smiley replied.

"That's twenty-four percent unsold, sites which have to have something on them, sites on which we pay rent and rates and maintenance – for what, for God's sake?"

"The same sites might not be unsold next month?" Everton suggested.

"Ah," Sir said, removing his feet from the desk, and pointing his finger at them. "Do we know which sites of the twenty-four percent never sell at all?"

"About a hundred of them," Everton answered.

"Thank you. Would you please list them for me, show the rent and rates paid and maintenance costs against them, and calculate what we would save if we gave them up, and how our profits would therefore increase?"

"But Sir, some of these sites would sell if we did something to them, improve them like."

"What, touch them with a magic wand?" and Sir laughed, trying to force a joke.

"We would have to look at the sites very carefully, we would - ," but Sir broke into Everton's developing proposals.

"When you've listed these sites, I will of course look at them very closely; you can leave that to me."

Everton knew that it was hopeless trying to make any explanations; either he would be shot down in flames or Sir would present them to the Meadows' as his own idea.

"When do you want this by?" Everton asked.

"Say by the end of the week," Sir suggested.

"You can have it now," Everton said as he withdrew a pile of papers neatly bound from a drawer in his desk; he winked at Mr Smiley as he handed it over.

"You've already done it!" exclaimed Sir. "How did you know I wanted it?"

"I thought you might ask for it," and Everton smiled. This had been his baby for some time, but he'd never got it further than Mr Colins' desk. The Meadows' had the habit of ignoring anything which was defeatist.

"And why did you think I might ask for it?" Sir persisted.

"Because I thought that someone of your intellect was bound to ask for the obvious, sometime or other," Everton lied, but following Mr Smiley's advice of buttering Sir up.

"You are a very strange person," Sir said, unwinding his long legs from the chair, and leaving the office in a less bustling manner than when he'd arrived.

"You didn't give him your suggestions about how we should improve some of those sites, did you?" Mr Smiley asked.

"Yes, but Sir won't act on them, it would cause delay."

Everton knew that the whole exercise would be hopeless. Father would never give anything up, particularly as he'd proved himself right by not giving up Horley Cross. On a separate list he'd made proposals of how many of these sites could be improved and made saleable, in some cases increasing the potential revenue tenfold. Mr Colin had never fully understood his calculations, so if Colin couldn't grasp it, what chance would there be of Father understanding it. But a plan was slowly forming in his mind.

"Why doesn't Mr Colin give the sites up when Father is on holiday?" Mr Smiley asked.

"He's not going on holiday," Everton said.

"How do you know?"

"I heard Gillian on the telephone cancelling all the arrangements."

"Wouldn't you know it," Mr Smiley laughed. "I can't but admire the old man. He knew that something was about to happen and he wants to be around when it does."

"No, I expect he wants to save some money. Buy himself another Roller, the other one is at least four years old. Save on the holiday and stop our Christmas bonus' and he might have just enough."

Everton allowed his mind to drift far away. He saw a way of trapping Sir, and then the final nail would be driven in his coffin.

CHAPTER FIVE

JACK PURVIS STUDIED THE figures which Everton had given him with a great deal of interest. He was no fool, this Everton, but he'd have to watch him. Sometimes he was so sharp he might cut himself one day.

The figures spoke for themselves, apart from a separate list suggesting improvements on sites which were already 'dead'. Perhaps he should go out and look at all these sites, but as soon as he'd thought that he dismissed the idea just as swiftly. It would cause delay. Impress Colin by the speed at which he gathered information, and keep Everton out of it for the time being. He withdrew the schedule of suggested improvements, then found the last sheet and appended his signature. He pressed Colin's button and heard his voice, "Mr Colin here."

"It's Jack, can I have a word?"

"Come right up Jack."

Colin read through the figures slowly, sometimes making calculations on his pad. "It all looks very familiar," he said.

"I did obtain Everton's assistance," Jack replied.

"Ah, of course…so what do you want to do now?"

"Over to Father, I suppose."

"Could you do the explaining? Don't let him look at the figures in detail, just go through the summary very slowly, telling him clearly how our profit would be increased. I do congratulate you; this summary is very clear. He's bound to be impressed."

Father went missing for a few days. To make up for his postponed holiday he stayed at home. Any excursion was no further than with his wife for tea at The Prince of Wales Hotel in Southport. Here, he could enjoy the luxury for which he'd worked hard for all his life, and of course, the cream cakes. Returning home late one afternoon, he saw one of his favourite poster sites on the road into Liverpool being dismantled. So that was it! The vultures had arrived! He stopped the Roller at a Taxi rank and sent his wife home in a cab, then, breaking all speed limits, he hurried into the office. They would not be expecting him and he'd show them who was boss! As he walked heavily and noisily past reception, Gillian was about to shut up for the day and already had her coat on. Breathlessly, she started to buzz offices, saying, "Mr Meadows is here." Others were also thinking of calling it a day. Now they thought otherwise.

Colin buzzed Jack. "Are you ready?" he asked.

"Quite ready."

"Let's go then."

As they entered the great man's office he looked up and said, "Just the two I want to speak to. Site number seven three one six, leaving Southport for Liverpool – why are we removing it?"

"I don't know, Father, I haven't issued any removal instructions."

"Find out then, now."

Colin rang the Estate Manager's office and there was a short exchange. "Father," Colin said, "the owner is redeveloping and there won't be room for us. We managed to squeeze another three months beyond our notice, but it has to come away now."

"Are you sure?"

"Quite sure."

"Oh, very well, what are you drinking?"

After sorting out their drinks Colin raised the subject uppermost in his mind. "Jack has a presentation here that he would like to take you through."

Jack took his cue and handed over a bundle of papers. "What's this?" Father asked, "You know I don't like paper."

"You know the way our clients buy campaigns," Jack started, "they take a package of chosen and hand-picked sites which are all priced the same?"

"Yes."

"Whereas some of the sites should be valued more than others, but they're all lumped together on a common price?"

"Yes, of course I know, it's my company, I should know."

"Our buyers purchase the best sites and leave the others."

"Well, it's your job to sell 'the others' ".

"If the sites were classified," Jack continued, warming to his subject, "some buyers would be happy to pay a premium for the good sites, and might still buy the poorer sites if they were cheaper."

"And?"

"We would get more money for the campaigns we sell."

"And you think that our buyers would be happy to pay more for the same?"

"They would if they knew exactly what they were buying and the sites were properly described, or classified."

"Listen," Father said, raising his voice to an excitable screech, "you're here for five minutes, and you're telling me how I should run my business. For years our clients have been buying our sites, so many at a set price, and of course some sites are better than others, so what! If some of these sites don't get bought you'll have to think up some way to sell them, not tell me how I should run my business. Next, you'll be telling me that part of your scheme is that we should give up some sites altogether."

"Well, just a few, not very many, but our profitability would - ."

"The answer is 'No'", Father fumed, and lifting up Jack's presentation he dumped the lot in the bin. "My profitability would be much increased," Father continued, "by saving on your salary and expenses. Now get out of here and sell, from door to door like you left Everton to do in Horley Cross. I thought you were up to something which is why I postponed my holiday. Is there anything else?"

Jack sat there fuming, and in desperation he turned to Colin, waiting for him to back him up, but Colin had retreated to the window, watching the traffic and distancing himself from the row. "I'll discuss it further with Jack," he said. "No, nothing more for the moment."

"In that case I'll go home," Father said, draining the last of his gin and tonic. He lifted his bulk out of his chair and stumped noisily out of his office, the floor boards creaking in protest.

After he'd gone Jack turned to his old mate, Colin. "Well, thanks a bundle," he said, "we agreed all this and not a word of support do you give me."

"Father was tired," Colin said, "you can't talk to him when he's like that. I still support you, but we've tried to rush it; be patient."

They left Father's office together, voices raised in argument. As they passed Mr Smiley's office, Everton heard Jack say, "I can't sell these sites, nobody can, not even your precious Everton, so don't expect me to. If Father wants to continue to pay rent and rates on them, then that's up to him."

The next day, Everton eagerly waited for Father to come in. He knew that he would because he'd shown that he was on a roll; he regarded many of his staff as 'the enemy' rather than faithful servants paid to be on his side, and he liked nothing better than ramming a message home when he thought he had an employee on the run. At the moment his eyes were on Sir, and he, Everton, could do no harm. Strike while the iron was hot. Everton knew Father's shortcomings; he was impatient and too lazy to understand new ideas, but hidden away there was a gut feeling that everything was not quite right. Everton knew that Father didn't think that some of these sites would ever sell, but that if he delayed in giving them up something would eventually turn up, but once the sites were gone, they'd be gone for ever. Everton had the answer so he would be listened to.

Sir grumbled all day, sometimes to the staff and sometimes to himself. Everton kept well out of his way. As expected Father came in, but Mr Colin was nowhere to be seen. Gillian said that he'd taken the family to his cottage in North Wales.

Everton heard Sir slip into Father's office, the floor boards creaking through the ceiling above his head. He heard them talk quietly, and then voices were raised. At five o'clock other staff left to go home, but Everton sat quietly at his desk, a folder at the ready. Then he heard Father's door bang and Sir strode out and clattered down the narrow stairs out into the street, muttering as he went. Everton lifted his folder and climbed the stairs. He knocked gently on Father's door. "What is it?" Father called out, then, "Oh, it's you, come in lad."

After Everton had sat down Father asked, "What is it then?"

"You told me, Sir, to come to you if I had any bright ideas."

"That's right. What have you got in that folder?"

"It's the details of a site in Borough Road, Birkenhead. There are seven sixteen sheet panels on a wall, and only one panel has been sold in the last three months."

"Why is that then?"

"The panels are on a wall near a cinema. When people queue there they get bored and they pick away at the posters, leaving them in tatters. Also the bottom of the panels touches the pavement and muck gets thrown up from the street. The site looks a mess. I've put it on every availability list and nobody will touch it."

"And you're going to tell me to give it up, I suppose, like everyone else has?"

"No, Sir."

"No?"

"Yes."

"Why?"

"Behind the wall is a gable facing the tunnel exit. The gable is owned by the same landlord. If we removed the panels on the wall and fixed one forty-eight sheet panel on the gable, we could sell that at ten times the maximum revenue the site can earn at present. Mind you, we would probably have to pay more rent, and it would cost something to convert. I have it here, Sir, in my folder. I have a photograph of the site as it is at present, and I have superimposed on it where the new panel would go. I even have an Advertiser who has expressed an interest in booking it long term."

Father snatched at the folder and started to examine it. Everton could see that he could understand it all only too well. He had the habit of pretending not to understand something which he disliked, but in this instance he did not disguise his excitement.

"Why haven't you told Mr Purvis then?"

"I have."

"You have?"

"It was on a separate list attached to the list of sites he wants to give up. Have you got it, Sir?"

"I put it all in the bin," and Father peered into the waste paper basket. "Yes, it's all here, fish it out lad."

Everton could see that the list of suggested improvements was not there, but the list of sites to be given up was, and it included Borough Road, Birkenhead. When this fact had been established, Father's attention was once again focused on Everton's presentation folder. "Well, what are we waiting for?" Father asked.

"You want me to do it?"

"Yes, and if it works you can apply the system to the other sites."

"What about Mr Purvis?"

"Leave him to me."

Jack Purvis did not go back to his digs, but he rang Mrs Biggs to excuse himself for his evening meal, and then went to the cocktail bar at The Adelphi to consider his position. The relationship with the Meadows' was not working out, and the time had come to review it. He still had his flat in London and there were always jobs in the city for the likes of himself; perhaps he could return there. Besides, Liverpool was in a shambles. It was dirty and shoddy, row after row of boarded up houses waiting for demolition, and it was always raining. Yes, that was what he would do, and he ordered another whisky. A pity, though, he'd had his eye on a little bungalow in Parkgate on the Wirral, with a view over to the Welsh mountains. It was pleasant there, only half an hour to the office. There was a local tennis club and a Conservative Association he could join; they would both be glad of his help and organisational skills. Could he go back to that long travelling each day in a crowded and dusty tube train, because although most people had a car, there was no room on the streets to use it? But how was he going to resolve his position with Father? His mind lingered on that for some time and then he realised that his glass was empty, so he had another. Best to ignore the man, he thought. He could do business with Colin, and they were old mates. Encourage him to be more his own master and take up the leadership reins; after all, he was Managing Director. That's it, he thought, I'll align myself with Colin. He needs someone like me to give him confidence, and he really could do his old mate a great favour. But what about Everton? Well, he'd have to keep him on a very short leash, and forbid him to go to Father to spill the beans. I'll have another drink, he thought, life wasn't all that bad, only if you made it so.

The next morning Jack had a hang-over and was late into the office. He detected a quiet hush about the place, as if everyone knew something he didn't. To cap it all, there was a curt note to see Colin as soon as he came in. "You're late," Colin said, in an unfriendly tone.

"Sorry, a bit of a long night last night," replied Jack, trying to laugh it off.

"Father rang me last night and asked me to go round to his house."

"Last night?"

"Yes; you know that list, the sites you wanted to give up?"

"The sites WE wanted to give up, you mean."

"Whatever. Why didn't you attach the further list of proposed site improvements?"

"You mean Everton's ramble and pie in the sky ideas?"

"Everton's considered judgment. Father is impressed and has instructed him to implement at least one of the suggestions, see how it goes. Why can't Everton and you co-operate a bit more?"

"I wish he would; he seems to be a law unto himself. Father threw my presentation into the bin. And where did he get Everton's further list?"

"Father pulled the stuff out of the bin, and Everton added to that the improvement list which you seemed to think so important to hide from everyone."

Jack was furious; it all seemed like some kind of conspiracy, not only Everton working against him but also his old mate allied to his brainless father. What sort of company was this, a Chairman who threw presentations in the bin and then took them out again, and a Managing Director who was a mouse? "I've had enough of this," Jack screamed, "you can all stew in your own juice and manage on your own, delay coming into the twentieth century. I'm going back to London where I know I'm appreciated."

CHAPTER SIX

EVERTON HEARD SIR COME in late, then hurriedly walk out of the building to go to the part of the separate building which housed Mr Colin's office. He didn't think that Colin would be there; he'd left yesterday with his wife for North Wales, as was his habit whenever relations with Father cooled. However, Gillian said that he was in early before the rest of them. Father had called for him last night and Colin had come back, all the way from Wales and left his wife behind there. That meant that there'd been a crisis, and Sir, rushing out in an agitated state, was something to do with it, and perhaps what he'd been up to was also part of the trouble. The atmosphere in the office had been electric all morning, and there'd been a general hush. It was like waiting for the thunder at the end of a hot afternoon, with storm clouds on the horizon. With half his mind on his work, Everton kept an eye and an ear open for Sir's return, and he didn't have long to wait.

Sir strode out of the other building and into the main block. He paused outside Mr Smiley's office as if he was coming in, then apparently changed his mind and rushed up the stairs. Everton and Mr Smiley looked at each other but neither of them said anything, so they waited.

A few moments later, Sir appeared with his coat on, his brief case bulging with papers, the fastener barely holding it shut. Again, he paused outside the office, then briskly pushed the door open and stood there, glaring. "Satisfied then?" he asked.

"I beg your pardon?" Mr Smiley replied.

"Not you, Everton there."

"Yes Sir?"

"Satisfied, carrying on your own pointless crusade behind my back? You didn't like me from the start, I could see that."

"What's all this about Jack?" risking not calling him 'Sir', partly to annoy him, and partly to find out if he was at long last departing.

"All chummy now, are we? Let me tell you something. You work for a dithering old fool who's going senile and won't last more than a year. Then what? Mr Colin will have to pay death duties and how's he going to do that? He'll have to sell part of the company to the city, and it wouldn't be long before they realised how unsuited Mr Colin is in running a company of this size, so then the city would gobble it all up. And they'd gobble you up too, because you're small minded and old fashioned. Then will you be satisfied?"

"Are you leaving, Jack?" asked Everton.

"How did you guess?" and with that last quip he turned around and left, without a backwards glance.

"Why do people underestimate Father?" asked Mr Smiley. "He's worth ten 'Sir's' any day."

Shortly afterwards, Mr Colin left. Gillian said that he'd gone back to North Wales. "He can't have had," Everton said, "because he's left us without a Sales Director."

"Oh, I expect Father will be in this afternoon, he'll sort it all out."

Father was in early and no sooner had Gillian buzzed the news around than there was a call for Everton to go up. "Why doesn't he want me?" Mr Smiley asked.

"Perhaps I'll be able to tell you when I get back?" Everton suggested.

Father appeared to be in a good mood, and already had the gin and tonic's poured out. "I have to tell you," he said, "Mr Purvis has left. He wasn't any good anyway."

"So who is going to be Sales Director?" asked Everton, with a glint in his eyes.

"Just at present, nobody. Mr Smiley is too old and you're too young." Everton's heart sank, surely he'd earned promotion, or some kind of promotion? This was the moment he'd waited for, and now there was nothing. "Don't you have confidence in me?" he asked angrily.

"Of course I do, but you still have to prove yourself. You've bet your reputation on selling the unsold sites, so let's see if you can deliver. It's all very well showing me your plan, on paper, but can you deliver?"

"But to whom do I report?" asked Everton.

"To Mr Colin or me, and not in any particular preference. I'm not advertising for a replacement for Mr Purvis. We don't need one and we can't afford it." Everton grasped the situation at once. The position of Sales Director was vacant, but he had to fully earn it – the title, prestige, a car and a better salary and even more promotion in the distant future. Well, he'd show them. This was his chance. Father was no fool, no ditherer, nor was he going senile; he knew exactly what he was doing. Everton got up to go, but Father hadn't finished yet. "And another thing, you get another two hundred a year, and I suppose you better have the use of Mr Purvis' car while you're doing your survey – only temporarily, mind."

Mr Smiley was not pleased. It was all very well not replacing Mr Purvis who was only a nuisance anyway, but to give Everton free rein on his survey work meant that he wouldn't be available to help him. Who was going to do all that work? He went to see Father about it. "I'm not going to manage," he said.

"It's only for a couple of months," Father said.

"It doesn't matter. I'll get so far behind I'll never be able to catch up again."

"You'll just have to put in some overtime," Father suggested.

"You don't pay overtime," Mr Smiley snapped.

"Oh, don't be such a misery. We'll give you a two hundred pound bonus, how's that?"

And with that Mr Smiley was stopped in his tracks. It was a typical bit of Meadows' technique; you have a problem so you just throw money at it. He would have asked for Mr Purvis' car as well, but he remembered that Everton had been promised that. "In that case – ," he started to say.

"Gin and tonic?" asked Mr Meadows.

Everton lived with his Mum on the front at Meols, facing a long expanse of sand and mud which was sometimes covered by the sea. The house was mainly grey pebbledash; indeed, everything was grey around it. Everton's Dad had died when Everton was doing his National Service in the army. He was an only child and he and his Mum were left to fend for themselves. She had no full-time employment, nor needed it. She lived on the proceeds of her dead husband's lifetime of toil. The unearned income was enough but no more than that. As inflation began to outstrip her resources she began to take part-time jobs, so she worked as a waitress in the café at the end of the street on Wednesdays and Saturdays. For most of the time she applied herself to Everton's welfare and comfort; she had nobody else to fuss over, and Everton paid her a few pounds a week towards household expenses. Sometimes they went to the cinema together, and less seldom to the Lighthouse Bar in West Kirby for a meal, usually to celebrate something. Everton's mother was sad that Everton had not yet had any kind of serious relationship with a young lady that would include trips to cinemas and restaurants; she would have been happy to do without their social trips together in favour of a normal, healthy relationship between her son and a girlfriend; sometimes she thought that he was so hell bent on furthering his career with Meadows' that he was unable to enjoy himself, and you are only young once.

Everton's mother was popular at the café with both staff and customers. Still only in her forties she could pass as being ten years younger. She remained most attractive, petite and slim, with large blue eyes and a smile that had left creases between her mouth and ears, and she enjoyed flirting with men. A serious relationship was out of the question. She'd been there and done that and besides, she would never feel comfortable with anyone else, she was still treasuring a relationship which was cut short only too early. But Everton wished that his Mum would find a relationship with another man, so each of them encouraged the other to make a move, but while that did not happen they were content in each other's company; Mother, spoilt child, and the child buried deep in his work.

On the day Everton was given temporary use of Jack Purvis' Ford Zephyr, he left early to surprise his Mum. The garage at home once housed a pre-war Morris ten and had since filled with household junk. He would park the car in the driveway and hope that driving rain and salt from the Irish Sea would not spoil the beautiful polish and sheen of the dark blue paintwork.

As Everton drove into the concrete driveway he hooted, then gathered up his newly acquired briefcase and made for the front door. He'd seen his Mum peer out of the kitchen window and she rushed to meet him on the doorstep. "What is that?" she asked.

"Tonight, Mum, I'm taking you out to dinner at The Adelphi, and we'll go by car, through the tunnel. When were you last at The Adelphi?"

"You haven't bought that thing, have you?"

"No, it's a company car."

"You mean you have it for the night?"

"For a month, maybe two."

"You've been promoted?"

"Not yet."

"Oh, come on John, something's happened; stop teasing me. And we're not going to the Adelphi, it's too expensive. What's wrong with The Lighthouse?"

"Not far enough away, and no tunnel to go through."

"Then we'll go through the tunnel and eat at The King's Head, it's much cheaper. And what's the briefcase for?"

Everton worked as he'd never worked before. The Meadows' gave him the green light to do what he liked with the hundred sites to be examined, even if it meant giving up those which everyone knew were useless. It was the first time he'd been given such responsibility, so he was off in the car day after day, to Manchester, Preston, The Potteries, seeing Landlords and negotiating planning permission where required, then selling the re-vamped sites to clients at outrageous prices. He still managed to help Mr Smiley, and the two of them worked together at night, catching up on the routine bookings. At the end of three months, he'd been able to report to the Meadows' that about a third of the one hundred sites had been termi-nated, but the rest had been sold at most attractive prices, much more than anyone had expected, perhaps enough, Everton thought, for Father to get that new Rolls Royce? On the afternoon he'd made his final report, he waited anxiously to be called; this was going to be his moment, the job of Sales Director must be his, surely?"

"You've done well, lad," Father said, then there was a silence.

"What do I do now?" Everton dared to ask. "Shall I hand the car back"

"Yes please, leave it in the car park. We have a new Sales Director arriving next week."

Everton couldn't believe it. A new Sales Director! Another Meadows import from the city? What had he done all this for? Why had he both-ered? Was he expected to go back to the boring old routine with Mr Smiley? It was never boring before, but it sure would be now.

"New Sales Director?"

"A Mr White. Has been with Taplows in Leeds, and they've been bought out by a city conglomerate. He doesn't like it so he's coming here."

Everton knew about Taplows and even Mr White. He was a gentle-man and everyone liked him, but the timing of his availability couldn't have been worse. Mr Colin said, "Everton, we've told you before, Mr Smiley is too old and you're too young, but we have something else for you."

"Something else?"

"We're making you Branch Manager of Birkenhead and North Wales."

"We haven't got a branch in Birkenhead."

"We have now. There's too much there for us to manage from Liverpool, so we're hiving the area off. You'll be in complete charge."

The news began to excite Everton, but there was still something worrying him. "Will I have a car, Sir?"

"Sure will, you wouldn't be able to do the job without one. There's one of those new Morris Minors, bright red, in the car park now," and with that remark he handed over the keys. "And you'll have another three hundred a year, back dated to the first of last month. We know you've been working hard and we reward that. Gin and tonic?"

CHAPTER SEVEN

DOREEN LIVED WITH HER Mum in a rented terraced house in Claughton, Birkenhead. Doreen's elder sister had flown the nest, for better things – she'd married a Yank and was somewhere in the States. Her brother had taken a Manual Engineering job somewhere up North where employment prospects were brighter. They were not a close family and didn't communicate. Doreen's Mum was in two minds about her younger daughter, still living at home. Her husband had smoked and drunk heavily and died of lung cancer ten years back. She thought that he had been pretty useless, apart from the strict discipline he had exercised over their children. Doreen does what she likes now, she thought, out all hours and only seventeen, not yet a bread winner and therefore a drain on their resources. But if Doreen left she would be on her own and she wouldn't like that. Doreen was at Secretarial College, the only one of her siblings who had attempted to get any kind of training, but already she was attempting to opt out of that. A prospective employer was interviewing for a Man Friday for a new office, and three of the students had put their names forward.

The other two were Amanda and Patricia Bottom. Amanda was a striking blonde bombshell, but her secretarial skills were not up to anyone's standards, and nobody expected her to be hired. Patricia Bottom was small and plain, dark hair with a fringe cut in, and large reading glasses, but her typing and shorthand were brilliant, and Doreen expected the man to choose her. Doreen's own skills were good on her day, terrible if she wasn't concentrating. The man would either hire Amanda for her looks or Miss Bottom for her capability. Yes, thought Doreen, Miss Bottom would be Mr Smyth's new secretary.

"You'll go in together, "Miss Townsend said, "and I'll introduce you to Mr Smyth. He'll see you together first and then give you all an exercise, something to copy. When you've finished hand the work to me, and remember, it's not a race. After that Mr Smyth will see you individually, and make his decision on the quality of your work and how you present yourselves. Doreen, do you know you have a smudge on your collar?"

"Is there?" Doreen replied, trying to get a sight of the offending mark.

Miss Townsend continued, "Mr Smyth tells me that there is a starting wage of six pounds a week." Six pounds a week! A small fortune, thought Doreen, this was an interview she'd not mess up. Without further thought she peeled off her blouse and retired to the washroom. "Where are you going?" Miss Townsend called out.

"The smudge," Doreen replied, "I've got to clean up, won't be a mo."

They all trooped in and sat in a line at a long table, opposite Mr Smyth. The first thought Doreen had was how young he looked, not much more than a boy. He had long hair, some of it burying his small and neat ears. His face was chubby and impish, rounded off with a pink turned up nose. He had shaved too well that morning and there was a cut on his chin. He wore a good quality suit but it was well creased, probably a sign that he lived in a car so no wonder he wanted a Man Friday. A lone strand of hair hung over an eye, and she longed to reach out and put it back in its place. He had stood up when they first came in, and he was about the same height as she was. Her boyfriend, Hank from the States, was short, and she had to persuade him to stand on something when he kissed her goodnight at the doorstep, but…she was running ahead of herself.

They were all given a typed letter and clean sheets of letter headed paper, and they were asked to go away and type a fair copy. "Come back when you're finished," he said, "but not all at the same time," and the girls giggled. Doreen noticed that Miss Bottom fairly raced through the typing, without any panic or concern; she finished before Amanda had done the first line and while Doreen was rubbing out and making any corrections, adding her trademark smudges to an otherwise clean sheet of paper. Doreen decided to do it all carefully and take her time, so she scrumpled her first effort up and put it in the bin, then started again. Her third and last effort was the best, only two smudges; she was good at smudges. Miss Bottom had already gone in with her effort, and came out fairly quickly, still expressionless. "Your turn now," Miss Townsend said to Doreen.

"Let's see then," Mr Smyth said, and Doreen smiled broadly while she handed over her work.

"Two copies?" Mr Smyth exclaimed.

"I was unhappy with the first."

"Are you happier with the second?"

"A bit."

"Doreen, if you come and work for me how many copies of everything will you be doing?"

"Dunno, till it was right."

"You could be expensive on paper," and Doreen giggled; this man
could be fun. Mr Smyth studied the letters with considerable attention.
"How do you spell 'receive'?" he asked.

"R E C E I V E."

"That's funny, you have it right on the first copy and wrong on the
second."

"You had it spelt wrong on the original, so I corrected it, then on the
second copy - ."

"You forgot."

"Suppose so."

"Well, it at least proves that you know something about spelling, but
your typing could be improved, Doreen."

"Oh, I know, and it will I assure you, but I can work at it – I'm very
keen."

Doreen felt that the interview was slipping away and she wanted the
job, so she'd have to make a better effort, she'd have to take the initiative.

"Can you explain precisely what I would be doing?" she asked.

"You would man an office while I was out, you'd answer the telephone and deal with client's queries; you'd assist in the bookings and the
billposters' worksheets, you'd make the tea and sweep the floor, and I'd
expect you to take an interest in the company and what you're doing.
How are you on the phone?"

Doreen stammered out, "Oh, I think I'm very good."

"Have you got a phone?"

She hadn't – her Mum couldn't afford one. "Yes," she replied.

"I suppose you chat on it?"

"Yes."

"Well, a business phone is not quite the same; it's for passing on urgent information; you answer it and then you get off it. I think that's as far
as we can take it for now, Doreen. Have you any more questions?"

The thought that she might have to ask anything more floored
Doreen. She was beginning to fancy this man, and she suspected that he
liked her. She would have to ask him something, but what? What were
men interested in? Football, of course, sex and football. "What team do
you support?" she asked.

Mr Smyth appeared surprised, and then smiled. "You mean, football?" he asked.

"What else? Yes."

"That's my cue," he said.

Doreen didn't know what he meant, so persisted. "Which team?" she asked.

"Everton, and have you heard something?"

"What do you mean?"

"That my nick name is Everton; have you been doing some research?"

Doreen still didn't know what Mr Smyth meant, but it sure sounded good that she'd been doing some research. "Yes, sort of," she said doubtfully.

"Well, we'll be in touch Doreen, you can go now."

The girls decided to go for a coffee and exchange notes. "I think he's lovely," Doreen said.

"Lecherous," Amanda said, "I noticed the way he looked at me."

"Is it any wonder," Miss Bottom said, "your skirt's half way up your bum. What a way to come for an interview."

"He'll employ me," Amanda said, "and I may not accept it."

The next morning Miss Townsend phoned Doreen. "I'm afraid Mr Smyth is not taking you," she said, "but I can keep you on the list if you're interested?"

"I'm interested," Doreen said. She was disappointed, but not at all surprised. She didn't have the looks or the skill. Why should anyone employ me?

Later that day Miss Townsend phoned again. "Are you still interested in working for Mr Smyth?" she asked.

"Yes, of course."

"Amanda has decided not to take the job."

"Amanda? What about Patricia Bottom?"

"You were second choice."

"Oh, wonderful, but I don't understand, why - ."

"I don't understand either, Doreen, but report on Monday morning, nine sharp, and for God's sake wear a clean blouse, wash the ink off your hands and don't wear a pelmet skirt, otherwise by the end of the week Miss Bottom might have the job."

After Miss Bottom's solemn looks, Everton was pleased to see a more cheerful looking girl, not matching Amanda's beauty, but nevertheless very pleasing on the eye. She was taller than the others, about his height. He first noticed her bright red pelmet skirt, and her long shapely legs which soon disappeared from view behind the table when she sat down.

On top she had a white blouse, smudged on the collar, and her long hands appeared to be ink stained; there might even have been an ink smudge on one cheek. She had an oval shaped face, large brown eyes and long brown hair. Her mouth was turned down at the edges, making her face look serious, but when she smiled her whole face lit up. No beauty, but interesting; very interesting. Why had she asked about his football team? Had she really been doing her homework and contacted the Liverpool office to find something out about him? He decided that she could be good on the telephone and chatting up clients. A possibility, but not his first choice.

After seeing Doreen, Everton had already made up his mind. It would be Amanda. He knew it should be Miss Bottom, but with a name like that his office would become the laughing stock of the business. Amanda's typing was terrible, but could improve, whereas Miss Bottom's looks would always be the same. The important thing was that Amanda's looks would be an asset to his office, and buyers would surely give Birkenhead office extended calls. Besides, sharing an office with such a beauty excited him. He rang Miss Townsend. "I've chosen Amanda," he said.

"Are you sure?"

"Yes, quite sure."

"What about Miss Bottom'"

"Yes, very capable, but I've chosen Amanda."

"Very well, it's your decision."

Two hours later Miss Townsend rang him. "I'm sorry," she said, "but Amanda has opted out. She was nervous about being the only other employee in a small office."

"Nervous?"

"She's very young, Mr Smyth, this is a big step for her. Besides, I don't think she's quite ready; now I know that Miss Bottom would measure up very well."

Everton began to wonder what the interview had been about. Miss Townsend had decided, not him. "I would prefer Doreen," he said.

"Are you sure?"

"Quite sure."

Finding a miss Friday had been Everton's first task. Creating a new branch office before Doreen turned up on Monday morning was the next priority, and he had three days to do it in.

Six billposters already worked from the yard behind the large hoarding at the corner of Hind Street, Birkenhead. Attached to the yard was an end terraced house, the ground floor converted to a Bill Room. Here, the posters were stored, and drawn by the billposters for their daily work rounds. In the yard, Everton observed a filthy toilet and a tank where paste was mixed. The remains of strippings off old posters from the hoardings, before new posters were pasted up, floated around the yard with spilt paste. It was an unpleasant site. Everton had a look upstairs in the house, and saw the empty room was used for storing any old unwanted rubbish that should have already been taken to the dump. It was here, in this dirty room, that Mr Colin had told Everton that there should grow an active and lively new branch office. He had relied upon Everton to create order out of disorder – and do it quickly.

Everton spoke to Sam, the young and new Billposting Foreman. Sam hadn't noticed the sorry state of the yard and toilets, but when it was pointed out to him he agreed that it was messy. "It was messy when I came here," he said, "and I suppose I've got used to it."

They managed to assemble an overtime squad to deal with it that weekend, and take all the rubbish away from the room which was to be an office that very evening. Everton looked at the empty shell and the dirty walls which otherwise were in good condition. With the limited budget which Mr Colin had given him, and the Billposters working on the yard, he realised that he would have to paint the office himself, so he bought some paint, brushes and an overall.

Late on Sunday evening Everton inspected the transformation of the Hind Street premises, starting with the toilets. There would be a girl sharing this now, and newspaper cuttings for toilet roll were not acceptable. He put in a roll of proper toilet paper, borrowed from his Mum, and had an extra scrub of the pan.

Upstairs, Everton looked at the bright blue walls which appeared clean and clinical. Along one side of the square room he had put a long tall bench-type desk which he'd won at auction together with a typist's chair and desk, and a second-hand roll-top desk for himself. The only new thing was a four drawer steel filing cabinet; he'd already got a spare typewriter from the Liverpool office. On the floor was new lino which he'd tried to fix himself and had got into trouble, so he'd persuaded Sam to finish it off for him. He was proud of what he'd achieved in such a short time, and with Doreen at her desk on Monday, and the Morris Minor at the door, he would be in business, his first real job, and boss of a small empire spreading to as far as Chester and Holyhead.

At nine o'clock he waited for Doreen to arrive so he could brief her for the first day's work. At a quarter past nine she still had not arrived. He anxiously watched the double deck buses arrive in the Square, hoping to see a sight of her hurrying along. At nine thirty he lifted the receiver to ring Miss Townsend to ask her to send for Miss Bottom. While he was dialling he heard rapid steps come up the narrow stairs, and Doreen burst in on him, with an anxious, red face and un-brushed hair, wearing the shortest ever pelmet skirt. "Oh, I'm so sorry, Mr Smyth," she started, "you see…"

CHAPTER EIGHT

"Just hold it there, Doreen. I don't want any excuses or explanations. I will overlook it this once, and only once."

"Yes, of course Mr Smyth, I'm so sorry."

"It so happens I have an appointment in Preston at lunchtime, and I'm taking Sam, our Foreman, and as I have to leave very shortly I have that much less time to brief you."

"I'm so sorry, Mr – ."

"And stop saying 'you're sorry'. We've established that. Take your jacket off and I'll tell you as much as I have time for."

Everton showed Doreen to her desk and typewriter. He said, "If you have spare time practice your typewriting while I'm out; there's plenty of paper. Write a novel if you want to."

Doreen smiled for the first time and her previous penitent face lit up and Everton's mood lifted. He had time to show her the plan book on the big desk, and how to make bookings from the order, then left her the Oxydol Contract to mark up. Answer the telephone, 'Meadows and Sons, can I help you?' Take careful note of any calls and leave it on my desk. If any buyer comes in, find out what they want and leave a note of that too. Make them a cup of tea, and now I must fly," and as Everton ran down the stairs he yelled, "Toilet in the yard, pink toilet paper," then, "Sam, Sam, we're late, we've got to go now."

Sandy, curly haired Sam and Everton hurried away in the Minor and made for the tunnel. Everton joined the slow lane; it was always quicker. This first appointment was vital and he was looking forward to it. When he'd been out and about doing his survey, he'd noticed how well the local Preston Contractor had posted his bills. They were flat and clean, no smear marks on dark colours, and absolutely no creases. He'd called in at Preston Posters and talked to Roy who showed him their rolling machine, an idea poached from the Americans. He said that he was converting to an electric machine and Everton could have the old one. At that time he'd put the matter on his long finger, but when he'd heard that he was going to Birkenhead he'd raised the matter with Mr Colin. "I'd like the Birkenhead men to do rolled dry brush posting," he'd said. "Roy will let me have an old machine. He won't even charge us for it."

"Merseysiders don't like new ideas," Colin had said.

"No, you're thinking of Liverpudlian's, we across the water are more adventurous."

"And what does it matter how the posters go up? We get the same money however it's done."

"I agree, but buyers are already noticing the difference; if they can put more weight of bookings with Roy they will do. It's really a matter of dragging ourselves into the twentieth century. We've posted bills the same way for a hundred years, so isn't it time we modernised?"

"If it's not costing us anything, but if the Billposters go on strike, drop it."

Everton had smiled. He already knew a way of persuading them.

"Is that the new girl?" asked Sam as they sped out of the tunnel onto Scotland Road.

"Yes, it's Doreen. I'll introduce her to you all this evening."

"She's a bit of a good-looker."

"You should have seen the other one who got away," Everton said, and they both laughed, a bond between them beginning to form.

Roy showed them into his Bill Room. The machine stood at the short end of the Bill Room table. It consisted of a water trough and spindle which clamped the end of each poster sheet. With the electric motor engaged the sheet spun round through water, then the other sheets followed until there was a complete poster rolled, each roll resembling an oversized damp white cigar. Roy said the billposters started at the top left corner of a pre-pasted panel, unrolling and pressing in with a handle less dry brush. The water stretched the poster and so the sheets lay flat, with no smear marks or creases; it's also quicker.

Sam said, "Do you waste a billposter's time preparing the days work?"

"We don't use a billposter. Tim here has just left school and he'll do the job for a year, and then go out onto the streets billposting. At present he also mixes paste, sweeps the yard and makes the tea."

Sam continued, "If the machine you're letting us have has no electric motor, how does it work?"

"By foot pedal."

"Is that slower?"

"Much."

They arranged for Sam to collect the hand operated machine the next day by a hired van. On the way back to Birkenhead, Everton raised the matter of how they were going to introduce the scheme to the men. "I want *you* to try it first," Everton said, "We'll go out in the evening to some quiet spot. Till you've tried it you can't discuss it."

"Good idea."

"Tell you what, I'll have a go too."

"You?"

"Yes."

"You're Management. Have you ever posted a sixteen sheet in your life?"

"Never, and neither have you. This way we start evens."

"I don't like it; billposting is still a seven year apprenticeship; if any monkey can post them up where will experienced billposters come into it?"

"It's called progress, besides 'experience' is overrated. Billposters only spend five percent of their time billposting, and the rest of the time getting from site to site — you don't need any special skill to drive a van."

"You call it progress — it could also mean trouble."

"I think not. I already know how I'm going to sell it."

Doreen was ashamed of herself for being late. She had pinned everything on this job, a decent salary, financial independence, an interesting occupation and a dream of a boss. He'd looked even sexier when he'd been mad with her, but she couldn't always be late just to wind him up. Indeed, she hadn't intended to be late and it was all her fault. 'Sunday nights' are home nights, watching Gilbert Harding on 'What's my Line' on the telly — Pauleen had come round later and they'd chattered. Then she'd made herself some Horlicks but didn't wash her mug. After she'd gone to bed and fallen asleep her Mum had stormed into her room and demanded that she come to wash the offending mug and put it away. She'd refused and it had ended up in a shouting match, then of course it took her ages to get to sleep again, and in revenge her Mum did not tell her that she'd overslept. Her Mum better watch out or she'd withdraw the two pounds a week she was paying her out of her wages. She and Pauleen could always rent a flat together. It was after nine before she realised what the time was. She'd thrown her clothes on and dispensed with the lipstick — a nice short skirt would make up for that. She had run after the bus and had jumped on. She hoped that Mr Smyth might not be there, but he was. She'd enjoyed watching him trying to be cross; his ever grinning face just wouldn't make the required adjustments to signal anger, and all that happened was that he looked real sexy.

Her mind had been in a whirl while Mr Smyth had been explaining everything, but she'd tried to take it all in; then there was that funny remark about toilet paper, so she made it her first task to look for the toilet in the yard and inspect it. She was surprised to find the bog spotless, most unusual for men and there were seven of them here. They tended to miss if they were in a hurry and not bother to clean up afterwards. The toilet paper was pink, most unusual and hardly used. Mr Smyth must have put it there himself, bless him. Workmen didn't appear to mind wiping their bums with newsprint.

On the way back she noticed one or two of the billposters hovering around. Surely they should be on the road by now. They called out cheerfully, and one of them, Mike, had a query and asked if he could come up to sort it out. "I don't think I could help you yet," she said.

"Oh, I just want to check the plan book," he said.

"Come up then and have a look." He followed her up the steep stairs and she pressed her pelmet skirt well into her thighs. Best not to show them too much at this stage; Amanda would have had a field day here. Mike showed her his worksheet and pointed to a Persil over a Bovril on site number 117 on the Borough Road. "I don't think there's a Bovril there," he said. Together, they turned the pages of the plan book and found the site record. The instruction sheet was correct. Amazing, thought Doreen, she'd always taken for granted posters on hoardings, with never a thought as to how they got there, and here she was right in the centre of operations.

Doreen was just starting a bit of typing practice when the phone went. Nervously, she lifted the receiver and in as posh a voice as she could manage she said, "Good morning, Meadows & Son, how can I help you?"

A man's voice said, "This is Colin Meadows, is Everton there?"

"Gosh, I mean…golly…do you mean Mr Meadows of Meadows & Son?"

"Yes."

"Goodness, well what do you know."

"Well, is he?"

"Is he what?"

"In?"

"Who in?"

"Everton."

"Who?"

"Sorry, my mistake, is Mr Smyth in?"

"Sorry, he's gone out to Preston."

"Of course he has, I remember now. Are you Doreen?"

"Yes Sir."

"Are you settling in?"

"Yes, thank you."

"What have you been doing?"

"Looking for the toilet."

"Did you find it?"

"Yes, it's spotless."

"Anything else?"

"Anything else what?"

"Have you been doing anything else? Its ten thirty now."

"I've checked that there's a Persil to go over the Bovril on site number 117, Borough Road."

"Sounds interesting. I'll come over now and introduce myself."

"Golly, I mean, yes Sir."

Doreen was flustered. The man would want a cup of tea, and she hadn't tried to find the kettle, or located the biscuits yet.

In half an hour a big man appeared, squeezing up the narrow stairway. Doreen noticed that he eyed her interestingly, a glint in his eyes. "Well, that's something," he said, "last time I saw this room it was a wreck."

"I can still smell the paint," Doreen said. "Would you like a cup of tea?"

"Yes please."

Doreen boiled the kettle but could not find any biscuits. She would have to speak to Mr Smyth about that. Mr Colin drank his tea quickly and then shook hands with Doreen. He said, "I hope you'll be very happy here," then squeezed down the narrow stairway. Doreen noticed him stumping about the yard, and he went into the toilet, so he would discover the pink toilet paper.

Doreen was about to take a break for lunch when another man arrived up the stairway, a look-a-like Jimmy Edwards and he was sporting a handlebar moustache. "My name's Callahan," he said, "Is Mr Smyth in?"

"I'm afraid he's out for the day," Doreen replied.

"Oh dear, I want to book twenty forty-eight sheets for OXO. Can you help me?"

"I'm afraid that this is my first day. I don't know my way around yet."

"That the plan book?" and he eyed the big record book on the large desk.

"Yes."

"Well, let's go through it together; we can mark bookings in pencil."

"Would that be all right?" Doreen asked doubtfully.

"Of course it is. I've been booking from Mr Smyth in the Liverpool office for years. I understand the plan book; we can make pencil marks only in case Mr Smyth wants to alter it."

"Ok then."

Together, they went through the big book, and then Mr Callahan took out his Reservation pad and wrote down all the sites he'd booked. "Mr Smyth can confirm the prices," he said. "Thing is…the form is that I call to make a reservation, then someone takes me out to lunch. Have you got a petty cash box?"

She had and Doreen peered into it; there was a float of ten pounds. "That will do," Mr Callahan said gleefully. "Right, where shall we go?"

Doreen returned to the office at about four, slightly drunk but in rattling good form. She'd had two gin and tonic's and a brandy, but wasn't used to it. She put paper into the typewriter and attempted to write, 'Dear Sir, We are in receipt of your letter of the 5th Inst, Yours Sincerely.' It did not look quite right, so she tried again, and again, and then Mr Smyth and Sam arrived back from Preston. "Hope you haven't been bored?" he asked Doreen.

"I've had a smashing day," she said, and grabbed the desk to keep her balance.

"What have you been doing?"

"I've been to the toilet, then Mr Colin Meadows called for tea, then Mr Callahan came and gave me an order for twenty sites for OXO, and I took him out for lunch, and I think I had too much to drink. My typing has got worse and there's no money left in the petty cash box and I can't find any biscuits. What sort of a day did you have?"

It was Everton's turn to say, "Golly!"

CHAPTER NINE

DOREEN WAS ONLY SEVEN minutes late next day and she avoided apologising. Everton decided not to say anything. Seven minutes was not so bad, and it was clear that time keeping was Doreen's weak point and he'd have to put up with it. Otherwise Doreen appeared to be a star performer. The order for OXO was far bigger than expected, and it was clear that Mr Callahan had given them a generous share of the total order. There was no receipt for the lunch; Doreen said that it was more than ten pounds but Mr Callahan had paid the balance and kept the receipt. The crafty old beggar, thought Everton, he'd probably charge it up against his own company even though he hadn't even paid for it. Liverpool Office said that without a receipt the ten pounds would be disallowed, so Everton had made up the money himself. Doreen, bless her, said that she'd save up the amount out of her salary, but it might take a few months as she had to pay her Mum for her keep. It was a generous offer but one he couldn't accept; he'd winkle the money out of Mr Callahan, the old cadger, whenever he saw him next.

On the plus side, Mr Colin had rung to say how self assured Doreen was, and funny, whatever that meant. As Everton watched Doreen glide like a model across the office floor, he felt he'd made the right choice, so he put up with the smudges on her typing – it was what she did best!

That evening Everton introduced Doreen to the Billposters when they came in to clock off at five. He'd flunked showing Doreen off the night before; she wasn't really in a fit state then. As the meeting broke up there were one or two low key wolf whistles. Everton knew what they meant. It wasn't that Doreen was a ravaging beauty, it was just her smile and the way she moved. He was beginning to have his doubts about having employed her as it was a situation he might well find hard to handle. Miss Bottom would have been safer.

After everyone had dispersed, Sam and he struggled with the rolling machine, man handling it from the back of the van to the end of the billposting table. They then laid out two sixteen sheet Persils and successfully rolled them through water. Everton then got his overalls on and they drove off to Mill Road, Wallasey. Sam took one end of the hoarding and Everton the other, and both of them finished posting at about the same time. They stood back to admire their handiwork; it was then that Everton noticed that his poster wasn't quite straight, but otherwise it was faultless. "Any problems?" he asked Sam.

"I'm rather taking to this," Sam replied, "and I can imagine that when there is a strong wind blowing, which is nearly always, it would make it easier to control the sheets; they couldn't fly away."

The next morning the Billposters were astonished to find a strange machine in the Bill Room. "What is it?" they asked.

Everton replied, "Come in this evening half an hour early and I'll tell you."

At four thirty Sam gave a demonstration of rolling sixteen sheets through the machine, then Everton explaining the reasons for doing it, and how the rolled poster would be unrolled and posted on the hoarding. There were immediate objections, and Mike asked why the dry brush didn't have a handle, and how could you reach the bottom of the poster when the angle of ladder was against you. Everton replied, "It's a disadvantage for short armed billposters, but it's quite possible. With a handle you can't put the same pressure on rubbing the poster sheets in."

"Why can't you brush the poster in with the wet brush?" another asked.

"Because dried paste on top of dark colours show as smear marks."

Everton sensed that the mood was hostile, then Mike asked, "It's all very well for Management to tell us how to do a job, but Management have never posted a bill, so what do you know about it?" and then added, "Sir," as if to soften his anger.

Everton was grateful for Sam's immediate reply, "That's where you're wrong, Mate. Last night both myself and Mr Smyth posted sixteen sheets at Mill Road, Wallasey. I congratulate Mr Smyth on his effort. It's perfect, other than it's not straight, but perhaps after a seven year apprenticeship he might get that right?"

There were gasps and some laughter from the men, and Sam added, "We have Management here who is not afraid of getting his hands dirty."

Everton decided that this was the moment he would go in with the kill. He said, "I want you lot to show the way. Why is it that the Liverpool Billposters aren't doing it? I'll tell you, they're inferior to any Birkenhead man. I want you to try this, then I can boast to Mr Colin, 'Look what they've done in Birkenhead'; all the Liverpool Billposters would say is that 'it's an interference of working practices'". Everton knew full well about Liverpool and Birkenhead rivalries. The spell was broken at once, and the men agreed to give it a try. Those with wives who were not fussy about what time they came home took the bus to Mill Road, to see Everton's handiwork, and had a good laugh at the crooked poster.

Doreen had always found it hard work to get up in the morning. The alarm would go and she'd turn over onto her back and resolve to get up in five minutes time. She'd be just about to pull back the bedclothes when her Mum would bang on the door, shouting, "Get up then, you lazy sod." That did it. She wouldn't get up for that; another five minutes was nothing, but she'd fall asleep again, to be woken again by her Mum in ten minutes, then she would *have* to get up. On her second morning of work she had time for one piece of toast and a mouthful of lukewarm tea, and then was lucky enough to catch the bus as soon as she arrived at the stop. The clock in Central Square was a five minutes past, so she'd say nothing to Mr Smyth unless challenged, and then she'd say that the bus was late or had broken down – No, just 'late' sounded better.

Doreen felt sorry for Mr Smyth because he was being made to pay for her lunch with Mr Callahan. She hoped that she might have other opportunities for lunch out because she'd enjoyed that, but she'd be careful to hold onto the receipt next time.

Doreen soon fitted into the office routine. Mr Smyth appeared to work half the night, and first thing in the morning he left a pile of letters in his hand writing on her desk; they were so neat that Doreen felt that they should go out as they were, rather than have her mess them up by trying to type them. She still found typing a trial, and as she was getting so much practice she felt that continuing her studies at night school would be pointless, even though she'd promised Mr Smyth that she would. She wouldn't mention the subject unless Mr Smyth did, and he didn't.

At about eleven she would have finished her typing, so she'd make the tea, either for Mr Smyth and herself, or herself only if Mr Smyth was out; if he was she'd drop downstairs to see if Sam was about, which he frequently was, usually playing with that funny rolling machine they'd got from Preston. She liked Sam because he talked to her as equals; she was always very much aware that Mr Smyth was her boss, and unfortunately that would be the way it would have to stay. She would have liked to talk to him about his family, his hobbies and love life, if he had one which she doubted – he was always too busy. Although he wore smart clothes he was always a mess, suit well creased in the wrong places and crumbs and stains on it, and his hair hardly ever combed. There was one occasion when she had her own comb in her hand, and moved forwards to comb his hair straight, then realised what she was doing and drew back. She longed to straighten his tie, one end was so much longer than the other, and tuck the long piece into his trousers; but she always remembered her place, and slipping a hand into the top of his trousers was much too personal, and she giggled at the thought of it.

Doreen was always glad to get the typing part of her day over with because she so much enjoyed her other duties. Poster buyers came in frequently, and if Mr Smyth was out she would have to attend to them, and sort out their queries and mark in bookings. She'd now been given the job of writing up the instruction sheets to the billposters, and it was fun arranging their work in route order; her geography knowledge of Birkenhead and Wallasey improved daily. If the billposters had queries they would come up to sort it out. Once in a while she deliberately wrote down site numbers which didn't exist on Mike's list, then he would have to come up and see her and that was fun; they would exchange banter unless Mr Smyth was there.

She certainly did not feel Man Fridayish. There were always people trooping up the stairs, and sometimes the telephone never stopped, so there was always someone to talk to. But how she wished to have a meaningful relationship with her boss. She admired his commitment to the job, his loyalty to his employers, and his consideration of her dreadful typing, and patience with her inexperience. Above all else she wished she could get under his skin, to find out how he ticked and where his heart really lay. She promised herself that she'd do all that, in time, and she had plenty of that.

Everton had never felt so happy and confident. To hell with the Sales Management job. Here, he was King. He had his own office and staff, six billposters and a secretary, not to mention the gleaming Morris Minor at the door, but he was also getting results. He had already achieved the impossible. Sam and his merry men had discovered the benefits of rolled dry brush posting; Mr Colin had been amazed at the transformation of the billposting appearance, neat and flat posters and no smears, and the apparent ease with which he controlled his staff and commanded their loyalty. But Everton's real success was in site acquisition. For many years his employers and opposition had put all their effort into Liverpool, Bootle and Waterloo, that side of the Mersey. Everton was working in virgin territory, and he appreciated Colin's wisdom in starting up a branch in Birkenhead, so near to Liverpool, but because of the river was considered by most as being far away. He discovered countless little pieces of land, good for nothing other than hoardings, and gable ends exposed by blitz damage and demolition. The planning department at Birkenhead Town Hall was flooded with applications; to Everton it was all as easy as falling off a log.

When Everton wasn't totally captivated by the job in hand, he silently and unobtrusively watched Doreen, her movement across the floor to the filing cabinet, like how he imagined a model would move; her sudden consideration like producing a cup of tea when he needed it but hadn't asked, and biscuits to go with it, bought out of her own money. At times he noticed her look at him in a motherly sort of way, and on one occasion she moved towards him with a comb and he was sure she was going to use it on him, and then she drew back and combed her own hair instead. Another time, when she was standing in front of him, she lifted the long end of his tie, and he was sure that she was going to tuck it into his trousers, then she let go of it, muttering, "You need to tidy up a bit if you're going to see the Planning Officer." He could have taken that as a slur, as an invasion of employer/employee relationships, but he accepted it as a friendly gesture. In truth he would have liked her to tuck in his tie, and he was beginning to feel it hard to keep his hands off her; he wondered whether she felt the same way? The trouble was she was an employee. He would have to watch himself.

Amid such mixed emotions Everton got an opportunity of a lifetime, a chance to prove that he was a cut above everyone else. Mr Colin Meadows had sent out a circular to all Branch Managers, advising them that there was now an opportunity to acquire advertising sites from the National Rail Authority. In Great Britain, roads cross railways in all urban areas, creating natural opportunities for advertising hoardings, also, there were bits and pieces of 'left over' railway property suitable only for advertising sites. Most of these opportunities had already been taken up, but there were still a lot which hadn't been. Here was a cry of help from the National Rail Authority to maximise this source of revenue, and it was to be done on the basis of the early bird catches the worm. It was up to the Contractors to find the sites and apply. Mr Colin had said, "We need to identify such locations, photograph them and prepare the required plans. It is a case of first come, first served. Get out into your areas and get looking; let me have full details and speed is vital."

Doreen was late again, seriously late. Mr Smyth was at his desk, fuming. "I've said very little about your timekeeping, Doreen, because you've been so useful to me, but this has to stop. Have you a problem?"

"Problem?"

"Yes, problem. Can you not get out of your bed in the morning? Have you an alarm clock? Does it work?"

"Oh, I see…I have a clock, but I go to sleep again after it's buzzed."

"For God's sake, if you're that tired you must go to bed late. What time do you do that?"

"About midnight, but if it's after a dance at Sealand, about three."

"Sealand?"

"Yes, the American base there; they have dances which run late, but there's transport provided back to Liverpool and Birkenhead."

"And then you get back at three?"

"Yes."

"You'll have to make up your mind, Doreen, either you give Sealand up or give your job up."

"Oh, I can't do that."

"Can't what?"

"Give Sealand up. I have a boyfriend, you see, an American. I could lose Hank if I didn't go to all the dances."

"And if you don't, you'll lose your job."

"Mr Smyth, I promise, I really promise, I'll not be late again."

"How can you promise that?"

"I'll get up when my Mum bangs on the door."

"And don't you anyway?"

"No."

"Why?"

"It's the way we are. I don't like being bullied."

Everton suddenly roared with laughter and the tension was eased. Doreen allowed a little snigger to escape.

"Are things that bad between you and your Mum?" he asked.

"Oh no, we just understand each other."

"I don't want to pry into your domestic life, Doreen, but just at the moment I have something serious to do, and I'll need your help."

"Yes?"

"I have a big job tomorrow. I have to cover the whole of our area including Chester and North Wales, taking photographs and doing plans; I'll need you to hold the other end of the measuring tape, and to rush into Town Halls and take tracings of their road maps. We'll be out all day, on the move all the time, no time for meals, you'd have to take sandwiches. Can you come with me?"

Doreen's mood picked up at once. What an opportunity, in a Morris Minor all day, with Handsome here – all day! "Of course I can, Mr Smyth. I'd like that."

"I can't afford to be late. I'll pick you up at home and you'll need to reset your alarm clock."

"Reset? To what?"
"Six o'clock!"

CHAPTER TEN

DOREEN KNEW THAT THERE wasn't any point in asking her Mum for sandwiches. She didn't do them. She did a hot meal once a day, usually in the early evening; if Doreen wasn't there at the proper time she did without, and as her social life came first she frequently did without; she therefore lived on Mars Bars and bottles of ginger pop.

"Can you bang on my door at six tomorrow morning?" Doreen asked her mother.

"What time?"

"Six."

"What on earth for?"

"Mr Smyth wants me for a big job; it'll take a full day."

Doreen's Mum's attention was immediately alerted. "All day did you say?"

"Yes."

"How much overtime will you be paid?"

"Meadows' don't pay overtime"

"Then don't do it."

"Mum, this is part of my job, it has to be done."

"The buses don't even run at that hour, do they?"

"Mr Smyth is picking me up, at six thirty."

"And will he be banging on the front door?"

"No need, I'll be waiting for him."

"And how are you going to get yourself up at that hour?"

"You're going to bang on my bedroom door at six."

"Let Mr Smyth pay me compensation, then I'll think about it."

Doreen set her alarm for six. She couldn't rely on her Mum to cooperate, so she went to bed early, but because she was so excited she couldn't get to sleep. Eventually, in the early hours, she nodded off. It seemed like only minutes before the alarm went off. She couldn't trust herself to rest for five or ten minutes, so she got up at once and made herself a cup of tea and some toast. With five minutes in hand she was outside the main door, carrying her Mars Bar and fizzy drink in a paper bag. With two minutes to go Mr Smyth came round the corner, and without the need for him to honk she waved him down, and she jumped into the front passenger seat, practically before the car had stopped.

Doreen wasn't sure what was expected of her. She thought that the whole exercise might amount to a leisurely drive into the country, an opportunity to get to know each other, and a picnic beside the road. It was not long before she grasped the magnitude of the task, and they soon combined into a team. They first sought potential advertising sites on railway property, and then they measured up, Doreen holding the other end of the measuring tape. In Chester they both called at the Council Offices, and Mr Smyth showed Doreen how to take tracings from the street maps of the plots they'd identified; later Doreen did that job on her own while Mr Smyth drew up sketches and took photographs on location. After he'd done that he went back to collect Doreen, then they went on to the next town.

After Chester they moved to Wrexham to repeat the process. They motored at breathless speed up to Queensferry and the Flintshire coast, then followed the coastline all the way to Caernarfon, Mr Smyth pressing his foot hard on the accelerator; the Morris Minor tried hard to respond, chugging up the steeper hills flat out in second gear. Doreen was longing for a piddle, but they didn't seem to pass any conveniences. Along a country lane, Mr Smyth suddenly stopped, and getting out of the car muttered, "A man has to do what a man has to do," then disappeared into a field, presumably to relieve himself. Doreen needed no second invitation and got out at her side of the car, hitched her skirt up, pulled her pants down and then relieved herself. She was still in a crouched position when Mr Smyth returned, at the run. He got in on his side of the car, and without any hesitation started up and roared off, leaving Doreen still crouching.

Horrified, Doreen stood up and yelled. Mr Smyth did not hear and the Minor quickly disappeared round the next bend. Doreen felt like bursting into tears, but then began to see the funny side of things. She wondered how long it would be before Mr Smyth realised that she wasn't there. In a couple of minutes the car returned, with a screech of brakes as it rounded the bend.

"God, I thought I'd lost you, what were you doing? We haven't time to look for wild flowers," he shouted.

"I was doing the same as you."

"Why didn't you say?"

"You didn't exactly give me much opportunity," Doreen replied.

After a pause they both burst out laughing. From then on they both became more relaxed with each other, and after leaving Rhyl Mr Smyth pulled in to the side of the road for lunch. He produced what appeared to Doreen to be two rounds of egg sandwich, "made by my Mum", he said, and added, "What have you got?"

Doreen produced her Mars Bar and a bottle of fizz.

"Is that all?" Mr Smyth asked.

"That's it. Have you a bottle opener?"

"Sorry. Is that all you've got to drink?"

"Yes."

"In that case you can have some of my tea; I've a spare mug."

"Oh, I couldn't, I - ."

"And take one of my sandwiches." Doreen looked longingly at the moist and fresh sandwich. "I will if you'll have half my Mars Bar," she said.

"It's a deal."

They proceeded with their mini feast, then Doreen, wondering what to say to her boss with whom she normally only talked business, said, "You're a very good driver."

"I like driving."

"What else do you like?"

"I like getting up early in the morning, walking along the prom 'til I can see the sun rise over the Welsh hills."

"Have you any hobbies? Football or something, girls even?" Doreen dared to ask.

"I've not had much time for girls."

"You must have fancied someone by now, someone you've seen, perhaps not talked to...yet?"

"I'm a man, I fancy nearly every young girl – unless they're ugly."

"Am I ugly?"

Mr Smyth's face reddened and he turned to face her. "Why did I choose you out of the three I interviewed?" he asked, "it wasn't for your typing."

"You didn't, you chose Amanda," Doreen snapped back, "and it wasn't because of her typing." They both laughed loudly.

This was the longest conversation they'd had all morning, and now it was time to move off because the Council Offices in Colwyn Bay would have had their lunches, and they would be able to get in now.

They finished up in Caernarfon at about five thirty, and then Doreen said, "Do we do Holyhead?" She reckoned that if they went further there

wouldn't be time to return that night, so they would have to book into a
hotel, and that would be interesting.

"No point in going further, Doreen, it would be too far for the billposters, and we haven't got any sites there to add to. We'll make for home
now; I reckon we've done enough for one day, and you've been splendid."

Doreen blushed, then settled down into her seat; she was dead beat
and felt sleepy, so perhaps she might be able to nod off for a bit. Well, that
was her intention but her companion started to drive like she imagined
a racing driver in a Grand Prix did. She had seldom been in a car before.
Hank didn't have one and neither did her Mum; her only experience was
in taxis, and this was no taxi. She was sure that Mr Smyth was a good
driver, but perhaps it would be better if she stayed awake. It was only a
little car, but he overtook everything on the road. Doreen noticed that
as soon as he came up behind a heavy lorry he would drop back, then at
the start of a straight piece of road he would charge, so by the time he
reached the lorry's back end he was doing twice it's speed. "Why do you
do that?" she asked.

"I have very little acceleration," he replied.

They arrived back in Hind Street at about seven thirty. They called
in at the office in case Sam had left them any notes, but there were none.
Mr Smyth asked, "Can I give you a lift home?"

"Yes please."

"Will your Mum have a meal ready for you?"

"You're joking."

"What are you going to eat? Surely not another Mars Bar?"

"Probably."

Doreen hoped that she hadn't sounded as if she was begging, but
even so the next question took her by surprise.

"You've worked hard all day, Doreen, and you must be starving. Let's
go out for a meal together; we could try The Victoria in New Brighton."

"Oh, I couldn't afford that, Mr Smyth."

"Don't be silly, Doreen, I'm treating you. It'll be a pleasure."

"On expenses, like?"

"No, Meadows' don't do that, only customers."

"You could say I was Mr Callahan."

"I could, Doreen, but it wouldn't be the same. I want to treat you."

"I'm not dressed up," Doreen continued, now nervous about the unexpected night out with her Boss.

"Neither am I."

Doreen paused, and then said, "I would like that very much."

"Would you do something for me, Doreen?"

"What?"

"When we leave the office now, could you call me 'John', just for the evening, like?"

"John?"

"Yes."

"Not Everton?"

"You can call me Everton in the morning, everybody else does."

"Ok Johnny."

Everton had been so wrapped up in the job in hand, he hadn't noticed what Doreen was wearing. He now saw that she had one of her pelmet skirts on, navy blue with a frill at the bottom; then he noticed that she'd had lipstick and makeup on which she'd never had before and which she now wished to renew. Standing in front of the small mirror above the sink in one corner of the office, she now applied more lipstick. Then, in exasperation she looked at her feet; her cheap outdoor shoes were caked in mud, as a result of plodding about on plots of North Welsh turf, while holding the other end of the measuring tape. "I can't go like this," she said, "just look at my feet."

"I can call at your house if you want a change of footwear, if you like," Everton said, "and you could get me a change of shoes and all."

"You don't matter, you're a man; they're expected to be dirty."

They briefly called at Doreen's house, time enough for her to change to high heeled evening wear, and she put on a clean blouse and left the top three buttons undone. In a flash she'd become most attractive and sophisticated looking. Everton's heart beat quickly.

They entered the main dining area of The Victoria, with dimly lit little tables surrounding a small dancing area. Everton was determined that before the evening was out, he would dance with her, holding her tightly around her waist; there was bound to be a slow romantic tune, and if there wasn't he would ask the band himself.

They ordered a meal, Everton helping out with a translation from the French. Doreen said that she was sticking with something she knew, tomato soup and a steak with chips. Everton couldn't be bothered to choose so he ordered the same and a bottle of red wine.

Everton made the first move towards familiarity. "This is amazing," he said, "to have you here on your own, away from Billposters and lecherous Poster Buyers." The wine was talking.

"But you'd rather have Amanda, wouldn't you?" Doreen teased.

"Not now. Amanda was striking, but perhaps she's a dumb blonde; you've got character."

"What sort of character?"

"You're chatty, you use your initiative, and you - ," and Everton hesitated.

"Go on."

"No, I can't."

"Yes, you can," and Doreen gently laid her hand on his wrist. Everton's heart beat faster again. He was on a roll; well, he'd let it continue and something good might emerge.

"It's the way you move," Everton said.

"Move?"

"Yes."

"How?"

"When you walk from your desk to the filing cabinet, you don't walk or run, you float, head held high, like a model; it's most sexual."

Doreen giggled, so perhaps she was enjoying the wine too. "I shall never get up from my desk again," she said.

"I shall make you by asking for things from the filing cabinet, then you'll have to."

"Here I was trying every day to look my best so that you'd notice me, and you were doing that all the time."

"Are you pleased?"

Ignoring the last question Doreen said, "This is nice music, are you going to ask me to dance?"

"Of course."

They got up and Everton held her gently, Doreen resting her head on his shoulder. He moved his hands around her waist and they smooched, barely moving on the crowded dance floor, neither of them saying anything. Everton wished that Doreen would pull her head away so that he could look into her eyes and maybe get some kind of message, and give her a light kiss. Other partners were also being amorous; it was that sort of place, so everything was being made easy for them. But Doreen was content the way they were, and only too quickly the band ended the music with a flourish, indicating they were going to take a break, and for the moment the magic was over.

When they returned to their table Doreen became talkative. She seemed reluctant to talk about her family, but kept on asking about Everton's. Everton steered her back to her life and he again asked about her Mum. He said, "If the two of you are on your own, you must have become very close; it's the way it is with me and my Mum anyway."

"My Mum doesn't care less about me."

"But she loves you," Everton said.

"Does she?"

"She must, every mother does. Does Hank love you?"

"Hank is a forbidden subject."

"Why?"

"It's personal."

"Do you love Hank?"

"I said it's personal."

"Sorry."

After that the evening became a little strained, and Doreen was less willing to open up. When they'd finished eating and drunk all the wine, Doreen said, "This has been lovely, but can you take me home now, Johnny?"

They were silent in the car. When they reached the terraced house in Claughton, Everton took her to her front door. "Thank you ever so, Mr Smyth," she said.

They stood facing each other. Her face was held towards his. Everton was in a torment. Was it too soon? Did he dare kiss her, and if he did would she think that he was taking advantage of an employer/employee relationship? Tomorrow, would she think that he'd given her too much to drink so as to obtain easy favours? While he hesitated she drew back a little and held out her hand and he took it; on an impulse he held it to his face and kissed it. She giggled, then turned to put her key in the door and was gone. 'Johnny' had vanished into the night and Mr Smyth had returned.

CHAPTER ELEVEN

DOREEN HAD WANTED TO slip quietly into bed, but her Mum was waiting for her. "What time do you call this?" she asked.

"Late," Doreen replied.

"Have you been with this Mr Smyth, working, all this time?"

"That's right."

"God, he's some slave driver. Are you going to take tomorrow off?"

"No."

"Well, your supper's all dried up; it *was* a lovely stew, but you'll eat it all the same, now."

"Mum, you never keep my supper, so why now? Anyway, I've eaten."

"What have you eaten?"

"You're not going to rest 'til I tell you - we've had a long day, all the way out to Caernarfon and back. Mr Smyth let me have one of his egg sandwiches. It was late when we got back so he took me out for a meal at The Victoria in New Brighton, then he ran me home. Satisfied?"

Doreen's Mum sat down, almost as if the account had exhausted her. She said, "The Victoria's posh; it's not for the likes of us. Is he having it off with you?"

"No, Mum."

"Did he kiss you?"

"No Mum, and now I'm going to bed."

"Where does this all leave Hank?"

"Mum, Mr Smyth is my boss, Hank is my boyfriend, now Goodnight."

Doreen didn't bother to wash, or even set the alarm. She peeled off her clothes and left them in a heap on the floor. She was exhausted physically and confused mentally. She shivered under the bedclothes until she warmed up, and pondered her Mum's last remark. Where does this leave Hank? She'd been courting him for six months now, and she'd recently been wondering where the relationship was going. Americans usually proposed after three months, and Hank had not made any commitment. He said he loved her and she believed him. Did she love him? She didn't know. What was love? To her, it was a free passage to The States, the land of plenty, a modern home and all the little luxuries of life, an end to the dismal Merseyside and England, lack of money and tolerating shortages. Hank had plenty of money and was generous, frequently giving her unexpected presents. He talked of Iowa and his home town, but never said anything about taking her there one day. Perhaps if she got pregnant that would force the pace, but Hank had never done anything much more than kiss, and she was still a virgin; his kissing was fantastic, but she didn't have much to compare it with. She quite fancied him even though he was small and had a large nose; he could have been a Jew but he said that he was an atheist. She'd recently considered dumping him, but there weren't any other unattached Americans at the camp and Hank was her passport to the social functions. Now Mr Smyth had brought a new dimension to her life.

She fancied Mr Smyth. She thought him clever and he'd probably go to the top. She admired his kindness and tolerance towards her, and he was her type physically, just like an untidy and cuddly teddy bear. The fact that he was her boss made it difficult for either of them to move towards each other romantically, so what was going to happen? She'd given him an opportunity to kiss her, and she sensed him waver and she'd drawn away; it could have spoilt their working relationship, and it was enough to know that he'd wanted it.

She didn't care that she'd overslept, and it was a quarter past ten when she got to the office. Of course Mr Smyth was already there, making finished drawings of yesterday's work; he could well have been there all night! "It's a bit late, Doreen," he said.

"I'm sorry, I was tired after yesterday and I overslept."

"Yes, you did well, but let's get back to normal now, and that means in by nine, at the latest. And there's another thing, a letter from Mr Colin this morning, complaining about your typing. Are you still doing that evening course?"

Doreen's heart sank; she hadn't been for a month and it was so boring. She blushed and said, "I've let that slip a bit, I'm afraid."

Mr Smyth looked hard at her and Doreen felt embarrassed. She hoped that he wasn't going to make an issue of it. After a long pause Mr Smyth said, "That's not good enough, Doreen. You go back to evening classes and I'll check that you have. If your typing doesn't improve you'll have to go. Do you understand?"

Doreen understood only too well, and tears started to form. She'd weep buckets if she didn't get a grip of herself. "Yes, Mr Smyth," she stammered and turned to his notes on her desk.

Everton felt pleased with himself after he'd dropped Doreen off at her home. Pleased with the day's work, pleased with the way Doreen had helped him, pleased with her company, and above all pleased that he'd resisted doing what he'd wanted – to grip her round the waist and give her a long kiss. He knew that she'd wanted it, but at the moment that was enough. She worked for him, that was all. Let's just see how things develop.

Everton's Mum was waiting for him. "What on earth have you been doing all day, son. You said you'd be late, but not this late. I've a cold supper ready for you, so I'll switch on the kettle now."

"Sorry, Mum. I've eaten already, but I'd like a cup of tea."

"Eaten? Where?"

"At The Victoria in New Brighton."

"The Victoria? That posh place? What on earth did you do that for? You know I can always cook you something, whatever the time."

"Doreen's Mum is not as considerate as you so I took her out; it was more for her benefit than mine."

"Doreen? The girl who works for you?"

"The same."

"That was spoiling her a bit, wasn't it?"

"She deserved it. She's been most useful all day."

"Son, Doreen works for you. It's not right that you should get too close to her. You might have given her all sorts of ideas."

Everton was irritated by his Mum's old fashioned standards, so he replied, "And what if it did? I like her. I enjoy her company."

"I hope you didn't kiss her or anything silly. I want you to have a girlfriend and you're far too backward in that department; but choose your own sort, for God's sake."

"Mum, I said I enjoy her company. I didn't say I'd proposed. Well, not yet anyhow," and he chuckled.

"Oh, stop teasing me, son. Seriously, keep your distance, and next time you keep Doreen late, let Doreen's Mum feed Doreen."

Everton went to bed with a tired mind, so he didn't sleep. Perhaps it had not been so clever to have had Doreen out with him all day. He was getting far too fond of her. If only she didn't work for him, they would be able to take their relationship to its natural conclusion, whatever his Mum might think of her not being his sort. He'd never had a steady girlfriend;

he'd always felt uneasy in female company. Whenever he'd been attracted to a girl he'd go through the same procedure as on his first date; take her out for a meal, to The Victoria perhaps, then on the next occasion go to the cinema together, and as a last resort to The Plaza Ballroom, but his dancing was terrible. By then, he would have a sense that the girl was becoming bored with his company; no wonder, because his entire life was centred on his Mum and his work. Sometimes he'd kiss the girl in the back row of the upper circle, but there were never many opportunities – he'd lacked a car, until now. What he liked about Doreen was that she wasn't his usual sort, and he'd got used to exchanging light banter with her, rather than having a serious conversation. He'd like to sweep her off her feet; he'd like to take her out for another meal, and afterwards to the big car park at Seacombe where the courting couples gathered, where they'd scramble into the back seat of the Minor...Dream on!

Everton was not surprised that Doreen was late, but he was irritated by her considering it excusable because of the work done the day before. He was also worried about the letter he'd received from Mr Colin, enclosing a selection of badly typed letters from Birkenhead Office. They were pretty terrible. Mr Colin did not mince his words, either Doreen would have to improve her typing or she'd have to go. Then, when he'd found that Doreen had been skipping her evening classes, he was both sad and angry. The magic of the day before, and in particular the evening before, had vanished. What a mercy he hadn't kissed her.

Everton was desperate to prove himself, faster and more successful than any of the other managers, so producing his railway site schedule first was essential. But could he trust Doreen to do the typing? He could not. He would have to do it himself, on two fingers. Doreen was typing away on some internal mail, so the first priority was to get her off the typewriter onto some other mundane task. "I want you to go down to the Bill Room and help Sam," he said to her.

"But I've got this typing to do, Mr Smyth," she said to him.

"You can do that later."

"I might not have the time."

"Then you'll have to make the time," Everton snapped.

Doreen's face dropped. She'd no makeup on and her complexion was pale. She looked disappointed. "What am I to do downstairs?" she asked.

"Help Sam arrange the sheets for the next rolling."

"I am not employed to do that," she said.

"You were employed," Everton said, "amongst other things, to type and you can't. You won't even try, and you've given up evening classes in favour of Hank, so you can now go downstairs. Do I make myself clear?"

That seemed to do the trick. Doreen got up without any further word and started to put the cover over the typewriter.

"And you can leave that, I've got some typing to do."

"But I can do that," Doreen said.

"I wish you could," Everton snapped again.

Doreen hurriedly left the room, and Everton noticed that she was beginning to sob, so he felt bad.

For seven hours Everton typed. Many sheets had to be discarded and he was surrounded by scrumpled up paper. Doreen came up at five o'clock to put her coat on and leave, but saw the chaos. "Please let me try," she said, "anyway, what's the hurry?"

"The hurry, Doreen, is that I have to be first, and just at the moment I can't trust you."

Doreen appeared to be overcome. She swayed on her feet, then the tears came and she blubbered, "I've let you down, I know I have, I'm so, so sorry."

Everton relented, and moved towards her, and without hesitation, put his arms around her and held her tightly.

"Please stop crying," he said, "it's just that I'm wound up and I want to do this right, and quickly. I felt that I couldn't rely upon you."

"I know, I know," Doreen said, "I'll sign up again for that class, to-night, and I will really try, I know I will."

"I know you will, too."

"And now I'll make you a cup of tea," Doreen said.

Mr Colin Meadows prided himself on keeping a pulse on his Managers, their strengths and weakness'. To do that he had to communicate, and Colin used Saturday mornings for that. The company had not yet adapted to a five day week, a habit now creeping into the commercial world. Only Civil Servants worked a five day week; Saturday mornings had therefore become a bit of a farce, employees arriving late and leaving at mid-day. Most of the time was taken up with a prolonged coffee break in the café up the road, sometimes with clients and sometimes without.

Colin had been determined to make Saturdays count, so he allocated the time to seeing his out-of-town Managers by rotation, two Managers per Saturday morning, one at ten and the other at eleven. For this particular Saturday Everton had the early slot, to be followed by Cyril Watson of Manchester.

Everton arrived at ten sharp, and Colin was ready for him. "What have you got for me this morning?" he asked.

"You know the work you asked us to do on Railway sites?" Everton asked.

"I do. Have you made a start?"

Everton didn't speak. He had not brought his usual small brief case, but in its place he bent down to the floor to open a suitcase he had brought in and which Colin had wondered about, and thought that perhaps he might be going away for the weekend? Everton produced a thick pile of plans and pages of neatly typed schedules. "What on earth is this?" Colin asked.

"I've completed the task. These are the plans and detailed lists."

"Completed?"

"Yes."

"You can't have, there must be months of work here."

"It's kept us busy this week, but it's done and Doreen helped."

"God Almighty, is this it?"

"It is."

Colin started to browse through the plans and photographs. Many of the locations were know to him because they were on the route to his family cottage in North Wales. "I don't understand," he said, "did you do all of this work on your own?"

"Doreen helped."

"Yes, the typing seems to have been improved. I take it all back."

Colin put the documents to one side and looked at Everton. This young man never ceased to surprise him. It had been an impossible task and yet he'd done it. Everything he touched turned to gold, and in the fullness of time he would have to be rewarded. He was sad that he'd not produced a male heir to take over the business, and so when the time came a stranger would have to do it. He hoped that it would be Everton.

Colin said, "When I have time I will look at all this in detail before sending it away; in the meantime let me just say, well done lad, and now send Cyril up to me."

"A top of the morning to you, Sir," said Cyril breezily.

"What makes you in such a good mood?" Colin asked.

"Well, I'm making good progress with the Railway schedule," he said.

"Where is it?"

Cyril paused and looked at Colin in amazement. "Well," he said, "I didn't exactly say that I had completed it. That would have been impossible."

"What have you done, then?"

"I was at Hyde and Glossop on Tuesday and noticed five locations. I shall have the plans ready next week."

"And?"

"I noticed a couple of sites south of Manchester."

"And?"

"I'm hopeful of producing quite a list."

"Hopeful?"

"Yes."

"But nothing you can show me yet?"

"Well," Cyril laughed, "that would be impossible, given the time it takes."

"Impossible?"

"Yes."

Colin then slowly pushed over to Cyril, Everton's huge pile of plans, and then said, "When I ask for something I expect action, not blarney. And top of the morning to you too."

CHAPTER TWELVE

ON LEAVING THE LIVERPOOL Office, Everton felt elated. Driving through the tunnel he smiled when wondering about the reception Cyril would now be getting from Mr Colin, who would be showing off his plans to prove that the impossible is possible; news would then travel fast through the managerial ranks, and wise ones would be saying, 'You watch Everton, he'll go far.' With those thoughts uppermost in his mind the Minor popped out of the tunnel and there, immediately in front of him, was a disaster. On the gable end facing exiting traffic from the tunnel was a large forty eight sheet panel advertising Jaguar, 'Grace, space and pace' it said clearly. Above the panel was marked 'Rogan Sites', their hated competitor.

How could this be so? Three months ago he'd called on the owner and made an offer for the space, but it had been clearly rejected – 'Over my dead body' he'd said. Everton parked the Minor at the bottom end of Borough Road and walked back to the site. The gable was above a hardware store owned by a Mr Williams, and Everton now remembered how hostile he'd been. He'd said that if any sign went up there it would be for himself. He'd been quite rude about it.

Everton went straight into the shop, a large chip on his shoulder. He asked the girl for Mr Williams and the girl said, "Oh, Mr Williams has left, he's sold the business to Mr Jeffries." So that was it! The property had been sold, and the Rogan man had been lucky enough to call after the event. "Do you want to see Mr Jeffries?" the girl asked. Mindful of the need in the trade not to poach each others' sites, he'd replied, "No thank you, you've already told me what I had wanted to know."

Everton went back outside to look at the little triangle of land joining the gable, then realised that to post and maintain the poster panel, Rogans would need access. After spending the best part of an hour he found the owner of the land, a Jim Webster who owned a paint shop in Borough Road. "I owned all the way down the street at one time," he said, "but I sold off a bit at a time, and I could never get any offer other than peanuts for that piece. Why do you enquire?"

Everton felt that he would have to proceed carefully, and not reveal that he wished to control the access. "I want somewhere to park my car," he lied, and then added, "It's so difficult to find anywhere now."

"You'd need not to get in the way of Rogans when they post their panel," he said.

"Oh, I didn't notice that, have they a wayleave?"

"No way, I'd never put that sort of impediment in the way of me selling. I just turn a Nelson's eye in the Rogan's direction." This was just the sort of news Everton had wanted to hear. "How much do you want for it?" he now dared to ask.

"Five hundred pounds and it's yours."

"Three hundred pounds," Everton said.

"Oh, you're one of them. Tell you what, four hundred pounds and that's an end of the conversation."

"Done."

Everton did not know where he'd get four hundred pounds from. He certainly couldn't involve Meadows and reveal what he was up to, as it broke the code of standards agreed between poster contractors. This was a personal matter, and once he had the land he'd enclose it with un-climbable fencing and a locked gate, and put up a notice saying 'Private parking, no access.' He would put the Minor there for as long as possible in case Rogan's tried to get over the fence. When Rogan's found that the site was useless to them they'd have to give it up; at that point he'd see Mr Jeffries and take the site for Meadows. If Mr Jeffries didn't play ball he would erect a panel on the land. He held all the best cards. He decided to ask his Mum for the money and so went straight home to seek her out.

"Mum, I need a favour," Everton asked.

"What is it?"

"I want to borrow four hundred pounds; it's an investment and I haven't got the capital."

"Investment in what? You're a man of substance now, a new improved salary and a company car. You must be flying?"

"Something has come up in business, and I need the money quickly."

"Business? Then Meadows must pay."

"Meadows doesn't know anything about it."

Everton's Mum paused and looked hard at her son, as if she didn't like anything he was saying. "Is that wise?" she asked.

"Not unwise, it's complicated."

"Is it legal?"

"Absolutely. Can I tell you about it?"

"Would rather not know, particularly if there's something funny about it, but you can have the money because I trust you. Do you want a cheque? I'll have to get it out of the Halifax."

"No, you'll need to pay a solicitor; you're buying a plot of land which will pay you a rent, it will have a better return than in the Halifax."

"Why are you doing this son?"

"I think I'd better tell you, it's to buy a piece of land down by the tunnel exit. I need it as access to a poster site."

"That's business, so why isn't Meadows doing it?"

"I don't want Meadows to know anything about it, only that they'll be paying you for access."

"I don't really understand and I don't want to try, as long as it's legal and you don't get into trouble over it, like."

"Perfectly legal, Mum, and thanks a lot."

Doreen found that the evening class was now oversubscribed, and there was no room for her. They said that she could start again at Easter, so she put her name down. If Mr Smyth asked her about it she'd be able to show that she was trying. But she couldn't afford to upset her boss anymore now, so she'd be early for once.

On her way she noticed something strange at the bottom of Borough Road, a gleaming forty-eight sheet panel of Rogan's advertising Jaguar. Now, that was very odd. She knew that Mr Smyth had been refused the site, so what was going on? As soon as she'd got to the office she looked up the file and found that her memory was correct.

"Mr Smyth?" Doreen said to attract his attention.

"Doreen, nobody calls me that. You may as well call me Everton, everybody else does."

Doreen was amused, so she cleared her throat and started again. "Everton?"

"Yes, Doreen."

"That site at the bottom of Borough Road, the one they refused you, there's a Rogan panel on it now."

"I know, Doreen."

"Why did they refuse you then?"

"The property has changed hands. A Mr Jeffries owns it now. The Rogan man had the luck to call in just as Mr Jeffries was moving in."

"It's not fair, Everton, and you tried so hard."

"I suppose we win some and lose some. But it won't be there for long. I happen to know that he'll lose his access."

Doreen only half heard because her mind was rushing ahead and she thought that she might be stumbling on something clever.

"So if you had known that the property was being sold, you'd have called in again?"

"Of course."

"Suppose," Doreen said, "you had a register of all the sites you'd been refused?"

"No point, I know them all anyway."

"Yes, but suppose you write to all of them once every three months, checking whether they might have changed their minds, or something?"

"If they've turned me down before they'll turn me down again."

"But that doesn't matter, if the man has died or moved on, or something, the postman will return your letter marked – 'Gone away', wouldn't they?"

Everton began to see what Doreen was driving at. He said, "Or 'not known', then I would know that there was a change of owner. Bloody brilliant, Doreen, you're not just a pretty face, are you? I'll make up a register today."

"You don't have to," Doreen said, "I can do it from the Refusal File."

"Yes, and don't bother to type, your handwriting is better, but even if it's internal, try not to leave any smudge marks on it. I might want Mr Colin to look at it."

Everton was ready for Mr Colin when he rang, which he did a week later. "Everton," he said, "you're slipping, how did Rogans get their site at the tunnel entrance? I was horrified when I saw it yesterday. It hit me right between the eyes as I came out of the tunnel."

"Don't worry about it," Everton said.

"I am. We just must not miss out on any of these prestige sites like this one."

"It won't be there for long."

"Why?"

"He has no access, and shortly that will be refused to him."

"How do you know?"

"I know that the land in front is not owned by the owner of the gable. Rogans presumed that there wasn't a problem, but a friend of mine owns the land. She won't let them have access, but she'll let us have it."

"We can't take the panel over, you know what sort of problem that would lead to in the Trade Association."

"The new owner won't allow the panel to remain if Rogans are denied use and aren't paying rental. He'll put it on the open market, but we're the only ones with access."

"You mean we're the only ones who could take it? You never seem to miss anything, Everton. Wait 'til I tell Father."

They all piled into a crowded bar in Chester, and Doreen didn't like that, as she wanted to be alone with Hank, and he was much too interested in the redhead in the corner. At least Doreen had been sitting next to him, so she had an advantage, but why did she have to fight for his attention? She touched his leg gently and whispered into his ear, "Can't you and I go off alone somewhere? Anyway, I'm starving."

"Hey Baby, they're our friends, and we're having a great time."

"You may be but I'm not. I want to talk to you alone, anyway I'm hungry."

"Come on Baby, you can say what you want to me here, and I'll buy you some crisps."

"Hank, I want a serious conversation, in private."

"Serious, Babe. What could be serious? Well, you're not pregnant, certainly not by me."

That remark infuriated Doreen, and something snapped. She spat at him, "I'm going, and you can come if you want." She got up to go, unable to work out how she was going to get home, and she'd no money for a meal. But she was angry, so she stormed out. The others were being so noisy they didn't notice, except that little bitch of a redhead.

Hank ran after her, thank goodness. "Sorry Babe, I didn't think that you were being that serious. Let's go to the Red Dragon, they do quite a good bar meal there," he said.

Forgivingly, Doreen linked arms with him, and in silence they moved off to the pub. After they had got settled, Hank said, "What is it then, Baby, what do you want?"

"When are you going home and out of the army – tell me again, Hank?"

"No precise date yet, about a month, I think, but we'll have a lot of fun before then. I have next weekend off, and I was going to suggest that we went off to North Wales, somewhere, with you of course, Babe, stay the night."

"In a hotel?"

"Yeah, nothing but the best for you," and he winked.

"And you want to sleep with me?"

Hank burst out laughing. "Well, I won't be taking single rooms," he said.

"I'm a virgin," Doreen said.

"I thought you might be and there's a first time for everything."

"Do you want to make love to me?"

"Well if I don't soon, I'll be gone."

"Then what?"

"What do you mean, Babe?"

"Will you just vanish, out of my life, or do you care more than that for me?"

"Babe, we'll be thousands of miles apart, what can we do?"

"I want to come with you."

Hank's expression changed and his wide grin disappeared. He looked embarrassed, then said, "Babe, perhaps you have the wrong idea, plenty of my mates want marriage, perhaps even to a Lancashire girl? I just want to have fun while I'm young, and you're too young too."

Doreen was relieved. Yes, she was too young, and her Mum would be mad, and maybe Everton was waiting in the wings, who knows? But she'd found out what Hank had been thinking and now she knew. She'd put Hank down to experience, but it was not with him that she wanted her first sexual experience, and certainly not during a pre-arranged trip to North Wales. When it happened it would have to be out of passion and surprise.

"Yes, let's have fun," Doreen said, "but I don't want sex yet, perhaps that little redhead will go with you? After we've eaten shall we go back to the others?"

CHAPTER THIRTEEN

"I DON'T GET IT, John," John's Mum said, "why must I call myself 'The Ajax Property Company'?"

"It's just a name."

"Why can't I use my own name, and why can't I lease the land directly to Meadows; why do I have to do it through an Estate Agent?"

"Mum, I'm not supposed to be interfering with Rogans' sites; if they thought I was doing that, they'd wreck Meadows' sites; we have an agreement in the trade, we - ."

"Aren't you getting into this too deep, son, why don't you let Rogans' have their site?"

"Because I want it."

"Hmmm, you haven't changed, I want, I want."

"I want to become Managing Director, Mum, so I must succeed in all things."

"Aren't you aiming just a little bit too high?"

"No."

As soon as the land was bought, Everton couldn't wait. He sent Mr Colin a wayleave agreement for the land, in the name of 'The Ajax Property Company'.

"Who are they?" Mr Colin asked.

"It's quite a new company," Everton replied, "we may be hearing a lot more about them?" Colin signed and Everton instructed contractors to enclose the land with high metal fencing. A gate was inserted at one end so that Everton could come and go and park his car, and it was securely padlocked.

During the operations Mr Jeffries came out, looking concerned. "Will the billposter be able to post the board?" he asked.

"Nothing to do with us," they said, "but we can leave you with the owner's telephone number, he'll be parking his car here."

"Parking?" Mr Jeffries did not look happy, but he took a note of the number and rang. "I'm worried," he said to Everton. "How is the bill-poster going to get in to post the board?"

"We can't let anyone in, someone manhandling ladders would be sure to damage my car. I'm sure we could make room for your car as well, no charge mind you, just being good neighbours."

"That's very decent of you, but if Rogans can't get in I'll lose my rental."

"I understand, but don't worry Mr Jeffries, if you lose your letting we'll take it over. I'm sure that we can agree terms. But I can't offer any-thing at the moment; I could be accused of trying to break a contract."

"What should I do then?"

"Just wait and see, but if Rogans approach you and wish to cancel their contract, we can take it from there."

Everton explained it all to Doreen. She would need to know in case Rogans tried to contact him when he was out. "Pretend to know nothing about it," he said, "just be a dumb blonde – I know you're neither dumb nor blonde, but you know what I mean."

Doreen's eyes twinkled. She was enjoying it all.

A week later Sam came running up the stairs, shouting, "Rogans' bill-poster is trying to post the Jaguar site; I can see him from here." Everton ran across the Square, and Doreen peered out of the window to see the sport.

When Everton arrived the Billposter's double extension ladder was against the gable, arched over the Minor at a wide angle. He had the board half posted and paste was dripping onto the Minor. "You - get down here!" he shouted.

"I'm busy," the billposter shouted back.

"If you don't I'll start shifting the ladder."

"You're mad you are; I'm coming down."

Everton waited patiently for the man to come down to earth. "That's my car," he said, "and you're dripping paste onto it."

"I'm sorry, Sir, could you please move it, then it'll be all right?"

"You're trespassing on my land. Can you not read the notice?" he said, pointing to the 'Private Property' sign.

"Oh, that," the billposter said, "nobody takes any notice of the likes of them."

"I don't think you fully appreciate the situation. This is private prop-erty and I have a lease of it. I don't want you here which is why I put the fencing up. I'll open the gate and you can go now."

"I've only posted half the board," he said.

Everton looked up at the sticky and wrinkled mess, the word 'Jaguar' half complete as 'Jag', and contemplated that if any of his billposters did work like that they'd be sacked. "That's not my concern, that's yours," he replied. "Are you leaving or do I call for the police?" he added.

"All right, all right, keep your hair on. Who are you and how can my boss contact you?"

"My name is Smyth, and the land is owned by the Ajax Property Company and that's all I'm telling you."

Everton waited until the Billposter was off the site, and watched as he went in to see Mr Jeffries; he saw the two of them through the window, deep in conversation at the back of the shop. Everton didn't wish to get involved with the Rogans man there so he went back to the office. "Well done," Doreen said. It made Everton feel good to have a resident cheer leader.

The following week an overnight storm hit the North West. Gusts of seventy miles per hour came in over the Irish Sea, accompanied by horizontal rain and a high tide. Huge waves broke over Meols promenade wall, and small boats were wrenched from their moorings in the Hoyle crashing against the concrete and were reduced to matchwood. Before turning in for the night, Everton went for a walk along the front, excited by the dramatic weather and dodging the heavy spray. His excitement was tempered by the time he got home to his bed, as he lay listening to the rain rapping against his window, and he began to worry about his hoardings. In his mind he made rapid calculations about the direction of the wind and which of the hoardings would be at risk.

The next morning he was wary when he drove into the office, passing broken off branches from trees and broken slates in the built up areas; in one instance a whole chimney had collapsed and half the street was roped off. He couldn't see any damaged hoardings and he was beginning to count his blessings, when...yes, there it was - his way into the car park space was blocked by a pile of broken wood and plywood board, all piled up below Mr Jeffries' gable. The wind had blown the board clean off; it probably wasn't very well built or attached very well anyway. Wonderful! Now he had them where he wanted them!

Everton rang the Estate Agent, and on behalf of Ajax Property, asked them to write to Rogans instructing them to remove the remains of the board, and giving them access for that purpose, and that purpose only. A deadline of ten days was to be given, after which the owner would remove and dispose of the wreck themselves, and send them a bill for costs.

Then he sat back and waited for the eruption, taking care at this stage not to contact Mr Jeffries.

Doreen was beginning to enjoy herself. Gone was the uncertainty of her relationship with Hank, and she was determined to enjoy herself with him for what little time there was left of his stay in England. She was also determined to protect her virginity. She had a fascination of 'doing it' for the first time, but the circumstances would have to be right. She would need to be slightly drunk and for the opportunity to suddenly emerge, and then to be driven by blinding passion. You couldn't plan for such an event, like going to a hotel in North Wales. You just had to wait for it to happen, and she knew that she would know when the time was right; it might be with Hank, it might not but it would be a moment to treasure because you can only have it for the first time once.

Her typing was slowly improving, mainly because she took more time over it, even though it was boring. One night, after Everton had gone home, her friend, Pauleen, came in and did some typing for her, with a great deal of panache. Everton was most impressed. He was less impressed by her timekeeping, although he now seemed to think that a quarter past nine was just about all right, and made no comment, but he made clear that twenty minutes was too late.

Doreen exulted in the cut and thrust of the business world, and although she was not directly involved in it she did, at times, have a ringside seat. The intrigue surrounding Mr Jeffries' gable excited her, and at times she was just a little bit sorry for Rogans. She thought that probably they'd met their match with Everton.

A week later Doreen was not so sure. A Mr Roy Thompson called at the office when Everton was out. She heard his heavy footsteps come up the narrow stairs, and was not surprised to see a big man, in height and width. He was thirty something and had gone to seed, with a beer belly to match and a bloated face, and she could imagine him propping up the bar on Friday and Saturday nights. "I want to talk to Mr Smyth," he growled.

"I'm afraid Mr Smyth is out," Doreen replied. "Can I help you?"

"I'm Roy Thompson of Rogans. I think you know why I've called?"

"No, I'm sorry Mr Thompson, I don't, but can I help you?"

"Look at this letter," he said, and flashed a sheet of paper in front of her.

"What is it?"

"What is it, you ask? As if you didn't know. A letter from an Estate Agent I've never heard of, on behalf of Ajax Property, a company nobody has heard of, telling me that my rights of access to Mr Jeffries' gable end are being denied."

"An Estate Agent?" Doreen said, keeping her cool. "Have you talked to them about it?"

"Listen girl," Mr Thompson started. Then he paused and asked, "What is your name?"

"Doreen, Sir."

"Listen Doreen, I'm no fool and I've found out. Ajax is Mr Smyth's mother, and your boss has bought the access, and he did it after we put our board up, so it's sour grapes. Your boss must be wet behind the ears if he thinks he can get away with this. It's gross interference with one of our sites so the Association will hear about this. In the meantime I'm pulling your railings down and I'm re-erecting the panel. The only concession I will make is to agree to post it when your boss' car is off site. Do I make myself clear?"

"Perfectly," Doreen said, on the edge of tears. "But you really must talk to Mr Smyth, and 'til you do I don't think what you suggest would be wise."

"What did you say?" Mr Thompson shouted.

"I don't think that course of action would be wise," Doreen repeated, now starting to cry.

"And why is that?"

"It's not your railing; you have no right to touch it."

"No right!" he snarled, "And you're lecturing me about rights, I'll - ," and then he stopped. Doreen had sat down and was gently sobbing.

"Serves you right for working for these crooks," he snarled. "If Mr Smyth puts you on sentry duty, then you're likely to get the flak, and I don't care."

Still muttering Roy Thompson made for the stairs.

Ten minutes later Everton found Doreen, now dry eyed but trembling by her desk. The sight of Everton started her up again. She felt that she'd lost all control. "What is it for goodness sake?" Everton asked.

"A horrible man, a Mr Thompson from Rogans has been in. He shouted at me and said that he was going to pull that railing down and post his panel. I was terrified; I even thought he might hit me."

"Doreen, I'm so sorry," and Everton put an arm around her. "I'll tell you what, I'll make the tea now, and you sit there while I serve you, for a change. Come to think of it, let's finish early, and I'll take you across to the hotel on the other side of The Square, and I'll buy you a brandy."

Doreen didn't answer, but she got up and put her arms around

Everton and said, "Why are you so nice…? Why do you always understand…? Why are you so good to me?"

"What about that brandy?"

"Yes please," Doreen said, and immediately felt more cheerful.

Doreen was experiencing all sorts of emotion; firstly Roy Thompson had reduced her to tears, and now she was excited about going across the road with Everton who was in one of his more considerate moods, and apparently ready to pamper her. A brandy? What would that do? Recent experience had taught her that she'd had a light head and had become emotional after more than two glasses of white wine. Well, now she'd see what a brandy would do.

There seemed very little at the bottom of the brandy glass. Everton showed her how to cup the glass and warm the brandy. "Take a little sip," he said, "a little goes a long way."

The first sip took her by surprise and gave her a warm glowing sensation all over her body. "Wow," she said.

Everton said, "You know, you're very precious to me. I can't have anyone coming in and bullying you."

"It's OK now. If he comes again I'll ask him to leave; I'll call the police if he doesn't."

"You shouldn't have to be put in that position."

"What will happen now?"

"Oh, he'll complain to the Trade Association, and they'll complain to Mr Colin, and he'll tell me to allow Rogans to have access. By then we may have our own panel up and possession is nine tenths of the law. I'll see Mr Jeffries tomorrow."

"It's quite exciting, isn't it? I never thought that this job would be like this," and with that she took another sip, her awareness of everything around her feeling as though it was becoming more incisive. Was she being seduced? She hoped that she was, and smiled at Everton, and giggled.

"How's your love life, Doreen?" Everton asked.

"Dead."

"Dead? What about Hank?"

"Hank has to go back to The States in a few weeks, end of story."

"Are you still seeing him?"

"Oh yes, I like it down there, at Sealand. Americans are fun, not as serious as the English. We're all good friends."

"You're very attractive, you know, you should find yourself a handsome and prosperous Englishman."

"I might already have?"

"Might?"

"I've found him but he hasn't found me." With that Doreen raised her glass and swallowed the rest of the brandy in one gulp.

"You managed that well enough, Doreen. Can I tempt you to another, but don't rush it this time?"

"Oh, I'm feeling better. Yes, another one would do me good. Will you be driving me home?"

"Of course."

They settled down to their second brandies and took their time. Everton made it clear that the second one was also their last, and said, "I'm not taking you home drunk, what would your Mum say?"

"I'll not be able to go right home, I'll need to let the brandy settle; perhaps I might be able to find some work to do in the office for an hour?"

Everton felt that he was being manipulated but he didn't mind. "No, no, you come with me to the prom at Hoylake. I'll walk you up and down there for a bit, and the exercise will do you good. What exercise do you take?"

"I dance...at Sealand."

"Indoors?"

"Of course."

"What outdoor exercise do you take?"

"I run for the bus," Doreen replied, and they both laughed.

"And you don't run fast enough," Everton added.

Everton did wonder if his Mum would spot them if they passed the house. She would probably be at the back of the house in the kitchen, preparing his supper. That reminded him, he'd have to call in at the office to ring her and say that he would be late. This was becoming a habit.

The nights were now getting longer, and there was the most beautiful sunset over the Welsh hills across the Dee. Doreen did not seem to notice it, and she struggled with high heeled shoes and repeatedly tripped, so they only got down as far as the slipway at the Lifeboat Station, and there they watched dinghy people return to shore on the high tide. "Do you sail?" Doreen asked.

"No, I haven't the time."

"You should make time, why live here and not sail?"

It was a good point. Perhaps he might join one of the local sailing clubs?

After about an hour they returned to the car and Everton drove Doreen home. She continued chatting, seeming to be sorry that the evening was ending so early. As Everton left her at the front door she put an arm around his neck and gave him a quick kiss on the lips. She held her mouth there for a couple of seconds, and with a curt, "Good night, Johnny Boy," she was gone.

Everton stood there motionless. Lights were going on and off in the house, and he heard raised voices between Doreen and presumably her Mum. Then he wondered whether he had gone too far? Would it be better to return to a strictly employer/employee relationship? Why did Doreen have to work for him? It would be so much easier for them both if she didn't, then she could call him 'Johnny Boy' all the time.

The next morning any thoughts about his relationship with Doreen were blown away in the wind. An angry Mr Colin demanded his presence with Father at four o'clock. "What about?" he asked.

"We'll tell you when you get here," was the short reply.

It was like old times, Father sitting at his desk with a weak gin and tonic, Mr Colin sitting to one side, not yet drinking. Mr Colin said, "Tell us about the Tunnel entrance site."

Everton realised that he would have to come clean and tell all, leaving nothing out. When he'd heard everything Mr Colin was furious. "Do you not see what you've done?" he said, "Rogans have quite rightly complained to the Association and demanded their rights of access. If we don't give it to them we'll be kicked out of the Association, and Rogans will retaliate; it'll be a bloody war."

Father intervened, "We're twice the size of Rogans, and if its war they want we'll win. I can't stand that bully, Roy Thompson. Can you get the gable?" he asked Everton.

"I was there this morning. Mr Jeffries wants one hundred pounds per annum. It's a bit steep so I decided to think about it."

"Think no more," Father said. "Sign up if you can Lad, and then put our own panel up. We'll check with Jaguar to see if they still want it."

"Father, I don't think – ."

"No, that's it. If the Association doesn't want us, let them kick us out, but they won't because they can't afford to do without our subscription."

By the time Everton had got back to Mr Jeffries he'd become greedier. He wanted one hundred and twenty pounds, but when he found out that Everton owned the land, his hostility was tempered.

"Do you want that land?" he asked.

"I park my car there," Everton replied.

"But you can park your car in your yard, can't you?"

"I can, but sometimes it's inconvenient."

"Thing is, I would like the land to park my van on. I'd like to buy it."

"We'd need eight hundred pounds."

"And if I give you that will you give me one hundred and twenty for the gable?"

"Yes, but with free access."

"It's a deal."

Everton's life with Doreen proceeded quietly. Every day he watched her and tormented himself. If only he had the courage to ask her out, away from business. He wondered whether he was still competing with Hank? One evening, after Doreen had gone home, he sat looking at her desk, her pen, her chewed pencils and rubber, and pieces of screwed up paper which had not yet found their way to the bin. He went over to the desk and fondled it all and looked at the inked messages on the rubber. One said, 'This is mine,' and the other side said, 'I love Ev'. Did she mean Everton? Perhaps there wasn't the room, there again perhaps she didn't mean Everton. He undid some of the paper and found various doodles meaning nothing, but hidden in the corner of one sheet was, 'I love Johnny Boy'. Everton's heart raced and suddenly he had an idea. With care he typed on a clean sheet, 'Meet me at Bidston Hill at two o'clock, Saturday. Love from an admirer'. He left his message on the roller and put the cover back over the typewriter. Tomorrow was Friday and he was due out in North Wales all day. He would not see Doreen until Monday, unless...

On Saturday, in fear and trepidation, he approached Bidston Hill. The windmill was a popular location for a good view. On a clear day you could look across to Liverpool, with the Irish Sea on the one side, and the River Dee and the Welsh hills on the other side. There'd be a few people about, but that would look better than Doreen being completely on her own. He'd convinced himself that Doreen would not be there, and if she was, he'd thought about what would they do and where would they go?

As he came in sight of the windmill he was aware of loud laughter and chatter, from many people. Doreen was there all right, but she was surrounded by many people, and he recognised Sam, the Foreman, five of the Billposters, quite a few from Liverpool Office and about three of the Buyers. He was horrified. What had Doreen done? Had she told everyone? Was she trying to teach 'The Admirer' a lesson? He didn't think that he'd been spotted, so he rapidly retreated along the way he'd come and got well out of sight, then he ran back to the Minor. He got in and lent over the steering wheel, in despair. He'd been a bloody fool. He should have just asked Doreen out, come straight out with it; she had only to say 'no' if she didn't want to. The overall message he'd got was that Doreen didn't want to get involved with him, and she'd chosen a very nasty and public way of telling him. What was he to do now? He'd work. He started the engine up and pointed the little car in the direction of North Wales. He'd do a complete inspection all the way to Caernarfon, leaving out Wrexham and Denbigh which he'd been to yesterday. In the evening he'd go to The Continental Cinema in Wallasey to see that film, 'Seven Deadly Sins'; alone.

CHAPTER FOURTEEN

DOREEN WAS LATE AGAIN, but her Master wasn't there, so there wasn't any problem. She didn't have much to do so she made the tea, for herself and Mike in the Bill Room, who was rolling himself some posters. She knew that Mike fancied her and she was quite fond of him, but her sights were set much higher. She had some typing to do so she took her own tea upstairs. She ripped the typewriter cover off and noticed a bit of un-finished typing, and started to read it, and then the full significance hit her. Perhaps it was a joke? Was it serious? Was it Sam or even Mike or one of the buyers? She dismissed the possibility of it being Johnny Boy – it would not be his style. If he'd wanted to take her out he would have asked, and she would have said, 'yes'. Excited, and with her tea un-drunk, she ran down the stairs with the piece of paper in her hand to see Mike. "Is this you?" she asked.

"Mike read it slowly. "Where was it?" he asked.

"In the typewriter."

"Who is it?"

"It's you, isn't it?" she said.

"Yes, I'm an admirer, but I can't type."

"So you got someone else to do it?"

"Don't be daft. What are you going to do?"

"Why, go, of course."

"You might be murdered, or something."

"Not if you're there, hidden in the background, like?"

"Gosh, will you really go?" Mike asked. "On Saturdays I normally watch Tranmere. They're playing Wrexham at home this week, but I'll give it a miss if you want?"

"Thanks a lot, Mike."

Doreen was not to know that she'd set a chain reaction of motion. Mike went over to the Liverpool depot to collect some posters. He mentioned it to the Foreman who was due to go to the Liverpool office to sort something out with Mr Smiley. A Buyer was with him, and buyers are gossips and so the jungle telegraph took over.

Doreen was unaware that the news had spread so widely. She was at Bidston in good time, and as she waited she was dismayed by the stream of well-wishers who had toiled up the hill to give her support. She now knew that she'd never know the identity of her 'admirer', so she made the most of a wasted afternoon, and chatted and laughed with the others. While doing so she saw a shadowy figure hovering in distant bushes, and then retreating. Who was it? Was it Everton? Then she began to wonder.

"I want to sell your land, Mum," Everton said.

"Whatever for? Could I get my money back?"

"You'll double your money. A Mr Jeffries has offered eight hundred pounds, so he can park his van on it."

"Eight hundred pounds?"

"Yes."

"Good grief. If it's increased that much in a couple of weeks, surely I can hang on and get more? I'm not in a hurry."

"No Mum, Mr Jeffries' offer is tied in with a Meadows deal with him – the two go together."

"What on earth are you up to now, son?"

"Don't worry, Mum, just take the money."

"Are there any other pieces of land I can buy?"

Everton was nervous about meeting Doreen on Monday. What would she say? Would she say anything? What if she asked him if it was him? Had she seen him? He waited anxiously for her arrival. Quarter past nine came and went, then twenty past. His anger about her late arrival was replaced by real concern. He had a pile of typing for her to do, and a late start would not help. She'd have to work through her dinner hour. Anxiously he peered out of the window, watching the buses from Borough Road emptying their loads in The Square. At last, there she was, half walking, half running, glancing up at the clock in The Square. She looked pretty awful, her hair all over the place, and as she got closer he could make out a strained and pale face. When she came through the door she started to plead, to get her word in first. "I'm so sorry, Everton, I overslept something awful this morning. I've missed breakfast. You see, I was down at Sealand on Sunday night for a special dance, and there was transport laid on but it didn't turn up. Pauleen and I had to walk along the Queensferry Road, hoping for a lift at one o'clock in the morning. Nothing came for ages, and then a lorry picked us up and left us in West Kirby. It was seven miles from there and we had to walk the whole way. It was nearly three when I got home, three! My Mum was furious, I - ."

"And so am I," Everton cut in.

"Oh, I'm so sorry; I'll work through my dinner."

"Next time you're seven miles from home in the early hours of the morning, all you have to do is to ring me," Everton said, sarcastically, then regretted it.

Doreen gave a half laugh, and then said, "Shall I make the tea?"

"No time for tea, Doreen, just get on with what I've left you on your desk."

"Yes, of course, Mr Smyth," she said. His adventures of Saturday afternoon were forgotten for a moment, and Everton hoped for good.

The next three weeks were the last three weeks before Hank left. Doreen decided that she was not in love with him, but he'd been an old and familiar friend who had been good and generous towards her, so she wasn't going to desert him in his last days in the UK. There was only one problem and that was the increasing pressure on her to have sex with him. He said that he hadn't had sex in the eighteen months he'd been at Sealand, and Doreen reckoned that he didn't want to go back to The States empty handed.

Doreen was in two minds about it all. She was generous and would have been glad to let him have his own way, but only to gratify him, not her, because she didn't feel ready for it. She was also worried about getting pregnant, and had discussed the matter with Pauleen. She said, "You should get some sheaths from the chemist; have them ready in your handbag, at all times."

"Have you got some?"

"Yes, of course."

"What, did you just go into the chemist and ask for them? Whatever they call them?"

"Contraceptives."

"Whatever."

"No, I've never bought any, my boyfriend keeps me supplied; he gives them to me three at a time."

"Three! How many times have you done it, and what's it like?"

"I've lost count, and it's all right."

"All right! Is that all? It's supposed to be heaven."

"Overrated. It's for the men; they need it. I like it when they start grunting."

"Grunting?"

"Yes, you know, like he's nearly there, leaving me a long way behind. But who knows, one day I may get a climax?"

"Climax?"

"God, Doreen, haven't you discussed this with your Mum?"

"My Mum!" Doreen exclaimed, "You must be joking; I wouldn't know where to start."

"Then you'll have to find out for yourself."

"The things you have when you go to the chemist?"

"Contraceptives?"

"Whatever. What do you ask for when you go to the chemist?"

"Oh, I don't know. Why don't you ask Hank for some? Haven't you discussed this matter with him at all? Every girl has some in their handbag, just in case. Men can be very persuasive when they want it. If you talk about it much more you'll give me the giggles. Really Doreen, where have you been? You'll just have to ask Hank."

"I can't do that; he would think that I wanted to do it."

"So would that be all that bad?"

"Yes, I'm only going to do it if it's special."

"Doreen, it's never special."

"Would you let me have one of yours?"

"Yes, I could. I only hope that Jim hasn't kept score."

Pauleen fished about in her handbag and produced a little pink sealed envelope. When she got home she went to the toilet and had a look inside. She examined the item with interest, and then sealed it up again. She hoped that if she did do it, Hank would know all about it, and now that she was so curious about the whole business, she decided that she'd have a go at the first opportunity.

A whole draft of Americans, including Hank, were all due to return home shortly, so it was partying time. One dance after another was held at the base, and in between there were pub crawls in Chester and Queensferry, and Doreen threw herself into the fray. Hank had hired a car for the last two weeks, and Doreen had new horizons opened up to her, trips to Llandudno and Shrewsbury, and picnics by the roadside. The only problem was that she was not due any time off, and evenings and weekends were the only time available to her.

The stress of burning the candle at both ends was beginning to show, trying to cope with an increased workload in the office, and maintaining her frantic social life. Her Mum did not bother to wake her if she overslept. She would get up in a panic, throw some clothes on and chase after the bus. She was arriving later and later in the office, sometimes twenty five minutes past nine, and then even ten o'clock. As luck would have it

Everton was in on that morning, and as she came through the door he snarled at her, "Forget the tea and sit down. I want to talk to you." She meekly sat down and waited.

"Doreen, this simply won't do, will it?"

"I'm sorry, so sorry; it won't happen again."

"But it does, doesn't it?"

"Sometimes, not always."

"Just look at you; you're a mess, your face is pale, your eyes bleary, your hair all over the place, and your stockings are laddered."

Doreen smarted; this was getting a bit too personal. She said, "I didn't think that personal appearance mattered in a crap office of this size."

"Of course it matters, and you're a wreck. Are you ill?"

"No, I'm just tired, it'll be OK soon. Hank goes back to America in five days time, and then I probably won't go to Sealand any longer."

"I hope not, because I'm giving you a final warning. If you're late again, you're out." Then, after a pause added, "And I would be very, very sad about that, Doreen."

She managed a smile, and thinking that the interview was over got up to make the tea.

"Just stay there, I'm not finished with you yet. I rang the agency last night. You were to have gone to evening classes last week and you didn't turn up."

Doreen's face fell. "Oh my God," she said. "I clean forgot. I intended to go; will do next week anyway, you see - ."

"I know - you blame Hank; he has a lot to answer for, hasn't he?"

Doreen detected a changed tone, for the better, and with difficulty she smiled. Everton continued, "Go on then, make us some tea."

After an exhausting day at the office, including her difficult interview with Everton, Doreen decided that she daren't risk annoying Everton ever again. Three days to go. She'd have an early night and be up in good time in the morning, do the same on the next day, then on Sunday she would see. Hank was due to leave on Monday. He had already asked her to stay on Sunday night, in the luxury of Blossoms Hotel in Chester. She now needed to talk to her Mum. She said, "You know that Hank is going back to the States, don't you?"

"Yes."

"He goes on Monday."

"What a shame. I'll not be getting those lovely boxes of chocolates again."

"Thing is, I'd like to stay overnight in Chester on Sunday. It'll be too late to get back to Birkenhead on Sunday night, and transport is hellish on Sundays."

"He's got a car, hasn't he; you told me?"

"Yes, but it would be easier to stay in Chester."

"Where?"

"In Chester."

"But where in Chester?"

"Blossoms Hotel."

"Is he paying?"

"Of course."

"What, in a double room, like?"

"No, singles," Doreen lied.

"No, you're not and I don't believe you, and even if he's booked singles it wouldn't be long before he would cuddle up to you; the next thing you know you're pregnant. Very sexy, these Yanks, in fact that's all they are, and generous."

"Mum, don't be silly, I want - ."

"You heard. You can come back here on Sunday night. Hank can drive you."

"Mum, it's only this once."

"Once is enough. *You* were made after only 'once'."

Doreen did not know this and it was interesting. She couldn't imagine her Mum as ever being passionate, but she must have been.

"Mum, please."

"No. I've said my piece. You come back on Sunday night; otherwise you're out on the street."

Doreen knew that she meant it. There'd have to be a change of plan.

On Saturday, Doreen tackled Hank. "I can't stay with you Sunday, Hank, I'm sorry."

"Why, Babe?"

"My Mum won't allow."

"Why?"

"I don't know, she just won't."

"Gee, Babe, I was looking forward to that."

"I'm sorry, Hank, there's nothing I can do, but I want to be with you on Sunday night."

"Oh, I suppose I can still," Hank said sulkily.

"I knew I could depend on you."

"We could book into Blossoms on Sunday evening, and then I could drive you home about midnight."

"Would you?" Doreen said enthusiastically.

"No problem."

"It's a date then."

They went to Blossoms at four o'clock on Sunday. Doreen was overjoyed at the sight of the room. Never before had she seen such luxury, and there was even a bathroom attached, and a corner of the toilet roll was bent over, practically inviting you to do your business. There was a coffee maker and biscuits, a drinks cupboard and a telephone, and she sank into the deep piled carpet as she moved about the room.

"Guess I'll have a shave," Hank said.

"Why?" asked Doreen.

"Don't want to prickle you."

"Are you going to kiss me?" Doreen asked, and then giggled.

"After we've eaten."

They went downstairs into the bar and Hank bought a bottle of champagne. This was a first, like the brandy Everton had given her. She drank it like fizzy lemonade, and then felt dizzy and slightly queasy.

"Dinner time," Hank said.

"Can we give it a miss?" Doreen said.

"You can, but I can't."

Hank ordered himself a steak, and Doreen contented herself with brown Windsor Soup, and felt better for it. Her mood improved but she still wasn't sure that she had control of herself.

After their meal they went back up to their room, Doreen's little envelope securely tucked in her handbag. Would Hank know what to do with it? Of course he would, he was an American.

Doreen watched Hank undress. She'd never seen him naked before, or any grown man for that matter. She hadn't known that he was so flabby around the waist; it had never shown when he was in his uniform. She tried hard not to glance at his crotch. In turn she peeled off her dress and bra, leaving herself in pants and stockings with suspender belt. Her stockings weren't laddered – she'd seen to that. "Come here Babe," Hank said. He pulled her towards his body and grabbed her buttocks, then found her mouth and kissed her in a new way, his tongue darting in and out.

Doreen groaned. "You will be gentle, won't you?" she said.

"Of course, Babe, bedtime now." He showed no sign of producing a contraceptive, so reluctantly Doreen moved towards her handbag. "What are you doing, Babe?" Hank asked.

"A little thing," Doreen shyly replied, and produced her little pink envelope.

"What's that?" Hank asked.

"You should know."

"Gimmee."

Hank undid the seal and looked in. He said, "You can't use that, it's so old fashioned, dry and covered in powder."

"It's all I could get."

"Won't do."

"Have you got one then?" Doreen asked.

"Don't use them," Hank said, and pulled back the bedclothes.

Doreen could only think of one thing. 'Don't get pregnant,' her Mum had said, 'It only takes once'. Hank would only take once, then he'd disappear to America, without a trace, and a child would be without a father.

"Can't do it," Doreen said.

"Come on Babe, don't be shy," Hank said and pulled her onto the bed, mounting her and trying to pull her pants off. Doreen was panic-struck. She grabbed the telephone beside the bed and struck it across Hank's head. "Jesus, what yer doing?" yelled Hank, and a voice could just be heard to say, "'Can I help you?'"

Some blood came from Hank's head, and slowly he raised himself and crept over to a chair. Trembling, Doreen fumbled with the telephone and put it together again, then looked at Hank.

"Sorry," she said, "are you all right?"

Hank felt his face and said, "Just a cut, say, you really know how to turn a guy on. Give me a minute and we'll start again, but no rough stuff."

"I'm sorry Hank, but I don't want sex; I'm not ready for it."

"Babe, I've spent all this money on the hotel and this room, it's my last night, I - ."

"I know you have Hank, but I can't and don't make me. I want to part as good friends." Frightened, Doreen began to dress, trying to appear that she wasn't in a hurry.

"What yer doing, Babe?" he asked.

"I think its better I go now."

"Oh fuck, go on then, get out of my sight."

After Doreen had dressed she said, "Sure you're OK?"

"Yes, yes, just go."

"Thank you for everything, Hank."

"Thanks for nothing, Babe."

Doreen fumbled with the door handle which didn't seem to want to work, then found the unlock catch, and left. She pushed the door shut behind her, then bolted.

Doreen left the hotel and in a daze walked around the town, quiet now on the Sunday evening. She started to make plans for getting home. She had no money for the train or the bus, so once again she wandered off to the Birkenhead Road and thumbed a lift. The first to stop was an American Serviceman, so she refused it. Much later on a lorry driver gave her a lift as far as Little Sutton, and she had to walk from there.

"You look awful," her Mum said.

"I feel awful," Doreen replied.

"Has Hank gone?"

"Good riddance."

"Any chocolates?"

"No chocolates, Mum. Can you make sure you get me up early to-morrow?"

"Why not sign off sick?"

"Because I'm not."

"What does that matter?"

"It does to me."

Doreen did oversleep, but she made sure that she looked a bit smarter; she combed her hair and put on lipstick, and found a pair of stockings without ladders.

Everton waited, and waited. When the clock hand moved to half past he made a decision. He rang the agency and asked, "Is Miss Bottom still with you?"

"Sure."

"Would she still be available for work?"

"She would be."

"Could she start next Monday, nine sharp, conditions as before?"

"I'll tell her, Mr Smyth. Was Doreen not satisfactory?"

"Not entirely."

At a quarter to ten Everton heard Doreen clatter up the stairs and she burst into the room. She stood by the entrance looking much smarter than she had been recently, almost cultured. This would make his task even harder. "Gosh, I'm so, so sorry, Mr Smyth, you can't imagine the hell I've had. I was with Hank last night, and we had a row in Chester. He was a beast;

he tried to rape me and I escaped. I had no money so I got a lift, and then walked the rest of the way. I was dead beat when I got home, dead beat. I could scarcely get up this morning."

It was all very convincing, Everton thought, a good performance but not good enough. He wasn't quite sure if his attitude would have been less harsh if she *had* been raped. Anyway, it was all too late now. Miss Bottom was coming next week; no chance of her being raped or even nearly raped.

"I'm sorry, Doreen, I did try to warn you. You're sacked. You'll have to finish at the end of the week."

Doreen stood motionless; it was as if Gold Finger had touched her. She said nothing at first, then tears began to roll, and she stammered, "Serves me right, I've made a proper mess of things, haven't I, and I've been so happy here, and I'll miss it terribly and you…you have been, you've been - ." She couldn't finish the words, so instead she flung her arms around Everton and wept.

Everton held her tightly, and then lightly kissed her on the cheek. He said, "I'll always remember you too, Doreen. I'll give you a fantastic reference."

"Better not praise my typing though."

"No, better not."

"Or my time keeping."

"Everything else though."

"Should I go now?"

"No, no, work 'til Friday evening. Miss Bottom comes on Monday."

For the next few days Everton found Doreen to be perfectly splendid. She was punctual and her personal appearance was transformed. She went back to wearing pelmet skirts which showed off her legs to their best advantage. Even her typing seemed to have improved, and Everton began to regret his decision. Perhaps with Hank out of the way she would have become more focused? If it hadn't been for the fact that he had already promised Miss Bottom a job, he might have relented, and kept Doreen on.

Downstairs, those in the Bill Room were stunned. Doreen was one of them; she'd spent many hours chatting up the boys, and Sam behaved as if she was a long lost daughter. "Does she really have to go?" he asked, "I mean would Meadows' employ both Doreen and Miss Bottom, now that there seems to be so much more work?"

Everton replied, "I'll miss her too, but we've got to move on."

Surprisingly Doreen's chief critic, Mr Colin, appeared broken heart-ed. "I know I've complained about her typing," he said, "but she's a character and a real good looker, an asset to have in any office. What does Miss Bottom look like?" Everton didn't tell him.

Bill Room conversation centred on Doreen's leaving present. Rather unkindly, Everton suggested an alarm clock, but they all thought that would be a bit too near the bone. Mike said, "What does Doreen like best?"

Sam replied, "What about a pelmet skirt?" So they got her a set of three, all in different colours.

On the Friday evening Doreen was asked down to the Bill Room to say goodbye. Everton thought she looked radiant. She wore a long yellow dress he'd not seen before, and had applied a generous portion of her favourite scent. Everton couldn't bring himself to make the farewell speech, so Sam filled the breach. "You're one of us, Doreen," he said, "and we'll always remember you…and your pelmet skirts," and they all laughed, then continued, "Speaking of which, we've got you a few more to keep you going."

Doreen seemed to be in complete self control. She said, "This has been my first job, and it's taught me a lot…like getting up in the morning," at which there was more laughter. Somebody produced a bottle of red plonk, and they all drank Doreen's health. At six o'clock she said, "Well, I'm off now lads, see you around." She'd already packed her personal belongings into a small bag which was by her side. She picked it up, and then she was gone.

Everton went back to the empty office. He sat on his own chair, and looked back at Doreen's empty chair and desk. She'd left her rubber, pen and pencil, but otherwise there was a clean surface; not like her. He went across and sat in her chair which was still warm. Everything about her was around him, her smell and feeling of hectic activity. He sat still and closed his eyes to imagine her still there, her long legs walking to the filing cabinet and back, her wild gesticulation of her arms and hands when she was describing something, her painful and laboured typing, and screwed up pieces of paper when she had to start all over again. Speaking of which, thought Everton, as he opened his eyes, that typewriter cover is all crooked, just like her. He moved to straighten it out, and lifted it off to smooth out the wrinkles. There was something typed on a piece of paper on the roller. It was Doreen's work, all right, untidy and smudged, but the message was clear – 'I'll know you'll not resist lifting the cover off to straighten it and therefore see this note. Meet me at Bidston Hill at two pm Saturday. I'll be on my own unless Mike gets at this message first."

Everton smiled. Worried that he'd perhaps made the wrong decision, he now knew that he'd been right. She was no longer an employee and

Hank had gone away, so nothing would now impede their relationship. Speaking aloud he said, "God bless you, Doreen, and don't you dare be late."

CHAPTER FIFTEEN

DOREEN HAD NEVER FELT surer of herself. She was convinced that Everton would see her note and act on it. She would be there on Saturday, and Everton would come. At first she wondered what they would do after such a romantic meeting? She supposed that Everton would take charge and would already have something planned. But suppose *she* take charge, just for once? What would she like to do? She'd already had her appetite whetted by a touch of luxury at the Blossoms Hotel, though of course she'd never go back there again; they'd probably charge her for a broken telephone. What about North Wales? The family used to go there when she was small, and she'd always admired the Commodore Hotel on the west shore, and its magnificent view across the estuary towards Conwy. She began to imagine her and Everton arriving in the Minor and walking up to the reception desk together, as if they were man and wife. She had a gold ring handed down to her by the family which she'd never worn. She would wear that as a wedding ring and they'd sign the register as Mr and Mrs Smyth, then they'd go up to their room, their cases carried by a porter. Everton would tip him and they'd be left on their own, in a luxury room with a wonderful view, and for two blissful nights they'd be there, together.

Doreen had her own thoughts of such an adventure. They'd kiss and cuddle, but there'd be no sex and that would be the condition. Unlike Hank, she reckoned that Everton was a gentleman and wouldn't object, but she'd have to make that point from the start so there would be no mis-understanding. Her experience with Hank had taught her that she wasn't ready for sex yet, and she'd be playing with fire, but she'd risk it.

There was another problem. How was she going to explain her ab-sence to her Mum? For that she needed Pauleen's help, so she went to see her.

"I've been sacked," she said to Pauleen.

"Never!"

"My own fault. I was late too often."

"Oh, I'm sorry Doreen. What are you going to do now?"

"I have an eye on that receptionist job in the hotel in Woodchurch, but there's something more important to do first."

"What?"

"Everton and I are going away for the weekend, and I've got to explain to my Mum why I'm missing. I'll tell her that you and I are going to a late night dance on Saturday, and I shall be staying with you Saturday and Sunday nights."

"You're joking. Everton sacked you, so you then go away together!"

"Oh, he didn't ask me."

"You asked him?"

"Not yet, but I know he will."

"Why have anything to do with him?"

"I love him."

"Never! How can he sack you if you're lovers?"

"I wanted him to. It's easier now."

"Does he love you?"

"I know he does."

"Has he told you?"

"Not yet."

"You're mad, both of you."

"Yes, quite mad, but will you cover for me?"

"Course, but what happens if your Mum calls round?"

"She won't."

Doreen's Mum was the next obstacle. "I'm going to a late night dance on Saturday," Doreen said.

"Sealand?"

"No, locally, but Pauleen and I are going together."

"That's nice."

"I'm staying with her Saturday and Sunday night, thought we might make a weekend of it."

"That's nice, I like Pauleen."

Doreen decided to say no more. There hadn't been any cross examination. Her cover was secured.

On Saturday morning she packed a little bag, with the minimum of stuff so as not to raise suspicions. When her Mum was out shopping she slipped round to Pauleen's as arranged, her whole being tingling with excitement.

"Bidston Hill, did you say?" asked Pauleen.

"Yes, at two o'clock."

"How do you know he'll be there?"
"Because he loves me."
"But suppose he isn't?"
"He will be."

Everton finished early on Saturday morning. He told his Mum that he might be late, and no questions were asked. He went across the Square for a beer and a sandwich. He had butterflies in his stomach and no appetite for anything more. While he sipped his beer he asked himself many questions. Would she be there? Was she playing a practical joke? What would they do if she was there? So he started to make plans. He knew that Doreen liked Chester, so he'd take her there to do some browsing; he might even buy her a present? Then they might have some tea, and be in time for an early showing at the cinema in Birkenhead or Wallasey. They'd come out at about nine, then they could go down to the car park at New Brighton and see if she fancied a little necking. She was a nice girl, only a child really, so he'd behave himself and be gentle with her. If this relationship was to work there would have to be a long-term courting. His Mum would have to get used to Doreen – 'not your sort' she'd frequently said. In time he'd introduce Doreen to her and they'd all be friends. Life no longer seemed to be only about work. It was time he started to relax and make friends, have a relationship and think of the future. In thirty years time would he still be on his own, his Mum gone maybe, slaving away for the greedy Meadows', still seeking promotion?

He set out for Bidston Hill early. There was a chill in the air and the car park was empty. When he came in sight of the windmill there wasn't anyone there, but he was ten minutes early. He lent against the structure, waiting for the future to unfold.

"Boo," a voice said behind him. The little devil had been there all the time, hiding. If he'd come even earlier he could have done the same. "I knew you'd come," she said.

"I wondered if you were joking," Everton replied.

"I was going to – I decided – I was going to tell you all sorts, now I'm just happy you're here."

"Me too, Doreen. I love you, you know."

Doreen blushed and didn't say anything more, or return the compliment. Everton had intended his remark to be a signal to move on from a childish prank to something more serious. She moved towards him and ruffled his untidy hair, and Everton kissed her gently, but held her firmly, not releasing his grip after the kiss, and they remained locked.

"I love you too," Doreen eventually said, "and I've got plans."

"Plans?" Everton exclaimed, now a little alarmed. He'd have to cool it.

"Just for the next couple of days, like," Doreen said.

"What sort of plan?"

"I've booked a room at The Commodore Hotel on the west shore in Llandudno. Do you know it?"

"A room?"

"A double room, for both of us."

Everton's heart raced. She had taken charge. Was he going to allow that? And a shared room for the whole night meant only one thing. He couldn't do it. "Doreen, you're very young. I mean, your Mum, what would - ."

"My Mum doesn't know."

"So what have you told her?"

"That I'm staying at Pauleen's for two nights."

"Two?"

"Yes, Johnny Boy, but there's something I want to explain first."

"Go on."

"I booked a double room because I want us to be together, a couple, like. But I can't make love to you; I'm not ready for that yet."

Everton's concern was at once eased. This Doreen was fairly something. She was in control and he'd let her be. He was in love with her, and now that her employment under him was over, they were free to do as they chose. She seemed to have sorted her Mum out, now he would have to sort his Mum out.

Still doubtful that this plan created the possibility of him being accused of abduction if it was ever found out, he cautioned Doreen. "You're very young; do you think we should go this far so soon?"

"Are you trying to talk me out of it?"

"I want you to think about it."

"I've been doing nothing else, Johnny, and I want this, please don't let me down."

"And it's our secret?"

"Yes."

"We better get along then. I'll have to pack a bag and have a word with my Mum, so you can keep out of sight while I'm doing that."

"Exciting, isn't it?" said Doreen, and giggled.

Everton's Mum was out, and that made it easier. Everton had always found it difficult to lie, particularly to his Mum, but she'd murder him if she knew what they were up to. She'd never met Doreen, but had judged that she wasn't 'their sort'. And her age…! Everton wrote, 'I have to go away for the next few days. See you Monday'. He knew that a further explanation would be required when he got back, and he'd just have to mumble something about a business trip to North Wales, to catch up on inspections. In the meantime that would stop her ringing the police and the hospital.

They arrived in Llandudno in the early evening. Silently they walked up the steps, through the revolving door, then confidently approached the reception desk, Doreen a respectful two feet behind and looking down at her feet. The reception girl was bright and breezy, and Everton felt more relaxed. "Would you sign here please, Sir?" she said. Then, "You seem to have brought the good weather with you. Will you be dining tonight?" Everton looked at Doreen who shook her head.

On the way up in the lift, Doreen asked, "Is that all right about dinner? It'll be too posh for me, and I haven't any other clothes other than this jumper and skirt."

"Quite all right, Doreen, we'll find something in the town."

"I could murder fish and chips," she said.

Doreen gasped at the view from their hotel bedroom. It was low tide and the evening sun was shining on the sand; in the distance they could see the ancient town of Conwy and the old suspension bridge, and beyond that they could see the stone buildings of the town, and a range of mountains sweeping up from The Irish Sea.

"Fancy waking up to that view every morning?" Doreen said as she pulled a chair up to the window and gazed out, appearing to be happy to stay there for ever.

Behind her, Everton unpacked his things, and then looked at Doreen's small bag. "Are you unpacking?" he asked. Reluctantly Doreen pulled away from the view, unzipped her small bag, and then pulled out a plain nightie and a wash bag.

"Is that all you've got?" Everton asked.

"I'm supposed to be staying with Pauleen," she said, "that's all I ever take when I go there."

After Doreen had inspected and enthused about every small detail of their room, they walked into town, hand in hand. They decided to go to the early showing of 'Love in the Morning' at The Roxy, and sat on the back row of the upper circle, along with other courting couples, and Doreen wept at the film. "I can't help it," she said, "I'm just so happy."

After the film they walked the full length of the promenade and back again, and then they bought fish and chips from a chippie van at the entrance to the pier. After walking back to the west shore they were both tired and ready for bed. Everton did the decent thing; he sent Doreen up to the room while he went to the bar to have a beer.

When Everton got back to their room, Doreen was tucked up in bed, wide awake but in darkness. "Can you manage all right?" she asked, "I don't want you to turn the light on."

"I can do everything from the light in the bathroom, and I'm having a bath first anyway. Don't go to sleep before I'm finished," he laughed.

When he returned Doreen asked, "Which side should I be on?"

"The left side," Everton replied.

"Why?"

"It's the same side as that girl was on in the film," and they both laughed.

Everton lay on his side and faced Doreen, and they kissed, and at the same time one of Everton's wandering hands found her bottom and pressed it.

"Don't please," Doreen said.

"Why?"

"It's private, but kiss me again," Doreen said, "then I want to get some sleep if I can."

They spent ages getting into different positions, and then decided that back to back was best. In no time at all Everton heard Doreen's gentle breathing. For a long time he remained very still, not daring to disturb her, and then he too drifted off.

They both woke at about six. As they lay there Doreen said, "This is the first time I've slept with someone."

"Snap," Everton replied, then added, "How have you survived the experience?"

"It's strange, but when I woke this morning and saw you there, I felt so content. I would like to wake up every morning with company next to me."

"You may have to wait a few years yet. Did you never sleep with Hank?"

"I was going to, but he was rough and it's put me off. I don't want to talk about Hank; it's you I'm interested in. I was scared of repeating my previous experience."

Everton laughed and said, "They say that if you fall off a horse, you should get straight back on again."

"What about you?" Doreen asked.

"What do you mean?"

"Have you really never slept with a girl? Have you ever made love?"

"No."

"Why?"

"I suppose I'm a bit of a loner. I never seem to have had time to keep a girlfriend. My Mum nags at me about it."

"Are you going to try to keep me?"

"I shall never leave you, Doreen, and I'll never let you go."

"You may say that now and you may mean it, but will it happen, like? You might meet someone more posh, perhaps?"

"I don't want anyone else."

"Why? You say you've never gone to bed with anyone else; you might want to sleep around and try it?"

"Doreen, I don't need to, I only want you, and come here…" They kissed with even more passion than before, but Everton was careful about where he put his hands.

They got up early and went for a walk, this time all the way to the top of The Great Orme. There was nobody else about and they were on their own on the peak, the tramway being idle at this time of day. They watched the sun rise over the headland. Doreen was getting cold, so Everton removed his jacket and put it on her, and then they briefly kissed, before starting the long walk back to their hotel.

Doreen was still shy about going into the dining room, but Everton explained that guests would have casual wear at breakfast, so they went in to have a 'full English breakfast' with all the trimmings. Everton noticed that Doreen was slowly gaining confidence in an environment to which she was not used. She said that nobody had ever called her 'Madam' before, and she started counting the number of times it was said to her. With every 'Madam' which was spoken she started to giggle. "Come on," she said to Everton, "you count the 'Sirs' and we'll see who wins."

The hotel was doing picnic lunches so they took one and drove up into the mountains, away from civilisation. Somewhere in a valley and beside a stream they found a place to park, where they enjoyed their sandwiches and red wine. Apart from the odd passing tractor and waves from friendly tractor drivers, they were on their own and in the sunshine most of the time. It was so peaceful that neither of them wanted to leave. "I would like to stay here forever," Everton said.

"Me too." Doreen replied, then added, "If ever I wanted to make love for the first time it would be somewhere like this, in the open, but private too."

Everton wondered if he was getting a coded signal; he hoped not. "Is that what you want?" he asked.

"Yes."

"What, now?"

"No, silly, I'm not ready for it yet. Do you mind?"

"Of course not, and you're too young; I could be accused of all sorts."

"If Hank was here he'd just do it. Men are animals – well, not all of them."

"Do you love me, Doreen?"

She turned towards him and smiled, playing with a long stem of grass over his face. "You know I do, otherwise I wouldn't be here."

"I love you too," Everton said.

"For how long?"

He looked up into the sky, pondering, and then said, "From the moment you came into that interview room."

"You were naughty; you should have chosen Miss Bottom."

"I have."

"I don't really believe that I don't work for you anymore."

"What will you do?"

"I think that hotel in Woodchurch is going to employ me as an Assistant Receptionist."

"Is that what you want?"

"It'll be a chatty job; I like chatting. I thought I was going to go to America with Hank and be an American housewife."

"Are you sorry?"

"Not now."

"Doreen, what's our future?"

"Marry, I suppose."

"Seriously?"

"Still, we can do that sometime – Do you think you might marry me, eventually, when I'm older, like, and my Mum gets used to the idea?"

"And my Mum too," Everton replied, "let's just take it one step at a time."

They stayed there all afternoon, lying on a rug on the grass, talking less but fantasising about the future. Everton didn't know whether Doreen was talking seriously, and only time would tell. Of one thing that was certain, now that Hank and her employment with Meadows' were out of the way, she was now his girlfriend, and this time he would make time for her. Eventually he would introduce her to his Mum, but he'd have to let her get used to their friendship first, get her on his side before they met. Doreen was still very young, and everyone would say that she was far too young for her to know her own mind. If she thought she was old enough to be an American housewife, then she was old enough to be his life's partner. There were problems ahead, but none that could not be solved. Suddenly he felt so content and happy; he lent over and once again kissed his loved one. "What was that for?" Doreen asked.

"I felt so happy and I wanted to share it."

The sun soon sank below the tops of the mountains, and the air immediately cooled. They packed up and left, driving back to the hotel in silent contentment.

They arrived back famished. Doreen stood in front of the menu card outside the dining room door. "Look at all that food," she said, "and its four courses."

"The helpings would be small. Do you want to eat there?"

"Yes, but I'm not dressed for it, just this jumper and skirt."

"It's a very modest skirt, Doreen, perfectly acceptable."

"Everyone else will be tarted up, like last night; some of the women even had long dresses on."

"Not tonight, it's Sunday evening and casual wear would be quite all right."

"Shall we then? Can you afford it?"

"You'll have to wait 'til eight."

"Then perhaps by then I'll be able to eat four courses?" she said.

At five to eight they were in their places, hidden behind large menus, written in French. "What does all this mean?" Doreen asked.

"It doesn't really matter, they'll cook you whatever you fancy."

"What do I do with all these knives and forks?"

"Work from the outside to the inside; I'll keep you straight."

"Just order for me, Johnny, I'm so hungry I could eat a horse."

"I don't think that is on the menu."

"What?"

"Horse."

"Don't be daft," and she playfully nudged him on the elbow.

Before they went to bed for the second night, Everton arranged for them to have an early breakfast. "If we can leave at eight," Everton said, "I can be in the office by ten."

"When will I see you again?" Doreen asked.

"Have you a phone?"

"No."

"Let's go to the cinema on Wednesday. Come to the office at about six."

"I'd like that, I can see how Miss Bottom is managing!"

When they arrived in Birkenhead, Everton dropped Doreen off at Pauleen's, to let her go home from there. Miss Bottom had been waiting since nine, but Sam had given her tea and had passed on Everton's message from Llandudno that he was going to be late. Even without any instruction she had opened the mail and arranged it in little piles on his desk, a good start thought Everton. On top of the pile was a note of a telephone call from Mr Colin asking Everton to ring as soon as he got in, urgently. He rang and was asked to call round at once. He and Father wanted to see him. "What is it about?" Everton asked Mr Colin.

"We'll tell you when you get here."

"Well, I mean, what file do I take?"

"Oh, you don't need any file. We just want to have a chat."

"Is everything all right?" Everton anxiously asked.

"Very much all right."

"I'm on my way, Sir."

Before he left he looked out some simple tasks for Miss Bottom to keep her busy while he was across the river. Why did everything happen at once, and on a morning he'd been late?

At first Everton had been worried that perhaps he'd badly slipped up on something, but the words 'Very much all right' reassured him. What could it be? Was promotion coming his way earlier than expected? He'd not heard of any management changes. In any case he was happy where he was. There was not much more to achieve, and he would just have to consolidate.

It was eleven o'clock in the morning. There was no gin and tonic, just coffee, and bone china cups and saucers from 'the important occasions' cupboard. Both of the Meadows' were there, looking very pleased with themselves, as if they'd solved a thorny problem. "How are you?" Mr Colin asked, in a very friendly way. "Miss Bottom settling in ok?"

"This is her first morning. I have high expectations of her."

"And what about Doreen?" So that was it, it was something to do with Doreen and their weekend away. They must have heard, but it was none of their business, anyway.

"I think she's taking a receptionist job," Everton said.

"Never could understand why you fired her."

"A matter of principle," Everton said. Surely they weren't going to run through that subject again. The matter had been dealt with and Doreen had gone, even though she had not gone from his personal life.

"Have you heard about Alf Nelson?" Father asked.

"No, Sir, should I have?" Alf was in charge in Ireland, both North and South of the border and based in Belfast. Where was this leading to?

"Dead," said Father.

"Dead? He was quite young, wasn't he?"

"Fifty," said Mr Colin, "massive heart attack."

"Oh dear, I'm so sorry, he was a perfect gentleman; everybody liked him."

"About all he was," Father said, "he was no good."

"Oh come on, Father," Mr Colin said, "he's done a lot in Ireland, just been out of sorts the last few months."

"Anyway," Father said, "there's a vacancy there. Place has been allowed to slip and competitors are getting the better of us. It's an 'area' rather than a branch like Birkenhead, has its own accounts staff and three branches of its own. Place needs an uplift, and there's only one person to do that, and that's you."

"What are you saying?" Everton asked.

Mr Colin said, "The job is yours at another thousand a year, bigger car of course. It's the next logical promotion and we need you there."

Suddenly Everton realised the twist his life was taking; he was being moved away from Birkenhead, away from Doreen, just at the very time they were making progress and needed each other. He'd promised Doreen and also himself that he would work at the relationship, and if he accepted the job, he would once again be giving 'work' priority. He couldn't do it, he decided. "No, I'm sorry," he said. Noticing the disappointment in their faces he quickly added, "I'm very grateful, Sir, but it's too early, and there's so much more to do in Birkenhead, and I've only been there for a few months. I have to decline, but thank you very much for offering me it."

CHAPTER SIXTEEN

MR COLIN WAS SPEECHLESS. It had never entered his head that Everton would refuse. Nobody had ever refused promotion in Meadows', and here was their brightest star doing just that. There must be a particular reason for this and he'd have to find out what. Just at the moment, he'd like to get Everton away on his own, far away from Father who would now become angry. "I'll pretend that I didn't hear that," Father said, "and it's been arranged to start you in Ireland on the first of the month. Young Stafford from Gateshead will take over from you."

"Have you spoken to Mr Stafford, Sir?" Everton asked.

"Not yet."

"Well, Mr Stafford can't take my job because I'm not leaving. There isn't a vacancy."

"Don't talk to me like that, lad, the company has been very good to you, you owe - ."

"Father," said Mr Colin, "I want a word with you on your own, so I would like Everton to wait downstairs for a moment."

Father didn't look pleased because he was used to being in control. "You heard that," he said to Everton, "you'll have to leave us while we discuss your future with us, if you have any."

A grim faced Everton left the room, and after his footsteps had died away, Mr Colin said, "You can't bully him into this, Father."

"But why is he doing it?"

"There have been rumours."

"What sort of rumours?"

"He may be carrying on with his ex-secretary, Doreen. Maybe that's why he sacked her, to separate business from personal matters."

"Why should that make any difference?"

"He wouldn't want to go to Ireland and leave her in Birkenhead."

"Ah!"

"Let me talk to him on my own and I'll get to the bottom of it."

Mr Colin retreated to his own office and asked Everton to come up. He'd never seen Everton look so sullen before, his characteristic wide grin now completely vanished. "What's the problem?" Mr Colin asked.

"I have no problem and I'm grateful for the offer, but I'm not ready for it yet. And you can't sack me from my present job."

"I know that and you won't be. Father was upset. Is this anything to do with Doreen?"

"A startled Everton replied, "Why do you ask?"

"There have been rumours."

"Oh."

"Well?"

"Doreen is my girlfriend."

"And you don't want to leave her?"

"Yes, that's right, not now, not just at this particular time."

"We can't delay Alf's death because he's already dead!"

They both laughed and the tension was relieved. "Look," Mr Colin said, "I understand your problem, and we can't make you go, nor can we remove you from Birkenhead, unless you fall down on the job, and you certainly haven't done that. But consider what you're turning down. You're on the fast track upwards, and who knows, you may eventually take over from me? Refuse this promotion now and your entire future could be damaged. If Doreen loves you, she'll put up with your move and wait for you. If not, she probably doesn't love you. So I don't want you to say anything more at present, and I'm asking you to go away and think about it, and in a week's time we'll need your final decision. OK?"

Everton paused before answering, his wide grin slowly returning. "You've been very good to me, Sir," he said, "and I must do as you ask. I'll speak to you in a week, probably earlier."

"Not earlier, unless it's 'yes'," Mr Colin said.

Mr Colin sat alone for some time and wondered what more he could do to persuade Everton. Suddenly a thought came to him and he rang Accounts. "Have you got Doreen of Birkenhead's address?" he asked.

"Doreen's employment has been terminated, Sir."

"Yes, I know, but I still want her address."

Mr Colin was given it, and after checking that she wasn't on the phone he immediately set off for Birkenhead. He found the house fairly easily, in a mean street, probably subject to demolition and redevelopment in the near future. There was no bell or even a knocker, so he banged on the outside of the door with his fist. There was no response, so he banged again, and he noticed a curtain tweak at an upstairs window, then heard a shuffling of somebody approaching and unbolting the heavy door. Mr

Colin faced Doreen, dressed in a white dressing gown and what appeared to be pyjamas under that. "Why, hello Mr Colin," she said, "Sorry, I was having a lie in."

"Sorry to disturb you, Doreen, but I need to talk to you urgently. Is it convenient for me to come in?"

"Is it about Everton?" she asked.

"Yes."

"Come in then, it's a bit of a mess I'm afraid."

Mr Colin was shown an easy chair, the most comfortable one in a cramped sitting room. There was little furniture or shelves or books, but a new seventeen inch television sat in the corner. The flowered wallpaper was faded and peeling in places. There was one small window which had partly drawn curtains, so they sat in semi darkness. "What abut Everton?" Doreen asked.

"We have offered him promotion, in charge of Ireland, based in Belfast."

"Wow."

"He's refused."

"Why?"

"I suspect it's because of you. He won't leave you."

"He must go, I mean, it's important, isn't it?"

"It affects his whole career."

"What do you want me to do?"

"Persuade him."

"How?"

"I'll leave that to you. I believe you know him well and you may be lovers, you - ."

"We're not lovers, but I love him."

Mr Colin was not quite sure what the difference was; in his experience, making love and falling in love were all done in one movement. He went back to basics.

"Will you try to persuade him to go? You're our only hope."

Doreen looked puzzled. "Everton is very forthright," she said, "he'll do what he thinks is right. I will, however, try to persuade him. I can see that it is important."

"When do you see him again?"

"Wednesday. He's a week to make up his mind and reconsider".

"Would you like some tea, Mr Colin?"

"Thank you so much but no. I think you've been very understanding already."

Doreen was in turmoil. She felt flattered that the great man had come to see her in their humble home, and she giggled at the thought that she only had pyjama bottoms on; I wonder whether he knew?

There was a rattle of the letter box in the hall and she went to see if the post offered any more drama. Yes, there was a letter from Hank. 'Hello Babe,' it said, 'Here I am back home, and I've got a good job lined up selling insurance. I'm writing to ask you to forgive me. I know I behaved very badly on our last evening. I don't want to lose touch. Will you write to me at the above address, Doreen, because I still love you, and I've found out how much I miss you? Love and kisses, Hank.'

Doreen's feelings for Hank hadn't changed much, but here was a life line if she needed it. She knew that it would not be any good telling Everton that he'd have to go to Belfast, yet she knew that he must. Mr Colin was right to come and see her, and she now knew how she was going to persuade him. Maybe later he would be grateful to her, maybe when he was installed in Ireland they could get back together again, maybe she could go to Ireland, maybe...?

There was only one way to force Everton to go, and that was to be cruel and to remove herself from all considerations. For this she'd need Hank in name, if not in person.

Doreen was punctual, for once. Everton heard her familiar steps come up the stairs. She looked strained and had no makeup on, but it was still Doreen, beautiful and graceful Doreen, his Doreen.

"Hello Johnny Boy," she said.

"Hello love, do you fancy a meal first?"

"No Johnny, I need to talk to you and we can do that here. Should I make tea for us both, a bit like old times?"

"You're very mysterious, but yes, all right, and I have some news for you."

They engaged in small talk while they waited for the kettle to boil, then when Doreen was settled in her old seat, Everton said, "I have news; they want me to go to Belfast, promotion like. But I've said 'No', I like it here."

"Is that wise?"

"Probably not, but it's what I want. What did you want to talk to me about?"

"I've heard from Hank. He wants me to go to America. I've decided to go for a while and I might stay."

A fearful dread entered Everton's mind. Was he losing Doreen so soon? "But Doreen," he said, "what about us?"

"I know and I'm so sorry, Johnny, and you've been so good to me, and there was that fantastic weekend in North Wales which I'll never forget."

"I thought we'd agreed on a long term relationship. Did what you said about us mean nothing?"

"It did at the time, honest it did, but then when I heard from Hank, I knew that's what I wanted all along. I want to go to America, away from this country, the wet, the grime and poverty. America is the country of the future and I'm young."

"If I went to Ireland, would you come with me?"

This appeared to puzzle Doreen. Her brow furrowed. "But I thought you weren't going?" she said.

"I might."

"You must go, on your own. Anyway, as I said, I want to go to Hank. If it doesn't work out, and you're still in Ireland, I could always join you there, if you still wanted me after all this?"

Everton now felt angry. The little Miss was seeing him as second best, as reserve, and was trying to leave her options open. He'd end this now and go his own way, without her. "You seem to have made your mind up already, Doreen, and I'm devastated and angry, so I think you should go now. Will you at least keep in touch because I care about you, and I still love you? I always will."

"Of course," Doreen said, and she got up to go, and gave Everton a kiss on the lips. "Thank you," she said, and then she was gone.

Doreen had found it hard not to cry. She could see the distress which she had caused. Then she'd been floored when he'd suggested that she went to Ireland with him, but there would have been too many complications, and she couldn't suddenly say that she didn't care about Hank any more; her Mum would have tried to stop her, and she couldn't marry Johnny yet because she was too young; she was really still only a schoolgirl, with romantic notions far beyond her years. At least she'd kept her virginity. If she went to Ireland she'd have to support herself, without the comfort and convenience of her Mum and her Mum's home. She would never let Johnny support her, though no doubt he would have made the offer. Could she go back now and beg forgiveness, say that Hank was an invention and she'd go to Ireland with him?

She was on her way to Pauleen's to get her sympathy because her Mum wouldn't understand. When she stopped at the traffic lights, waiting to cross the road, she decided to return to the office and tell Johnny about everything and about Mr Colin's visit, and say she'd either go to Ireland with him or join him later. She turned and ran. As she approached Hind Street she saw the Minor pull away from the kerb, Johnny's gaze fixed forward onto the road ahead, towards Meols. She frantically waved to him but he didn't see her. Out of breath she lent on a lamppost and let the tears come. It was an omen that she'd missed him and she'd just have to accept that. Maybe in a month or two she'd contact him in Ireland? She knew that she was taking a gigantic risk letting him go, but somehow it seemed right. She'd take that job in Woodchurch, but right now she'd go to Pauleen and pour her heart out to her, because Pauleen would listen; she always did and she was a good friend.

Everton's Mum could see that her son was in distress. His eyes were red and he toyed with his food. "Are you going to tell me," she said, "or are you going to bottle it all up?"

"I have mixed news, really. Mr Colin has offered me a good job in Ireland, and I didn't tell you because I decided not to accept it."

"Was it promotion and more money?"

"Both."

"For God's sake, John, have you taken leave of your senses?"

"Don't worry, I've changed my mind; I'm going now and I shall tell Mr Colin in the morning."

"Why ever did you refuse it in the first place?"

"Because I was going to lose Doreen."

"That young girl in the office you sacked?"

"Yes."

"What's she got to do with it?"

"I love her and she said that she loved me, but now she's going to America to marry a Yank or something."

John's tears started to flow. His Mum moved towards him and put an arm around his shoulder. "You poor boy," she said, "you're so lacking in experience, this sort of thing happens to every young person several times over before a permanent relationship is formed. Your problem is that you don't yet realise that your experience is not unique."

"I'm a silly fool, aren't I?"

"No, you're not, you're human, and I was beginning to worry that you weren't, with no girl in sight. You've been too busy and 'all work and no play makes John a dull boy'. Anyway, tell me about the Irish job; it sounds very interesting."

"I think it is, and I can't wait to get stuck into it."

"You'll be leaving home and that's yet another experience for you."

"Will you come with me?"

"No, my life revolves around here, but I'll visit. Will you buy a house?"

"Suppose I will."

"Great, then I'll come over and advise about curtains and carpets. It'll be great fun. I wonder what Ireland is like?"

It was Doreen's birthday in a week. He'd bought her a Yardley Compact, the sort that was currently in fashion. He'd chosen the shade with great care as it was the first present he'd bought her, and it had to be exactly right. After supper he went out to Meols promenade. It was low tide and there was plenty of sand and soft gurgling mud. When he'd made sure that nobody was watching he threw it into the mud. It landed with a satisfying plonk, and he watched the mud close in around it, before it sank without trace. One chapter of his life was over and another was about to begin.

BOOK TWO
MID SUMMER – 1956

CHAPTER SEVENTEEN
Mid summer 1956

EVERTON WENT ON THE deck of the 'Ulster Prince' and watched the ferry manoeuvre out of the Liverpool docks. The dirty water filled up the last basin, raising the boat to the level of the Mersey, then the big dock gates opened and they moved out. He went to the stern of the boat and watched the bright lights of Birkenhead and Liverpool gradually fade away. Behind him he was leaving all he knew, his Mum and home in Meols, Doreen in Birkenhead, and his bosses and workmates in Meadows'. The effects of the beer drinking in the Birkenhead Bill Room were beginning to wear off, and he began to feel depressed. He mused that in life there would be moments like this which he would remember with utter clarity, while the rest of his life would be just one long blur. One such memory would be the final minutes of the goodbye party, the keen and excited expression on young Stafford's face as he was about to take over the well knit organisation he'd created. Beside Stafford had been the serious face of Miss Bottom. In the last few days he'd grown quite fond of her. They would have made a good partnership.

Somewhere in the hold of the boat was the latest model of the Poster Rolling Machine which he was taking with him. He'd make that lot sit up and notice, just as he'd done once before. He was glad that Sam had taken him aside for a whole day so that he could practice dry brush posting. If need be he was going to have to demonstrate the advantages to the Belfast Billposters. Mr Colin had said that the Belfast men were a lazy and difficult lot, so he had obtained his permission to experiment on a bonus/incentive scheme for them. Father had not been consulted, "Because," said Mr Colin, "he wouldn't be able to understand it. As long as you don't increase billposting costs you can do what you like."

There was a chill in the air and a cold wind came through as the boat gathered speed. Trying hard not to think too much of the past, he began to contemplate the new challenges ahead, and then he went down to his cabin and turned in early. He would be disembarking at eight and he'd walk to the office and surprise them all by an early start.

Everton's first view of Belfast was in bright summer sunlight. Coasting slowly along the Lagan River he was aware of the clanging of Harland and Wolf's great shipyard, two new ships being cradled in scaffolding. He heard trams going across the bridges, and the general noise of a great city awakening. All around him in the distance were the hills of County Antrim and Castlereagh, the city appearing to nestle in a giant saucer.

In Liverpool, they'd given him a map of how to get to the office from the boat and he decided to walk, having previously spurned the invitation of a lift. In Linenhall Street, behind the City Hall, he found Meadows' office, a new, narrow, red brick building squashed in between taller office blocks. In time this would become as familiar to him as the cosy office in Hind Street, Birkenhead, and the group of buildings in Liverpool, which served the company as a head office. The outside gate was open, revealing a narrow entrance to the rear. Stuck in the gateway was a van with a puncture, blocking the way off to other vehicles behind. Everton decided to wait and watch.

There didn't appear to be any hurry to get moving. Far from being outraged, the men behind the crippled van had come out to join the punctured vehicle. They didn't help, but there was a lot of good natured banter. Although the wheel was being changed, it was all done at snail-like pace.

After half an hour the two man team who had done the work got back into their vehicle and drove off, at last releasing the other vehicles which now followed. They all turned left and sped off down the street. Odd, thought Everton, that they were all going the same way; they should by rights be spreading out into all quarters of the city. In the distance he noticed that all the vans had stopped. Why? Everton set off on foot to investigate, and then he saw a shop facia above a window declaring that business there was 'The Cosy Teashop'. Inside were the billposters, apparently having breakfast. It was time, thought Everton, to go into the office, and find out whether there was the same relaxed atmosphere in there as there was outside!

Nobody noticed him go inside, and nobody at the counter challenged him. He went through a door into a corridor, then up a flight of stairs. A sign outside the door on the landing was marked 'BILL ROOM', so he went in, and came into a large and airy room with a large Bill Room table in the middle, and poster racks around all the walls. In one corner there was a small office partitioned off with glass panels. Inside the office he spied an elderly man with a much younger one, enjoying their tea or coffee in large mugs. On the desk in front of them was a sugar bowl from which the elder man was taking large spoonfuls, the other man must have already helped himself because he was slowly and ceremoniously stirring. Everton burst into their reverie and asked, "Did you not see the shambles outside?"

They turned and looked at Everton, as if to say, 'you're disturbing us, go away'. For a moment they made no reply, and then Everton said, "Well?"

The elder man said, "Excuse me, who are you?"

"I'm your boss."

"Come again?"

"My name is John Smyth and I've come from Liverpool to run this area, and so far I don't like what I've seen. Now, who and what are you?" The atmosphere changed at once from indifference to nervous attention. They both leapt to their feet and the elder man said, "I'm Jim Waters, the Foreman, and this is Pete, my assistant."

"All right, Jim, I'll go back to the beginning again. Two of your men had a puncture this morning and were blocking the access for half an hour or more, preventing everyone else from getting about their work. While this was going on, where were you?"

"We were here, Sir," Jim said.

"Doing what?"

"Sorting out the day's work."

"And making tea?" suggested Everton.

"We're entitled to a tea break."

"So soon?"

"When we like."

"And were you aware about the events that were going on below? You must have known because I see that there is a large window looking straight down into the yard below."

"It often happens, Sir, a van doesn't start or something, and then everybody else gets stuck."

"So, you were prepared to let events look after themselves?"

"There was nothing we could have done."

"And where did the men go when they left?"

"To work, of course."

"You mean, you don't know?"

"Don't know what?"

"That they go to the Cosy Teashop for breakfast, the whole damn lot of them."

"You're joking!"

"Go out and see for yourself. I've been here for half an hour and know that; you've been here probably half a life time and know nothing.

Now, get out there and go down the street and expel them from that place and into work. And you, Pete, take me to your ex-boss' office, and I shall now want to see Don Wells."

"Oh, Mr Wells won't be in yet, Sir," Pete said nervously.

"Then I'll wait."

Pete took Everton back into the corridor and volunteered some information about the geography of the building. "The Bill Room is at one end of the passage," he said, "and yours and Don Wells' office is at the other end. In between are toilets and washrooms and the typists' office. On the top floor are 'Rents' and the Canvasser's office." Pete pushed open a door and said, "That will be your office, Sir, but I'll show you Mr Wells' office next door."

"Don't bother," Everton said, "I'll wait in my own office, and with the door open so that I can see people come and go."

"Can I bring you some tea, Sir, the morning paper perhaps?"

"That's very thoughtful of you, Pete; yes, I would like that."

Everton had taken an instant like to Pete. He had a perpetual smile and alert looking eyes. There was no hope for him while he worked for scowling Jim Waters, and Pete had volunteered useful information and he didn't have to do that. With satisfaction, Everton realised that if he sat behind his desk and left the door open, he could see down the corridor as far as the Bill Room. He presumed that the toilets, half way down the corridor, were the only ones in the building, other than for the Billposters in the yard. That would mean that everyone from upstairs and downstairs would have to visit them at some time during the day, and from this vantage point he could call out to anyone he might want to see. He would feel in contact here, and have a feel of the pulse of all that went on in the building.

At half past nine a tall but stooped man, slim with a good crop of grey hair, came along the corridor. He appeared surprised to see Everton through the open door. Looking in, he said, "I'm Don Wells."

"Call me Everton," Everton replied.

"Yes, of course, we've heard quite a lot about you, Mr Meadows' blue-eyed boy."

Ignoring that quip Everton said, "Come in and sit down, we have a lot to discuss." Don came in and moved to shut the door.

"No, leave the door open," Everton said.

"Open? Are you quite sure?"

"Quite sure."

Don had worked for Meadows' as a boy, progressing through the Bill Room, then to Accounts, and had promotion to the Chief Clerk when he was forty, then finally became an Assistant to Alf Nelson, for whom he'd worked for the last five years. He did not see himself as a high flyer, just a reliable and accurate worker which Meadows' could not do with-out. He regarded his partnership with Alf as comfortable and they had become good friends. When Alf suddenly died, Don was at mortified at first, then excited by the prospect of promotion and achieving his just reward for hard and loyal toil. The Company in Ireland would be safe in his dependable hands. When he'd heard that he had been bypassed by an unknown, he was bitterly disappointed and even considered resignation, but where would he go and what would he do? He made enquiries about John Smyth, nicknamed Everton, and heard that he was a young fellow in his twenties, once Assistant to Mr Smiley whom he rang to find out more. "He's a bright lad," Mr Smiley had said, "and so far lucky. He saw Jack Purvis off and did us all a favour, and he's been doing marvels with the Birkenhead Branch, in a very short time. But then if you have luck and Mr Colin backing you, how can you fail? At the moment he's flavour of the month."

Don decided to accept the situation, but he would watch Everton closely. If he discovered that 'Superman' was cutting corners, he'd pull him up, or report him, or both!

Don took his seat, opposite this youth, and said, "Why do you want the door open?"

"Because I can see the staff as they pass. Like I saw you, and pulled you in."

Don did not like the words, 'pulled you in', but nevertheless he ex-tended his hand and said, "Welcome to Ireland."

"Thank you Don. Now, to business. How many billposting rounds are there in Belfast and how many sixteen sheet units are there in each?"

"There are about one thousand five hundred units, and we employ ten billposters working five rounds."

"So that's about three hundred units per round and one hundred and fifty units per man."

"I suppose that would be right, but of course it varies round by round."

"No wonder they can afford to spend half the morning having break-fast down the street."

"I beg your pardon?"

"Oh, don't you know?"

"Know what"

"When the men eventually stumble out of here they go up to 'The Cosy Teashop' to have their breakfast, before a single sheet is posted."

"How do you know?"

"I watched them when I arrived this morning."

"Well, they might do it now and again; but I assure you it's not normal practice."

"Have you checked every day?"

"That's not my job, that's Jim's job. Have you met Jim yet?"

"Yes, and he said that he didn't know about the café and doesn't seem very interested."

"Jim is very sound and he's been here a very long time. He has my full vote of confidence."

"He hasn't got mine, but moving on, can you tell me why you have two men per round when one man would do? Eighty percent of a billposter's time is spent on travelling and only twenty percent on posting, probably only ten percent if you take off breakfast."

"It's normal practice. Always has been. Some of the sites are high and one man needs to hold the ladder when the other man is posting."

"How many sites are there of, say, over twenty five feet tall?"

"I can't tell you."

"Well find out. I suspect it's only a handful, and in those instances one billposter can double up with another."

"What are you suggesting?"

"I suggest five one man rounds plus one spare man for doubling up."

"But that would mean four billposters becoming redundant. What would become of them?"

"Natural wastage and sacked when caught out, like having breakfast in the firm's time. I could have sacked the lot this morning."

"You can't do this, Everton. You've been here for five minutes and you think you know all the answers. Ben Rice is the Shop Steward and you haven't had dealings with him yet. Any kind of bother and they're out – on strike. What would you do then?"

"They'll not do that. I intend that half the number of billposters will do the job at seventy five percent of the present cost."

"I don't understand."

"We'll put them on a bonus incentive scheme. We'll measure their work load and pay them the basic pay for a seventy five percent of target. If they achieve their target they get a twenty five percent bonus. If, for instance, they exceed their target by ten percent they get a thirty five percent bonus."

"My God, how complicated can this get? Who's going to work all this out?"

"You are."

"Me?"

"Yes. I have other work to do and I need to go down to Dublin and Cork soon. I'll see the billposters this evening before they go home. And there's another thing, I've brought a poster rolling machine with me. They start dry brush posting at once."

"They'll never do it," said an agitated Don.

"With a twenty five percent pay rise they'll do anything. Finally, we both need to keep an eye on Jim. I don't trust him."

"Jim is a fine man and there's absolutely nothing wrong with him," Don shouted.

"Only his attitude, and as I don't think he'll change that I suspect he'll leave."

"What then?"

"Pete will get the job; he's a good lad."

Don went next door to his own office, upset and visibly trembling. His secretary came in with his mail and noticed his demeanour. "Are you all right, Mr Wells?" she asked.

"Have you met Everton yet, Sarah?"

"Who?"

"Everton, our new boss. He's next door."

"Betty has been in taking dictation already. Says he's very bossy," and she giggled.

"We've got to learn to live with him, Sarah. Would you bring my tea in early, please?"

Don pushed his mail to one side and considered his position. He was feeling bitterly disappointed that he hadn't got the top job, and now he was going to have to live alongside this young tycoon who thought he knew all the answers. He would like to resign, in protest, but what good would that do? It wouldn't worry Everton, and he'd probably promote Pete and at fifty five where was he going to get another job? He would have to stay at his post and try to minimise the damage. There'd be an immediate confrontation with the Shop Steward, and Ben would crucify Everton. That was it, he'd try to steer a middle course and prevent a strike. He'd mediate between the combatants. He'd suggest that natural wastage would be the remedy, and to delay the new work rounds until that had been achieved. There'd be no sackings and there never had been before, so he'd prevent a strike. Somehow he'd have to warn the men not to go to that café, although he didn't see the harm if they got through their work. He'd speak to Jim to tell the men that the café was definitely out of bounds in company time. Odd that Everton had only been in the place for minutes and had stumbled upon one of their worst working practices. Talk about luck – Mr Smiley had been right.

Everton stared at the assembled billposters. They all looked a decent and jolly lot, except perhaps that wiry sharp nosed character in the corner, who was probably Ben. Don introduced Everton who now had the floor.

"I'm happy to meet you," Everton said, "and I wish to associate myself very closely with your work problems. I want you to know that I'm always approachable, and my door is always open, literally. The first news is that I've brought over with me, from Liverpool, a poster rolling machine. You will see that it's at the end of the table. It will make your life easier and, combined with dry brush posting, will improve the look of our sites. I'll not accept any arguments that it's not practical. It works well elsewhere, very well in fact –."

Ben cut in at once. "If you expect us to adapt to new methods we'll need more pay."

"Quite right, Ben – it is Ben, isn't it? Yes, I'll come to that." There were some mutterings and low whistles. They appeared not to be expecting any of this. Everton continued, "Sites have been lost and sheetage reduced, so your workload has been downsized. We must work towards a re-grouping and Mr Wells has been doing work on this all day. At present you have too little work to do and you take too long to do it and take home too little pay, so we must give you more work and more pay. In future there'll be five one man rounds – an extra billposter will be retained to double up on high sites."

The billposters loudly protested at this latest news, and Ben called out, "We're not going to accept staff redundancies."

"I'll deal with that now. We need a saving of four men, and all that will be taken up by natural wastage. Two of you are due to retire in six months time, so by then we'll be half way there."

"Will there be any sackings?" Ben called out again.

"Only for misconduct, like having breakfast in company time."

There was stunned silence. Everton continued, "You'll not be paid in the normal way. We're introducing a bonus incentive scheme. You will be paid by results. If, for instance, you achieve your target performance, you'll get a twenty five percent bonus. I shall be happy to discuss the proposals with Ben and your Union Representative, without delay."

"What about overtime?" someone asked.

"You'll not get paid overtime, but if you achieve a heavy work load by working overtime, the results will be reflected in your bonus. Now, one final point, this morning I watched a shambles while one van got stuck in the gateway and you all had to wait to have your breakfasts. Subject to checking security at your homes, you'll collect the day's work the evening before and take your van home, then you can go straight to work from there. You will not use your vehicle for private purposes and if you do we will know and you'll be sacked. If you're late in starting from your home, you'll have to work longer to complete your work. We won't mind when you do it as long as you do do it."

Again there were mutterings and low whistles. "Any more questions?" Everton asked.

"Yes," Ben said, "It's all very well for Management to tell us about dry brush posting when Management knows fuck all about it, particularly on high sites when you'll have to get in close on the bottom sheets and your ladder is angled away from the board. I'd like to see you do it."

Everton had been waiting for this one and hoped that Ben would fall into the trap. He couldn't have put it better himself. The days training with Sam in Birkenhead on high sites was about to pay a dividend. "What site do you have in mind, Ben?"

"Well, Hope Street, top line."

"What have we got on?" Everton asked Pete.

"Sixteen sheet Oxydol."

"Roll that for me and at eight tomorrow morning I want all of you to meet me in Hope Street, and I'll show you how it's done. I wouldn't dream of asking any of you to do something which I could not."

CHAPTER EIGHTEEN

WITH RESERVATION DOREEN TOOK the receptionist job. She had decided
in advance that she was not going to like it, and it was easy to do just
that once she'd started. How could she like it, she thought, after all that
excitement in Hind Street? And of course Everton had gone, probably for
good. There was no way that she'd try to contact him. Trouble was that
although she knew where he was, he thought that she'd gone to the States
and would therefore not try to contact her. Had she been too severe on
herself spinning all those lies, just to make sure that he'd go to Ireland and
safeguard his future?

It was therefore with pure delight that she received a letter from Mr
Colin. She read –

'Dear Doreen,

I would like to thank you for a neat bit of deception which ensured
that Everton went to Ireland. I asked him what had changed his mind,
and he said something about your telling him that you were going to the
States. I hope that your separation from him will not prove to be permanent and that no long term damage has been done to your relationship.

I now write to ask a favour. Our receptionist, Gillian, is leaving to
get married. I would like to offer you her old job, and I presume that you
are not really going to the States. You would not have to do any typing,
but of course we would need time keeping discipline. Before advertising
the job I would be grateful if you would contact me as soon as possible
and tell me your thoughts either way.

Yours sincerely,

Colin Meadows.'

Doreen instantly knew what she would do. She rang Mr Colin and
asked when she could start. He suggested that she come in next Monday
and work alongside Gillian to get some training. After two weeks she'd
be on her own. "I want to ask a favour of you now," Doreen said.

"Yes?"

"I don't want Everton to know that I'm still here, at least not yet. I don't want to be known as Doreen on the switchboard."

"What, a code name perhaps, 'Foxtrot Charley'?"

"No, just another girl's name," and she laughed.

"You tell me what you'd like."

"What about Hilda, my Mum's name?"

"Hilda will do very nicely, Doreen, but won't Everton recognise your voice, though he is likely to get his own switchboard girl to put a call through to various people here."

"I doubt it; it's not Everton's style. He likes to do everything himself, but I speak Liverpudlian, and nearly everybody else here speaks the same way."

"Hilda it is then."

Doreen turned up early for her first day's work. Gillian found another seat so that they could sit next to each other, and Doreen watched Gillian make all the connections. It was quite simple and made less boring than it could be by the playful banter between Gillian and the callers. Every few minutes a visitor would call in from off the street, and Gillian would have to find out the nature of their business and the person whom they wished to see. Sometimes she would offer them a cup of tea and Doreen would make it, something she was well used to from her Hind Street days. On one occasion, when Gillian had to go to the loo, Doreen took a call from Everton who wanted to speak to Mr Colin who was out. Doreen said, "Mr Colin is out for the day."

"Is that Gillian?" Everton asked.

"No, I'm Hilda. I shall be taking over from Gillian."

"Oh, hello Hilda. Are you new?"

"Very new."

There was a long pause as if the voice was considering something, and then Everton said, "Ok Hilda, I'll ring tomorrow."

Doreen breathed a sigh of relief; she had passed the first test.

When lunch time came Doreen was allowed to take over while Gillian had her lunch break. At five o'clock Gillian suggested that they go for a quiet drink where "I can tell you some things you should know, best told out of the office".

They went up the road to a quiet hotel and ordered two orange juices in the deserted cocktail bar. "I need to warn you about Mr Colin," Gillian said.

"He's nice, isn't he?" Doreen said.

"Too nice; that's the problem."

"Problem?"

"He fancies the girls. At the moment he's having an affair with Francis in Accounts."

"Affair? You mean he fancies her?"

"More than that. He takes her to London when they go on business."

"Christ! How does she get the time off?"

"Oh, he just says she's travelling as his secretary."

"Doesn't the staff think it odd?"

"Oh, we all know the score, and it's in our interest to say nothing."

"Does Mrs Meadows know?"

"Carol knows nothing but suspects a lot. If you're married to a rich man it's probably easier to put up with it."

"Do you know Carol?"

"She comes to the Christmas party and gets very drunk. Last time she cuddled up next to Mr Smiley. Well, you'd have to be drunk to do that, wouldn't you?"

"Thanks for warning me."

"You need to look after yourself."

"How do you mean?"

"You're a good looking girl and you're young. It's only a matter of time before he moves in."

"Crumbs! How? What do I do?"

"Go along with it if you want early promotion. If you don't mind about your promotion prospects being dented, fend him off on the first approach. That's what I did."

"You?"

"Shortly after I came here he would stop when passing through Reception, and if I wasn't busy he would chat me up. One day he invited me out to dinner."

"What did you say?"

"I just said that I didn't think that it was a very good idea, him being married and that. He said she wouldn't mind as long as we were discreet which he would be. I said that I didn't see the point and no thank you very much, and he said he was sorry he'd asked, but he just liked to get to know his staff well. I cheekily replied, 'What, male staff as well?'. He left me alone after that."

Doreen said, "I wouldn't mind a free dinner, but I'd die if it caused trouble with his wife."

"Yes, and he'd expect you to go all the way."

"How do you mean?"

"He'd take you to the Adelphi and spoil you on a slap-up dinner and wine, and all the time he's got a room booked upstairs."

"You're joking!"

"I have it on good authority."

"I'm not having sex with anyone 'til I'm married," Doreen said.

"Why not try it out first?" Gillian enquired.

"I might not like it," Doreen replied and they both laughed.

When Gillian left they all went round the corner to the pub to say their farewells. They presented her with a silver cigarette case with her name engraved on it. She lit another cigarette and coughed. Mr Colin put his arm around her and said, "Send us a piece of the cake, Gillian," and he ordered another round of drinks. The evening's entertainment was on him, or to be more accurate, out of the petty cash float. After a couple of hours the party began to break up, and Doreen noticed Francis cuddle up to Mr Colin. They made no effort to disguise their feelings towards each other, and they left together, hand in hand. Gillian turned to Doreen and winked.

Doreen was on her own in the office on Monday and at lunch time she felt exhausted. Her relief from Accounts took over so she could take an hour off for lunch. She went off to a Milk Bar in Bold Street, but felt lonely without Gillian's prattle. It was with relief that she returned to her desk, and to have the company of voices, if not of people in body.

During the next few days Doreen took several calls from Everton, asking her to put him through to various people. She even joked with him and that was a mistake. He said, "Do I know you, your voice is familiar?"

She replied, "I'm Hilda, the new girl who's taken over from Gillian."

"Oh well, Hilda, can you put me through to Mr Smiley please." Two minutes later Mr Smiley came back to her on the phone and said, "Everton wants to speak to you again."

"Hello again," Doreen said.

"It's not Hilda, is it?" Everton asked. "I've managed to winkle it out of Mr Smiley, you're Doreen."

Doreen's heart sank. She was not ready for this. "I'm Hilda," she said weakly.

"No, you're not, and stop messing me around, Doreen."

Doreen was silent, then Everton spoke again, "What are you doing there and why are you calling yourself Hilda?"

"It's just a temp job, Everton; I need the work. I didn't want you to know I was here because I thought it would upset you."

"I thought you were going to join Hank and that's why I'm here in Ireland."

"Are you enjoying it there? Aren't you glad you went?"

"Stop avoiding the issue, Doreen. Why aren't you in America or on your way?"

Doreen thought that it was time she came clean so she said, "I was never going to go to America but I wanted you to go to Ireland."

"So you lied."

"Yes."

"To make me come here?"

"Yes."

"I broke my heart on you."

"And I broke mine. And I didn't want you to know that I was still around, at least not yet. I thought that in time you'd forgive me, and I was trying to give you that time. Nothing is lost and I still love you and always will – I could join you in Ireland now or at any time you want, you only have to say."

"Oh no, not now. I've made my move and you've made yours, and I could never trust you again."

"You haven't thought about it, so please do that; I did it all for you."

"I know you did, Doreen, but it's too late. I've already got you out of my system, and I don't want to go through all that love sickness again. I want to bury myself in my work. It's best that we go our own ways."

Doreen knew that she was going to cry. She'd have to get rid of him and get off the line before she broke down. "Bye now," she said, "Mr Colin is trying to get an outside line," she lied before cutting him off.

Mr Colin found Doreen in tears. "Whatever is the matter?" he asked. Warned by Gillian of his amorous habits, Doreen said, "It's personal."

"You're not in a fit state to be at your desk. You need a break. I'll get some relief for you."

"I'm all right," Doreen snapped, then a thought came to her mind and she added, "Actually, I don't think I can stay on this job so is there another one I can do?"

"You've only been at the job for a few days. What's the matter? Can't you do it? Everyone is saying how well you're managing."

"It's Everton, Sir, he's recognised my voice. He's very angry and doesn't want to know me any longer. He comes through on the phone every day, and I don't know why he can't use his switchboard girl like everybody else. That's why I can't stay in this job."

"You're a good girl," Mr Colin said, "I'm sure there's something we can find for you. Tell you what, suppose we have a quiet drink after work? Come up to my office, and in the meantime I'll think about options. We don't want to lose you."

Doreen was caught off guard. Her relief that Mr Colin was taking her troubles seriously blinded her concern that Mr Colin might have another agenda. "Oh, thank you, Sir, I'd like that." It was only after Mr Colin had gone up the stairs that she realised that she might have been hasty. A drink? What sort of drink? His office, after hours? She'd have to make sure that Francis from Accounts did not see her.

At half past five Doreen crept up the stairs to Mr Colin's office, and knocked. "Come," he called out. Mr Colin was laid back in his swivel chair, his feet on the desk, reading The Times. He leapt to his feet and opened the drinks cupboard. "Well, I think we have a solution," he said, "and what would you like? A sherry perhaps?"

"Yes please, just a little one," Doreen said as she sat down.

Mr Colin poured her a full glass of sherry and a gin and tonic for himself, the same drink which Everton had once said that the Meadows' lived on. "Cheers," Mr Colin said, and took a sip. Doreen took a great big gulp of sherry, and felt better for it.

"Mr Smiley has got problems in his department," Mr Colin said, "and he's been on at me about extra staff. I don't think he needs it, but if you're available, so to speak, we could move you into that office. You'd be an assistant to his Assistant, and there'd be no need for you to be on the telephone to other staff. It's a sideways move, at the same salary, and presumably you can revert back to 'Doreen' again?"

That would do nicely, Doreen thought, certainly as a temporary measure. She didn't like Mr Smiley for having broken her cover, but she'd forgive him. "Thank you very much, Mr Colin, I'd like that, but have you anybody to take over from me in Reception? It's not a job you can leave empty. I've already discovered how essential it is."

"I have indeed, Francis from Accounts will work alongside you for a few days, and then you can move to Mr Smiley's office. Francis can let it be known to Everton that Hilda has left, and from his point of view you will have vanished."

"Has Francis agreed to this yet, Sir?"

"No, but she will. She's waiting for me in the car park at the moment. Francis always does everything I ask her."

Doreen was not quite sure whether Mr Colin had winked as he had said that. At once she felt more relaxed and took another gulp of sherry. There was no longer any need to fear Mr Colin who had Francis to give him what she quite definitely was not prepared to give. She would now be working in the same office Everton had worked in and she would have company, and more importantly, she would still be in employment. "Thank you ever so," Doreen said, and finished off the rest of her sherry.

"Like another?" Mr Colin asked.

"No thanks, Sir, you can't leave Francis in the car park any longer."

On Doreen's next natter with Pauleen, her friend asked, "And so Mr Smiley is not so bad?"

"He's a dear, but Debra, his Assistant, is a disaster. It's why the department is in such a mess."

"Will Debra get the job when Mr Smiley retires?"

"Afraid so."

"Then you'll be an Assistant to Debra and have to carry her."

"I'm not looking that far ahead at the moment."

"I'm glad to hear it because I wish that just for once, you'd think and talk about something else other than your flaming work."

"Sorry."

"What's your social life like?"

"You know what it's like, dead without Everton, therefore dead for good."

"Rubbish! How do you fancy a blind date?"

"What?"

"My boyfriend, Gary, has a friend, Eddie. He's a bit of a loner. Care to make up a foursome?"

"To do what"

"Oh, I don't know. We could go down to Chester for a meal, then the flicks. Make a night of it. Eddie has a car."

"What's this Eddie like?"

"As I say, he's a loner. He runs with Gary in the Harrier Club. Gary says' he's rather superior, and doesn't know what he's doing in the club."

"Running, perhaps?"

"Very funny. Yes, Eddie says he's a front runner and goes in for all the championships."

"Hasn't he a girlfriend?"

"As I say, he's a loner."

"Ok. What's there to lose?"

"Next Friday?"

"Next Friday it is then."

They met outside the Adelphi Hotel. Doreen knew Gary and thought him lovely. Eddie turned out to be tall and slim, with a narrow face, a small mouth and a sharp nose to go with it. He wore a well pressed suit and carried a neatly rolled black umbrella which made Doreen laugh. They all got into Eddie's car, a well polished green Riley, and drove at speed down to Chester. They had supper in a Milk Bar and then went on to the cinema. Pauleen sat entwined with Gary. Eddie sat bolt upright, his umbrella firmly positioned between his knees.

On the way home Pauleen and Gary sat on the back seat and cuddled up together. Doreen began to realise the object of the exercise, to get Eddie to drive them about in his car while they had the back seat to themselves. Eddie dropped Gary and Pauleen off at Pauleen's house, before driving Doreen home.

"Thank you ever so," Doreen said, "it's been a lovely evening."

"Jolly good," Eddie agreed. He had a plumb in his mouth at the time.

Doreen waited for the expected kiss but no movement was made. "I'll go now," she said.

"I say, would you like to come out for dinner some time?"

"Dinner?"

"Yes, the Adelphi maybe?"

"Isn't that rather expensive?" Doreen suggested.

"Oh, I'm paying."

Obviously he could afford it so Doreen said, "Yes, ok." After all, what was there to lose?

Doreen had never had a meal like it. They went to the Mal Maison in the hotel. Each course took ages to arrive so Doreen nibbled at the dinner rolls, and as soon as one was eaten a waiter would put another one in its place. She was not that hungry when the real food arrived, but was glad of her training with Everton because at least she knew which cutlery to use. Eddie said little. He obviously lived in another world, of high finance and stocks and shares, public school education and University, living in with his parents in a big house in the country. But she liked him. He was polite and considerate, with little mannerisms such as unlocking her side of the car when she got in and closing the door after her, and seeing that she left the room in front of him. He tried hard to amuse her, telling her jokes which she didn't understand and she wondered if they were dirty, so gave them guarded laughter. Everton had never behaved so regally to her as Eddie was doing, and it all seemed to come so naturally. She was sure that she had been unable to impress him; she wasn't bright enough for him for starters.

They went out several times, and Doreen began to understand him better and be entertained by him, she was impressed by his grandeur and self importance, his dress and articulate speech. She didn't fancy him but every girl likes a kiss and she never got one.

After about a month, Eddie announced that it was his birthday and to celebrate he would take her to Blackpool to see the lights. Doreen was excited about that because she had never been there before and was curious, and perhaps there might even be a bit of romance? They parked the car at one end of the prom and walked the full length, admiring all the illuminations on the way. Doreen was quite tired by the time they got to other the end, and was glad that Eddie had decided to go back on the upper deck of a tram, enabling them to admire the lights all over again.

When they got back to the other end they went to the Pleasure Park. Doreen was terrified by some of the rides, but Eddie sat bolt upright in all of them, with his umbrella still firmly fixed between his knees. Doreen told him quite truthfully that she had a headache and would like something more gentle, and longingly looked at the two-seater canoes at the love tunnel. Instead, Eddie took her to the shooting booths and won a large pink rabbit which she loved to bits. "And now to dinner," Eddie said.

"Dinner?"

"Yes, at the Metropole. You've deserved it." Doreen thought she had too, and pondered on all the good food she'd had for the past few weeks and the extra weight she'd put on; there was no chance of slimming while she went out with Eddie, but now she was ravishingly hungry, and could eat anything; perhaps tomorrow she'd start giving up lunches, which would save her money as well.

They arrived at the Metropole Hotel by taxi and much to her astonishment, Doreen discovered that he'd booked a full suite including a sitting room. What luxury! There was certainly something to be said for having a rich boyfriend; if they ever married she would be set up for life, and who knows, she might even start to love him, and she was already quite fond of him. She didn't see what he saw in her, particularly as he had never made any advances towards her. "What are we doing here?" Doreen asked.

"You can order your food and drink from room service, and they'll bring it up here; it's called gracious living."

Doreen was amazed. Eddie was spending a fortune on her. What would it be like to always live like that, without any apparent effort to obtain the means, unlike her or Everton who both worked like slaves?

They ordered food and two bottles of wine. After three full glasses of wine, Doreen was incapable of knowing what she'd eaten, and she felt slightly drunk; she waited to be seduced and surely now it would happen? She did not have long to wait. After the staff had cleared away the table, they retired to the couch in their private sitting room. Doreen was prepared for anything, and she realised that Eddie deserved a little something in return.

"Come here," he said, and drew her to him. They kissed passionately and Doreen responded to Eddie's advances. The man was human after all, but how far was he going to go? In alarm, Doreen had to fight to stop Eddie's hand starting to explore her thighs under her dress, and fumbling with her suspender belt. Doreen pulled his hand away but he was not discouraged; he moved to the top of her dress, skilfully unzipping it from the back and yanking her bra off, before he grabbed her breasts in an animal-like fashion.

Trying hard to push him off and screaming, she was still unable to stop him from mounting her while he pulled his trousers off; she was being raped. She pulled a knee sharply up against his crotch and he winced. Doreen took the opportunity to slide out from under him, and then she grabbed her bag, bra and coat and bolted for the door. She unlocked it and limped through it, leaving one shoe behind. In the corridor she didn't dare wait for the lift, so instead she found the top of the stairs and half ran and half fell down three flights to the ground floor. She replaced her bra, zipped up her dress and put her coat on. There was silence behind her; she'd got away.

She had been there before. There was only one man in the whole world she could trust and that was Everton, and he didn't want her any more. Trying to act as normally as possible, she went out into the street and started to limp her way to the Station. Wait until she told Pauleen!

CHAPTER NINETEEN

ON EVERTON'S SECOND DAY he ventured upstairs to interview Mr Hamilton, the site-getter for the Belfast area. He was met by a very fit sixty year old with thick grey hair and a big head on a slim body, all of which didn't seem to match. He was very well dressed and sported a bright yellow bow tie. He seemed surprised that Everton had come up to see him – no Manager had ever ventured up the final flight of stairs for as long as he could remember.

"Should I not come down to see you in your own office?" Mr Hamilton asked.

"Why?" Everton replied. "You have all your records here, so it's simpler this way."

"Records?"

"Yes – you must have some."

"My call sheets, perhaps?"

"Call sheets?" asked Everton. "What are they? Actually, you better start from scratch. Give me an example of a typical day?"

Mr Hamilton explained and Everton took great care not to interrupt him until he had finished.

"I come in at nine," Mr Hamilton said, "then I take my black book down to the typists' office." He showed Everton his book, rather like a large notebook in which he recorded, in neat longhand, all the calls he had made on each day. "I find a typist who is free and I dictate my calls from the day before, and she types it all onto a page of A4. Then I sign it and go out. I go to an area of the City I haven't been to for some time and I search for potential sites, gable walls with good visibility, or scruffy pieces of land which nobody else wants. If I sign anything up, I attach the agreement to the call sheet the next day. That's it, really."

"OK," Everton said, "I'll now ask you questions about that. Firstly, who sees your call sheet?"

"Top copy goes to the Manager and other copies to various departments if there's anything in which they're interested."

"What does the Manager want to see it for?" Everton asked.

Mr Hamilton laughed. "That's for you," he said, "and you'll need it to see that I've done a fair day's work."

"Don't I trust you?" Everton asked.

Mr Hamilton laughed again. "It's the only way I can tell you what I'm doing," he said.

"Mr Hamilton," Everton said, "the only thing I want from you is results. If you're not bringing me that, then you're not doing a fair day's work. Abolish call sheets, they're a waste of your time, and tell other departments anything they need to know which I don't suppose is very often."

"Abolish?"

"I don't want them; I just want agreements."

"Ah!" Mr Hamilton exclaimed.

"Ah, what?"

"There are not many of them, agreements I mean."

"Why?"

"It's the opposition. They are very strong here, and they offer more money. I'm not allowed to offer more than five pounds per annum per sixteen sheet."

"Your second order from me then," Everton said, "you sign up everything at what it takes, then let me decide whether it's worth it or not."

"Just like that!"

"Yes, but moving on, how do you get about? Does the company provide you with a car?"

"Dear me no. I've been here for thirty years and have never had a car. I take buses and walk. You see so much more by walking, and in any case I don't drive."

"Sounds good. It's all right; we're not going to force you to drive. Now, do you keep a record of refusals?"

"Refusals?"

"Yes, sites which have been refused, for one reason or another."

"They would be on my call sheets."

"Right, Mr Hamilton, for the rest of the day, go through your black book for the last twelve months and list all the refusals."

"Whatever for?"

"We'll write to them and tell them that we have a new proposition to make, and we'd like to talk."

"But some landlords might have died, or just moved on."

"Exactly – and what would happen to those letters?"

"They'd come back marked 'Gone Away'."

"Yes, and those are the ones we're interested in."

Mr Hamilton smiled. "Well, well," he said, "so those are the ones we call on?"

"You've got it in one."

There was a pause for a moment and Everton waited; there was something on Mr Hamilton's mind, then he said, "There's something personal, like."

"Go on."

"I'm sixty. Are you going to keep me? I don't want to go because I enjoy my work."

"Why shouldn't I keep you? If you bring in the results you can work 'til you're ninety."

Mr Hamilton looked relieved and he laughed. He said, "I'll tell you when I get tired."

Everton was well pleased with the interview. Here was a man who had been suffocated for many years, and he was sure that he could bring in the goods, more so if restrictions and systems were removed from him; what's more, he enjoyed his work. He stood up and shook Mr Hamilton's hand and said, "Both of us together will go places."

Two desks away, Everton had noticed the Canvasser, Clare Holden, strive to hear what was going on, so Everton moved across to her and sat down. "And you are Clare?" he asked.

"Yes, welcome to Ireland."

"Unusual to have a lady doing this job!"

"Is there anything wrong with that?" Clare asked tetchily.

"I don't care what age or sex you are as long as you bring in results."

"It's difficult at the moment."

"Why?"

"The opposition are taking all the best sites."

"That will change. What else?"

"We're not competitive; the opposition are cutting their prices and I'm not allowed to cut ours."

"By how much?"

"Sometimes by as much as ten percent."

"Right, get letters out to all the agents today offering a twenty percent discount for settlements within 30 days and subject to exclusive bookings on Meadows' sites, the offer will last for three months."

"Twenty percent! Will we make a profit?"

"Probably not, but it will get them into the mood."

"What happens after three months?"

"We'll play it by ear; maybe continue at a reduced discount. Anyway, by then, Mr Hamilton will, I hope, be producing some excellent sites. Clare, this is war and we've got to be on the winning side."

After Everton had left there was a stunned silence in the upstairs office. Everybody had heard and seen the hurricane move in and then out again. "Did you hear that!?" Clare said, "He's a fine young fellow in a hurry. I hope it all works out; and I rather fancy him."

"I haven't got that problem," Mr Hamilton said.

Within three days Everton had made himself known to all his staff and made clear to them what their targets were. He was beginning to establish favourites. Pete from the Bill Room was one of them; he was eager and quick witted. He had witnessed Everton's skill as a billposter in Hope Street, and Everton knew that he had won the respect of him and all the other billposters. He had taken them by surprise, and all those stored up complaints vanished overnight. Everton was not sure about Clare, other than she was a good-looker, and that must count for something. By comparison, Mr Hamilton was old fashioned, a hard worker and lacked good looks, but his heart was in the right place. Everton realised that his favourites were the oldest and the youngest in the building.

On the fourth day, Everton got into his silver Humber Hawk and drove off to the other offices, in Dublin, Cork and Londonderry. It was also a time to relax during the long hours of driving between towns on empty roads and admiring the beautiful scenery. In Galway staff at his hotel said to him, "Are you not going to Connemara?"

"Where is it?" he asked.

"Ach, sure, it's just up the Clifden Road, you'll be there in half an hour."

Everton took them by their word and instead of travelling back to Belfast he made his way to Clifden. The journey took an hour, an Irish half hour maybe. Soon after leaving Galway, he slowly drifted into hilly country, and with the sun shining he followed a twisty road at the foot of the 'Twelve Bens' mountains. Although there was a lack of trees, the bright light shone down onto the many shades of green on the steep slopes, dropping down to narrow lakes which reflected peat bottoms through the dark blue surface. It was picture postcard country, only spoilt by the haphazard placement of brand new gleaming bungalows, appearing at odds with the older thatched, whitewashed cottages of another age. Everton stopped at a wayside picture gallery where local artists displayed their craft. He bought a postcard of the 'Twelve Bens' which he sent to his Mum, and on it he wrote – 'Like Ireland very much. Have taken a few days off here where you can sit by the side of a lake, and not hear any sound, except for the birds. Heaven!'

When Everton returned he was glad to find that his new systems he had put in place had started to take effect and were running smoothly. Mr Hamilton was beside himself with enthusiasm, now hitting the road at nine each morning instead of waiting until mid-morning to get his calls recorded. He was already outbidding the opposition, which was a first for him. Clare was more cautious in her opinion of their new Master and cynical about getting results, but the morning after seeing Everton, she obtained a large exclusive order from a Bakery Company, so she had mixed feelings about Everton's initiative, and at this early stage, considered that the jury was still out.

Everton was pleased that he had made the giant leap of NCO rank to Officer. In Birkenhead he did all the work himself, apart from backup by Sam and Doreen. Here, he resisted the temptation of getting involved in the actual work. He set the policy and monitored the results. He kept his door open, and many a member of staff hesitated about going to the loo when they knew that their name could be called out loud and clear down the corridor, not that they dreaded any encounter with their new boss.

The only fly on the ointment was Doreen. When he discovered that she was working in the Liverpool Office, in disguise as Hilda, he was angry and sad at her attempt to deceive him. When he had had time to reflect he realised that the one element missing from his new life was Doreen. And she had sacrificed their relationship to safeguard his career. What sort of a heel was he! Could he not tear his thoughts away from work? He remembered that his last words to Doreen had been harsh and unfair. He decided to ring her, if only to say sorry. "Hello Francis," he said, "can I speak to Doreen?"

"She's not here any more," was Francis' brief reply.

"Not there? Where has she gone?"

"I don't know, Everton. Is there anybody else you want to speak to?"

"No thanks."

What was he to do? Had she left the country? Should he write to her at Birkenhead? Yes, that's what he'd do. He made several attempts at drafting a letter, but no matter how hard he tried, it didn't sound sincere. He gave up. If she was still in the country, then Doreen knew where he was. If she still loved him she would contact him. Besides, his own feelings for her were muddled. He didn't think that his Mum approved of her, and she was still very young. And, how on earth could he activate their old relationship of young love? He did nothing more and tried to forget her. There were priorities and the first was where he was going to live and in what? He had decided to buy a house and put himself at the bottom of the property ladder. But how as he going to find the time to engage in house hunting? Meadows' had generously paid for him to stay at the Crawfordsburn Inn, ten miles out of Belfast on the south shore of Belfast lough, but it was on the strict understanding that he did not delay in making other arrangements. He rang his Mum. "How 'yer doing?" his Mum asked.

"Fine, but I want to buy a house. I need your help."

"What sort of help?"

"Could you come over and find me one?"

"Just like that?"

"I haven't time, Mum, and I don't suppose I'm any good at that sort of thing."

"Son, do you expect me to drop everything and run? I have a job too, you know."

"Could you not take some leave?"

"And why do you suppose that I want to spend that in Ireland? Besides, at your age you should have a girlfriend or a wife to do that. Have you heard from Doreen?"

"Doreen and I are finished, Mum."

"I'm not sorry."

"Yes, I know, 'not your sort' you'll say next."

"Something like that."

"Well, can you come?"

"For how long?"

"As long as it takes."

"Don't talk to me like I was one of your employees. I'll come for a week. Where would I stay?"

"You can come to where I am staying, the Crawfordsburn Inn. I'm paying."

"You've talked me into it, Son."

Everton's Mum arrived at the same time as a work crisis had arisen in the Dublin office. He only had time to collect his Mum from the ferry and drop her at the Inn before he had to rush off again. He left her with a portfolio of lists of properties from Estate Agents. "How am I to get round all these?" she asked.

"If they want to sell they'll take you round."

"And what sort of a house are you looking for?"

"Two bedrooms, maybe three; detached or semi detached. Somewhere in this area would be nice. I'll leave it to your better judgement."

Everton's Mum was excited at the prospect of a diversion from her humdrum and predictable life. She arranged a week's leave and booked her passage on the Liverpool/Belfast overnight boat. She was tickled pink with her little single cabin – everything which you might need but it could all be fitted into a shoe box. She turned in early and lay on her back and thought of her son, the only tangible reminder of her marriage. She considered herself lucky. She knew many of her generation who had 'family problems', with out-of-work sons and daughters. John had got a job at an early age and stuck at it. He had made a success of his career, not because he'd had a university career, but because he'd applied himself to his work. But without a wife or even a girlfriend to share everything, what was it all about? If he'd arranged his private life a bit better another woman would be doing what was now being expected of his Mum, not that she wasn't looking forward to this little adventure. She didn't know Doreen, only by reputation, so perhaps she'd been unfair to her, but she was gone now anyway. She hoped that it wasn't because of anything she might have said about her. But she must be very shallow if she ditched him just because he was going to Ireland. No, she wasn't 'the right sort' and she'd always suspected that.

She slept fitfully, aware, in the middle of the night, of a gentle roll and creaking, and the throb of the engines. In the morning the light came through the portholes and she looked out. They appeared to be coasting up a river, the banks of which were bordered by other ships and cranes. She dressed quickly in case she might miss anything and went on deck. By the time she arrived the boat was docking, and men on the shore and on the boat were throwing ropes at each other. In the distance, above the roofs of a big city not unlike Liverpool, she saw green hills crowding in, enclosing a busy community in their grip, above which lay a distinct smog blurring vision. John had said that Crawfordsburn was ten miles out, about the same distance that she lived from Liverpool.

She went down below to have a hurried breakfast, and then went to her cabin to pack and wait for John in the reception area as already instructed. John soon arrived and bundled her into his Humber Hawk and drove at speed down to Crawfordsburn, against the flow of the traffic of commuters going to work. In less than half an hour they entered a sleepy village, a quaint and picture postcard place, not what you'd expect in Ireland, more akin to something in Shropshire. The Inn looked inviting and the staff were friendly. She took her key and John showed her to her room. She'd never seen such luxury. It wasn't like a hotel room at all, more like you'd expect in an old home, with curtains, carpets and bedspread all matching – if only she had the money to do up her own bedroom like that! She looked out of a window at a wood outside and could hear the noise of running water from a stream or river. She thought that not much house hunting would be done today because there was so much to see on her doorstep.

After John had left she took the portfolio of properties which he had left her and looked through them. She spied a red brick three bedroom detached house in a place called Blackwood Crescent in Helens Bay. She didn't know what John would do with three bedrooms, at least not yet; maybe he had some ideas?

She went to Reception and asked where Helens Bay was. "You're nearly there, Madame, it's just down the road, and you could walk there through the glen."

"Do you know where Blackwood Crescent is?"

"Certainly Madame. If you walk through the glen you'll come to the shore; turn left on the coastal path, then up beside the golf course to the Station Square; ask again when you get there. It's at the top to the left."

It was a fine day, so, after lunch, she took off on her adventure walk. In all her wildest dreams she'd never seen such a lovely spot. She came out of the wood onto a sandy beach with rocks and small children playing at the water's edge, and then walked along the path to yet another beach bordered by a golf course. As instructed she walked up to the Station Square and found the house for which she was looking very easily. It was a quiet and peaceful area, and so close to recreational activities; perhaps John could be persuaded to play golf and join the Golf Club? It couldn't be wrong and the house was a snitch. Although it was viewing 'By Appointment Only' an elderly lady living there took her round. Inside, the house was in perfect order and needed little in the way of re-decoration; she would enjoy coming over to Ireland every now and again and staying there, weeding the private garden at the back, and walking down to the shore – she might even swim? She had a feeling about this house, so she made an instant decision. She told the nice lady that John would be buying it, at the asking price. She could stay here for a month and not find anything more suitable, and if John wanted her back later to help with curtains and carpets she would come. In the meantime her job was over; she would stay one more night and be off on the ferry the following evening – no point in wasting any more money on her stay.

BOOK THREE –
MAY 1961

CHAPTER TWENTY
May 1961

EVERTON'S MUM LAY ON the beach enjoying the sunshine. Experience had taught her that May was the best month for Northern Ireland; there was more sun then, and she would miss the beating of the big drum and parades which came in explosive July. In May she could lie here and watch the children play, and talk to the regulars who came to exercise their dogs. In the last year she had spent so long in Ireland that she'd had to give up her job in the café. Now that John had done so well and had commanded a good and ever rising salary, she had reluctantly agreed to accept a small allowance from him; this enabled her to come every couple of months for long stays, and tidy up the garden, which she now considered to be her creation and so her property. John had tried to persuade her to come for good. She would have liked that, but she saw that she would get in the way if John found a girlfriend...If only!

The shadows started to lengthen so she decided to go. On the way up Church Road she noticed an Estate Agent's 'For Sale' sign in front of a big house with bay windows, with stupendous views across the golf course and the sea. She would mention it to John. It would be far too big for him, but it might prompt her son to take a wife and start a family. What a fantastic place this would be to bring up children, then another thought came to her. If John moved into a bigger house, she could take the smaller house in Blackwood Crescent. Her heart warmed to such an idyllic dream. If only...

The trouble with John was not only the amount of his time spent on work, but that now any of his spare time was crammed with sporting pursuits. He had a golf club four he played with once or twice a week, and on Saturdays he crewed for a friend in a Waverly class yacht in Bangor Bay. All his mates at the Golf Club and the Yacht Club were men. Since breaking up with Doreen he seemed to run a mile from female company, as if he was saving himself for someone, Doreen perhaps, if only...

Much to his surprise, John was home early and she hadn't even begun to think about what they would be having for supper. She knew that something was wrong as soon as he came in through the door. His face was white. "What is it?" she asked.

"Father Meadows is dead," he said.

In the late afternoon Everton had taken a call from Colin. "Its sad news," he said, "Father has died, quite peacefully in his sleep."

"I'm so sorry, Colin." There was a lump in his throat as he added, "I have a lot to thank him for; he gave me opportunities."

"He was always a fan of yours and admired your work style, as I do, of course. The funeral is on Thursday, family and friends only, and I'd like you to come. Stay overnight; there may be things to discuss with you the next day."

"I'm honoured, Colin. I'll be there."

"Oh dear, John, had he been unwell?" John's Mum greeted the news.

"I don't think so. Old, maybe, not far off ninety, but that need not be old now-a-days. I haven't really got my head round the news yet. I always regarded him as indestructible."

"We all go sometime. Are you going to the funeral?"

"Yes, I'm invited and have been asked to stay over. I'll travel on the ferry on Wednesday night. Will you be all right here, on your own?"

"It's time I went home, John, I've forgotten what it looks like, so I'll go with you."

"I'll book two single cabins then."

"Will this make any difference, John?"

"What do you mean?"

"To the management of the company? Will Colin be the new Chairman?"

"I haven't even thought about that. No, I think he'll make himself Chairman and Managing Director all in one. For years he's been stopped in his tracks on one scheme or another. Now, if he's Chairman, he just has to ask himself and he'll say 'yes'! Anyway, he doesn't trust anyone else – it's a Meadows' trait."

"But will it make any difference to you? Will he want you over there to hold his hand? Will you have to leave Ireland?"

"I shall never leave Ireland. I'm happy here. I run my own show, and I've fashioned it the way I want it. I love this house and the people. I get plenty of fresh air in playing golf and sailing. How could I go back to dirty old Merseyside?"

"But you're ambitious, John; you always said you wanted to go to the top. Perhaps this is it?"

"No, I don't think I'll be asked to move, and if I don't want to go they can't make me."

"In that case, there's something I want to discuss with you. A lovely house has come up for sale in Church Road, facing the golf course. I'm sure you could afford it."

"Yes, I know, I've seen it. It's a bit big just for me, but you could move in too, and sell your house in Meols."

"I've been thinking about that, but that might stop you finding a wife, and if you did find one she wouldn't want me around."

"I've given up on women."

"Don't be daft, John."

On Thursday morning Everton's Mum decided to find an answer to a question she'd been asking herself for an age. Where was Doreen? Was she still in Birkenhead and did she still work for Meadows? There was only one way to find out and that was to go to Meadows' office and ask while the funeral was taking place, only she would deliberately ask for Doreen by name, and they'd presume that she was a friend and fetch her. They might still be play acting in that place and be keeping Doreen concealed, but if she wasn't there they might know where she'd gone. When she got to the office it was shut, 'due to a family bereavement', the notice said. Of course, silly me. As she was still reading the notice she heard a noise inside, and a lock being undone behind the door. When it opened she faced an attractive young woman who said, "I'm afraid we're closed today, and I'm only here because I had some work to finish. Did you want anything?"

"I'm looking for Doreen," John's Mum said.

The woman appeared surprised and after a pause asked "Who wants to see her?"

"A friend."

"A friend? Is that you?"

"Yes."

"I didn't know you were my friend. I *am* Doreen."

"Oh, my God, but what luck, Doreen. I know all about you, I'm Everton's Mum."

Doreen stared and hesitated, then slowly smiled and held out a hand and said, "Pleased to meet you, Mrs Smyth."

"Can we talk somewhere?"

"Does Everton know about this?"

"No."

"What do you want to talk about?"

"Everton would be a good subject."

Doreen's face brightened. "Would it be our secret?" she asked.
"Yes of course, Doreen."
"Shall we go for a cuppa or something, then?"
"An excellent idea!"

They found a local teashop and settled themselves down in the bay window. She really was a most attractive person, Everton's Mum thought. She had light makeup on and had recently had a perm, beautiful curls crowning her head. She had the appearance of having spent money both on clothes and herself, and there was a trace of expensive scent. It was five years since she'd been an office girl; she'd probably done well and could afford to make something of herself. With relief she saw no engagement ring. She went straight to the point. "Are you married?" she asked.
"No."
"Boyfriend?"
"No, I've had bad experiences, not with Everton, mind."
"And you still work for Meadows'?"
"Yes, I'm Mr Smiley's Assistant now, and I'm to take over from him when he retires."
"Do you still love my son?"
"I've always loved him and always will."
"Well, why for God's sake, are you hiding away from him, all this time?"
"I'm scared."
"What of?"
"Of him rejecting me. I deceived him, you see, and he doesn't forget anything easily. I thought that if I hung around and he loved me he would find me; that would be easy and its not as if hasn't had time to do that!"
"But he loves you, he really does, and I don't know why he hasn't tried to find you; I think he thought you'd gone away."
Doreen's face lit up. "But he can't still love me," she said. "Has he told you?"
"He doesn't need to, I'm his Mum and I should know."
"Does he talk about me?"
"Seldom."
"So how can you know what he thinks about me?"
"As I say, I'm his Mum, and I know my son."
"I suppose Everton hasn't a girlfriend or anything?" Doreen asked anxiously.
"You know what he's like, he works hard, and when he's not working he buries himself in male pursuits."

"Pursuits?"

"Sailing and whatnot."

"He's over here now, for the funeral like, isn't he?"

"Yes, and I have this plan?"

"Plan?"

"I'm due to meet him for dinner tonight. You go in my place."

"Me? Without you, you mean?"

"Yes."

"Where?"

"The Adelphi."

"Oh dear, I don't have happy memories of that place, but yes, I will," then the tears started to flow.

Everton's Mum hugged her and said, "I hope, I do so hope I'm doing the right thing. He's a funny boy, but how can he possibly throw you over, not now, not after all this time."

Everton didn't enjoy funerals. It made him think of life's frailty and his own life span, and it annoyed him how so many others indulged themselves in mourning. Since being in Ireland he had learnt that when anybody died there, everyone else was off to the funeral, whether they knew them well or not; just to know of them was enough. If this was Belfast you wouldn't be able to park anywhere near the church, and in spite of Mr Meadows' stature there weren't more than twenty or thirty mourners, packing the rows at the back of the church, leaving the first row for Mrs Meadows and Colin.

Colin spoke kindly of his father and with a steady voice, he said, "My father built a business from nothing, and he was much loved by his staff who called him 'Father'. I will strive to continue to grow the company without his wise counsel, but in order to survive in the new business world of multi-nationals it might be necessary to find new partners and new finance."

Everton was shocked by these remarks and wondered what had made Colin refer to it all, unless he was up to something and was firing the warning shot. Colin had inherited his father's drive and vision, but they could murder him out there in the cold commercial world, without his father saying 'No'.

The mourners were invited back to the house, a big place on the outskirts of Southport, and at last Everton had a chance to speak to Colin, but not alone. A small, middle aged man, with a narrow face and long narrow nose, was continuing to shadow him, almost afraid to let Colin out of his sight. Colin said, "Everton, this is Neville Singer who looks after our finances."

Everton took hold of a warm and soggy hand, and dared ask both of them, "Finance? For the company, like?"

"Yes," Colin answered, "Neville has always managed to come up with the goods whenever there's been a need for capital injection."

"Someone useful to know," suggested Everton, then Colin swept Neville away to introduce him to somebody else.

Everton left early, with uneasy thoughts. He'd always regarded the Meadows' Company as rock solid, an employment for life. But Colin had no male children, unless there were some illegitimate ones scattered around. He might want out, take the money and run. What would the Meadows Company be like in the public domain, subject to strict financial controls? Where would all this leave him? He hoped that Neville wouldn't be around when he saw Colin the next morning, because he'd like Colin to reassure him. In the meantime he looked forward to dinner with his Mum at The Adelphi.

Everton arrived early and took a seat in the cocktail bar and asked for the menu. He ordered himself a large whisky and a sweet sherry for his Mum. He briefly looked at the menu, then sat back and relaxed, watching the to and fro of people crossing the foyer. His Mum didn't arrive immediately which was odd, because she was always early for appointments. He looked at his watch, and then gazed out at the foyer with a more eagle eye. He saw a well groomed woman, in an expensive suit and a crown of many curls, come through the main entrance. She hesitated, then appeared to spot the cocktail bar and rapidly moved towards him. There was something familiar about her walk, more like a glide as if she was a model. He kept his eye on her because she was cultured and beautiful – if he had to pick a date with anyone within sight, he would pick her. To his astonishment, almost as if she was answering his prayers, she walked right up to him and smiled, then said, "Hello Everton, sorry I'm late, but you know me; never could be punctual!"

Doreen of course, Everton realised, and he jumped to his feet and held out his hand which Doreen took and squeezed. "Doreen," he said, "this is fantastic; how did you spot me?"

"Because I knew you were here. Your Mum has stood you up and I'm here in her place."

"You've seen my Mum?"

"Yes, and I've taken the risk that you won't send me away. Will you give me dinner?"

"This is like a dream," Everton said, and then realising that they were both still standing offered her a seat.

"Can I stay?" Doreen asked.

"Of course you can "

"Is this my drink?"

"I bought it for my Mum. Do you like sweet sherry?"

"That'll be fine."

Further conversation was interrupted while a waiter appeared from nowhere to take an order.

"What will you have?" Everton asked.

"It reminds me of The Commodore in Llandudno," Doreen said. "Such a lot to choose from, will you decide for me please?"

Everton studied the menu carefully and ordered what he thought Doreen would like best, salmon for the main course, asking for two of the same, just like old times. Then they were left on their own again.

"It's been five years hasn't it?" Doreen asked.

"It feels more than that. How are you Doreen, are you married, or anything?"

"Neither married nor 'anything'. I wouldn't be here otherwise. I know you're not married either; you're too busy!"

"Something like that, but you must have had boyfriends, a good-looker like you?"

"Only one who was a disaster, and I said to myself, never again. I'm still a virgin, but only just."

"But where have you been, Doreen?"

"At Meadows'."

"They said you'd gone, after I talked to you at the switchboard."

"Gone from the switchboard. Mr Colin was very good to me, and he found a place for me in Mr Smiley's office. I had to work for a girl called Debra and she was hopeless so I carried her. Now she's gone and I've got Debra's job, with a prospect of taking over from Mr Smiley when he stops putting off his retirement date for the last time."

"But why hide away like that?"

"Do you remember what you said when we last talked? I was very hurt."

"Not really, but I don't think I was very nice, was I?"

"I was devastated because there was only one man in my life...you. I knew that if I stayed around with Meadows' you'd be able to find me if ever you had a change of heart. My mother no longer lives in Birkenhead; she's gone to a sister in Leeds. I share a flat with Pauleen now."

"I did try to write to you, but I gave up. I couldn't say what I felt."

"And what do you feel?"

"That I still love you and I know what a sacrifice you suffered to persuade me to go to Ireland. I should have seen that at the time, but I was angry, and I didn't want to admit that I'd been wrong, even to myself."

"For ever the perfectionist! What do you feel now, Everton?"

"I love you and I always have. I've not had any other kind of relationship because I wasn't prepared to accept second best."

"I know, your Mum told me."

He held out his had to her, and she kissed it, and said, "I'm not going to let you get away this time."

They went into the restaurant and celebrated their reunion with a bottle of bubbly. They talked about old days, the Hind Street office, Bidston Windmill and the Commodore Hotel in Llandudno. Towards the end of the evening Doreen said, "They say you've achieved great things in Ireland."

This was the moment Everton feared, to pop the question, but he felt fairly confident that she would accept. "Will you come back with me, Doreen?" he asked.

"For a holiday, like, or what?"

"Will you marry me, for God's sake, and come and live with me, in my new house which I'm going to buy, facing the golf course and the sea, and have our children there?"

Without hesitation Doreen said, "I thought you'd never ask, and I like the bit about the golf course and the sea. Yes, of course I will."

Everton lent over the table and kissed her on the lips; the waiter was arriving with the bill and decided to delay that for a while and went away again.

"Will you mind leaving here?" Everton asked.

"Mind? I'll not miss it, the filth and the dirt, the smog and the rain, the crowded streets and roads. I want fresh air; will Ireland give that to me?"

"In abundance, but there'll be one thing the same, the rain," and they both laughed.

It was late when Everton got to his Mum's house that night, but a light was still on downstairs, and he found her in the sitting room, waiting for news, so he teased her. Everton tried to look grim and scowled. "Where were you? I had to have dinner on my own," he said.

"On your own, you mean - ."

"You weren't there; did you forget or something? Are you all right?"

"Perfectly well, but did you not meet anybody else?"

"Who?"

"Doreen, perhaps?"

"Why should I have met Doreen?" His Mum looked embarassed, and he couldn't keep this ploy up any longer. He said, "Yes, of course I met Doreen, you scheming so-and-so, and we're going to get married. Doreen will come and live with us."

His Mum broke down and tears flowed. She seized her son and held him. "At last," she said, "and now you can go home as quickly as possible and buy that house in Church Road, and I'll take over your house in Blackwood Crescent and sell up here – and be available for baby sitting!"

"You've got it all worked out, haven't you Mum?"

The meeting with Colin was to have been at ten, but he didn't turn up until ten thirty, so he hadn't changed, Everton thought. He looked well and had already discarded his dark suit and black tie, in favour of a light summer suit and yellow tie. It was back to business as usual.

"I'm to become Chairman," Colin said, "so the post of Managing Director is vacant. I shall want to take it easy, and have time to explore investments with Neville Singer. The only person I can trust to do the job is you. Congratulations Everton, you're the boss now. I'll need you over here as soon as possible."

There was a long pause and silence. Everton's heart sank. It was what he'd always wanted, but not any more. Last night had changed everything, but even without that he knew that he would not want this promotion any longer. He was too happy where he was, too stuck in his ways, in complete control of Meadows' in Ireland, with nearly all their competitors either gone or reeling. He knew he was the right person, in the right job, at the right time. But more than that, he'd carved out for himself a social and sporting life, his golf and sailing, and now he was to have a new home and family. He couldn't possibly give all that up, not now. How was he going to refuse Colin, without it sounding ungrateful? He thought long and hard before replying, and then said, "I know it's what I've always wanted, ever since working for Mr Smiley, but things have changed. It's too early for me. Every time I get to grips with a new job, you move me on, but not this time. I've still got heaps to do in Ireland, and last night something happened which has changed my life for ever."

"Last night?"

"Yes, I met Doreen again – You've been concealing her from me. We're to get married and move into a new house in Ireland and be joined by my mother. I am astonished at the confidence you have in me, but let me go on in Ireland. In a few years time Meadows in Ireland will be bigger than Meadows in England."

At those last remarks Colin smiled and said, "You think so, do you?"

"You can count on it."

"Well in that case I shall be Chairman *AND* Managing Director, but I'll still need someone to lean on. Will you become 'Deputy Managing Director' and move onto the board?"

"Will I be allowed to stay in Ireland?"

"If you're so optimistic about continued growth there and you can do it, yes, that would be essential."

"And would I get a salary increase?"

"That goes with your extra responsibility. And congratulations on your engagement to Doreen; she's a good girl and we'll miss her here. So, do we have a deal?"

"We have a deal."

As the over night ferry glided up Belfast Lough, Mrs Doreen Smyth looked out of the porthole for the first sight of Ireland. It was raining. Well, my husband did warn me, she thought to herself.

CHAPTER TWENTY ONE

THE WEDDING HAD BEEN a quickly arranged and low key affair. Doreen had not wished it otherwise because she had no family home or much family support. Her sister in America wished her well but declined to come over. Her brother in Scotland also declined, so only her mother was present on her side of the family. There was little point in having the wedding in Leeds where her Mum lived with her sister as Doreen had no associations with that place. Everton's Mum, who regarded herself as the matchmaker, offered her cramped house in Meols for the reception for about twenty people, and they were married in the local church.

Pauleen agreed to be bridesmaid, but apart from her and Doreen's Mum, most of the other guests were from Meadows' Liverpool and Birkenhead offices. Sam from Birkenhead agreed to be Everton's best man, and much to everyone's astonishment, Colin Meadows stepped in and gave the Bride away. The Meadows Company had hijacked the wedding, but Doreen was happy about that; she realised that the event cemented a personal relationship between Colin and Everton. She was already deeply troubled by Everton's decision, without reference to her, of refusing the Managing Directorship. Events had come about full circle – she'd pushed him into the Irish job, but she couldn't very well disappear again so as to compel him to come back from Ireland and live in Liverpool, at Colin's side.

Everton and Doreen had briefly discussed the honeymoon, and Doreen had easily persuaded him to spend it in Ireland. She was disappointed that Everton had said that he was only taking two weeks, but then that was Everton – work came first, and when there was a honeymoon involved, work was downgraded to a very close second, only.

Doreen would have been happy to spend their first night in Liverpool in a posh hotel, in comfortable and luxurious surroundings, but Everton had insisted upon moving off to Ireland as quickly as possible, because, in his own words, 'there was so much to do'.

When they got onto the ferry Doreen was horrified that their cabin was so cramped, one narrow berth on top of another, and little room for one to dress and undress, let alone two. All her life she'd saved herself for this momentous occasion, fighting off Hank and that Eddie, so if nothing better could be found she'd insist on leaving the boat and booking in at The Adelphi; perhaps it would be the first row they would have? "How are we going to make love here?" she asked. "Is there not something bigger?"

"I'll ask," Everton replied, "but it would be a bit of a challenge to do it here," making it out as if that would excuse it all. They went off to the Purser's office.

The boat had two deluxe cabins, A and B. B was still available, so they took it. Two separate beds replaced tiered bunks, and there was generous space all around them and a shower and toilet off their room. It was not heaven, thought Doreen, but at least it was better.

Everton's Mum had flown over to Belfast from Speke in the late afternoon, to get to Blackwood Crescent so that she could welcome them the next day. They would all inspect the empty house in Church Road and make early plans for decorations and furnishings, before driving off to Dublin for the first stage of their honeymoon. As Everton had said, 'There was such a lot to do'. Perhaps in Dublin, Doreen thought, they could relax for five days and stop rushing around? Was life going to become one long rush?

The early morning rain, which Doreen had seen through the porthole, soon dried up, and by the time the two of them had had breakfast on board, the North Easterly wind was chasing the clouds away, and quite large blue areas appeared in the sky. As they turned off the Belfast/Bangor Road and took the narrow road down to the Helen's Bay peninsula, the sun was shining on the wet leaves which were the fresh green colour of early summer. It all took Doreen's breath away.

Doreen was excited enough about the neat and tidy house in Blackwood Crescent, but couldn't wait until they saw the older house which Everton had bought in Church Road. They walked round the big rooms, their steps echoing on bare floorboards. Doreen wondered how on earth they would fill this house, either with people or furniture. She tried hard to visualise how it would be in ten years time, perhaps looking worn and untidy, the cries of small children running from room to room, and both she and Everton working in the ample garden. Was it wise to dream so far ahead? Would life be kind to them, and would they receive the luck which everyone needed? Would they still be living even? Life was so uncertain, perhaps it would be better to take it one day at a time, so she contented herself with looking out of the big bay windows overlooking the bright green of the golf course, and the blue green of the sea beyond, disturbed by the occasional white horse. My God, what a view! She'd ask Pauleen to come and stay so she could show it all off. Perhaps even her Mum would come?

The decorator called as arranged and they chose paint colours for all the rooms. The kitchen was the problem. There were so many doors, including the cupboards, all painted a dirty grey. Doreen had a navy blue colour in her mind, but couldn't make up her mind about the right shade; eventually she marked one on the card and said, "That will do, but can you make it a little bit darker, please." The decorator said he would do what he could. Little did Doreen know that in the fullness of time the same blue doors would save their marriage.

In the early evening they left for Dublin, breaking their journey South by stopping at a wayside pub for a meal. It was late when they reached the Shelbourne Hotel in St. Stephen's Green. Doreen had encountered luxury before, but this was different. There was an old world charm both in the décor and the politeness of the staff. Their room was enormous, with windows overlooking the trees and ponds of The Green, and the cars going round the Square, mainly looking for parking spaces. Best of all there was a large and inviting double bed in the middle of the room. At last!

It was in this bed that Everton and Doreen began their first serious post wedding dialogue. After they made love Everton would fall asleep almost at once; he had got what he wanted, and Doreen stayed awake, wondering what the matter was with her sexual feelings and pondering the future. In the morning there was no hurry to rush to work, so when they were awake they lay together and talked. "When we've got the house done and move in and eventually have some time on our hands, how will we spend the weekends?" Doreen asked.

"Weekends? I will work 'til lunchtime on Saturday."

"Then we have a day and a half together, so what will we do?"

"I crew for my friend, George, for the Saturday points at the Yacht Club. I can't let him down just because I'm married now."

"Why not?"

"It wouldn't be fair on George; I've always crewed for him."

"Hey, what about being fair to me? Your life has changed now and you have to make adjustments."

"I can't let George down."

"How many crew is there in this boat?"

"Either two or three including the helmsman."

"Who's the other crew?"

"There isn't one, that's why I can't let him down."

"Well then, it'll be me, it's something we can do together."

"But you can't sail?"

"Could you, five years ago?"

"No."

"Well then?"

Everton was silent for a moment, thinking it out. "It depends on George," he said, "It's his boat after all."

"Then ask him when we get back."

"I'll do that; say, that's not a bad idea," Everton said, now in a more cheerful mood.

"Well, that's Saturdays taken care of, what about Sunday? Do we go to church on Sunday mornings?"

"Christmas and Easter, maybe, and on special occasions."

"We could start."

"Why?"

"'Because it's something we could do together, that's why."

"But it's boring."

"It needn't be. It's what it opens up for us, all sorts of church activities; it's a way of getting to know people, be a part of a community."

"I didn't think people bothered with church any more?"

"Well, we're going to. What about the rest of Sunday?"

"Well, err, that's difficult."

"Difficult?"

"I have a golf four I play on Sunday afternoons."

"Surely you're not going to keep that up."

"I'll have to; otherwise they'll make fun of me."

"Why?"

"Oh, you know the sort of thing – 'she's got you under her thumb, you've no time for your mates now'."

"And they're more important than me?"

"No, of course not, it's just a question of fitting it all in."

"Well, the weekend isn't long enough; anyway, why do you work on Saturday mornings? Not many people do any more?"

"It's quiet then; I can get quite a lot done."

"Quiet?"

"Yes."

"Why?"

"There's nobody else around."

"You mean the company is not working?"

"Yes."

Doreen jumped up in bed in surprise and glared down at her husband's face. "Well, I'll tell you something, John Smyth, you either play your golf on Sunday and don't work on Saturday, or don't play golf on Sundays. Now I know what your Mum meant by 'your manly pursuits'. You're married now, Everton, you've got to change."

Everton's determined expression gradually changed and he smiled. Then he said, "Is that what you call compromise?"

"Call it what you like. Because I'm married to you I will want to see something of you."

"You win," he said, "I'll not work on Saturday mornings."

"Good, we'll do the shopping together and have coffee out."

"You're lucky, you know," Everton said, "you have my Mum up the road so you won't be lonely."

"I married you, not your Mum," Doreen said, and playfully poked him in the ribs.

"Let's get up," Everton said, "before you start to organise my time from Monday to Friday."

Although Doreen and Everton had the whole of Dublin to explore and just five days to do it in, Doreen was mainly attracted to the park outside in St. Stephen's Green. They strolled through the trees, and scattered crumbs, saved from breakfast, to the over fed ducks. After they tired watching the birds they sat on a seat in the sun and watched the people, some of them rushing through the park, with briefcases under their arms, to keep an appointment, maybe, and some like themselves, sauntering with all the time in the world. Alarmed at their lack of exercise, Everton drove Doreen out to Dun Laoghaire Harbour where they walked out to the end of the harbour wall, sometimes racing the ferry to see who would get to the harbour exit first.

After five days they left Dublin and their luxurious hotel and large double bed, and drove to the romantic and up market Ashford Castle Hotel on the edge of Connemara. Each evening they sat in the dining room at their table with a small Union Jack displayed, and on other tables many flags of many nations were also displayed, making them realise the popularity of Ireland as a tourist destination all around the world.

It was during this last part of the honeymoon that they discussed their likely post honeymoon life, and how their lives would be changed. Sitting on a rock half way up a mountain of which they had failed to reach the peak, Doreen began to debate the mode of their newly married life.

"What am I to do all day?" she asked.

"Mum will be just up the road."

"I'm grateful for that, but I'll need friends."

"Give it time, you'll gather them up, on the beach and in the shops and the post office."

"I'll be bored stiff."

"You could take a job – I mean, you don't need to work, but you might prefer it?"

"Doing what? Would Meadows take me on?"

"No."

"Why?"

"Because it would be awkward. Sometimes I shout at my staff, and I don't want to shout at you."

"We could start a family?"

"We've been into all that. Yes, we will start a family, but when that happens life becomes one long rush and we'll have no time for ourselves. Let's have a couple of years of freedom first. We're both young and we have plenty of time."

Changing tack, Doreen suddenly asked, "What time do you get home from the office?"

"It varies."

"Why?"

"It depends what's on."

"And how do I know what time to get supper ready for?"

"You keep it hot, or something; Mum has always managed it."

"I'm not your Mum, and I need to know what target time I should work to."

"About eight."

"Eight! Listen, John Smyth, I'll need you home by six. Remember, I'll have been on my own all day and will want your company. You can be home by six."

"Six!" Everton shrieked, and Doreen thought that it was just as well there was nobody else within sound; then he added, more quietly, "I can't promise that."

"All right, six thirty, I'll compromise."

"What if there's panic at the office?"

"Is there panic every night? How often?"

"Oh, only now and again."

"Then you can ring me."

Everton did not reply. His face had set in a grim determined expression, almost like the rocks around him, Doreen thought.

"Can't you?" Doreen persisted.

"If I'm going to be late it will only delay me more if I have to ring you."

"You'll ring me," Doreen said crossly.

"Let's go," Everton said, "the sun's gone and I don't like the look of that black cloud."

They got up and in silence, started to slither down the mountainside. In normal circumstances they would have been laughing and shouting, but Doreen had decided to sulk, her first as a married woman.

That evening they only spoke briefly to each other. Doreen felt the need to keep the sulk going, and it would teach Everton a lesson, not to mess with her. At dinner they spoke briskly to each other and only when required, like 'please pass the salt'. Doreen began to realise that life was going to change so much that love alone would not be enough to cement their relationship. There was only one solution, and that was to start a family, with or without Everton's consent or knowledge. Up until now, when they'd made love they'd needed a condom, and as it had been in the middle of the month it had been essential. Doreen had been frustrated that she'd still not reached a climax, and fiddling about with a condom had been distasteful and she'd lost the natural flow, and besides, it had reminded her all too much of her unhappy experiences with Hank and Eddie.

They lay together in their fine double bed, a gap between them, both of them wide awake and unhappy. Doreen turned towards her husband and in a soft voice said, "Come here, you daft thing," and she began to touch and feel all the parts of his body she knew he couldn't resist. At the crucial moment Everton said, "The condom, quick, I'm bursting."

"Not tonight, love," she replied.

"But you must."

"It's safe, you chump, I'm in the safe period," she lied.

"Are you sure?"

But it was too late and Doreen had mounted her love and helped him to penetrate her. At the same time as Everton gasped with thankful relief she reached her climax, and the heavens opened. She'd achieved it! Yet had she also conceived?

CHAPTER TWENTY TWO

EVERTON HAD, AT FIRST, found Doreen compliant and ready to hang on his every word, but after the wedding he discovered that she had a mind of her own. Her dismay about the small cabin on the boat demonstrated that point. He had to admit to himself that he hadn't really given much thought to their first night. Once they had decided to go to Ireland for their honeymoon he had not seen any need to waste touring time and spend a night in Liverpool. He'd know of the existence of the deluxe cabins, so it was stupid of him not to have booked one of them in the first place. It was lucky that there had been one still available because otherwise he might have had to argue with Doreen about going ashore, and causing all sorts of complications about re-booking. His first attempt at love making in Cabin B could not have been better, only it seemed over so quickly, and shortly afterwards Doreen had agreed that he move into his own single bed so that they could both get some sleep.

Doreen took ages in choosing the paint colours in the Church Road house, and Everton found out about her indecisiveness for the first time. He'd readily agreed to the dark blue colour the decorator had shown them for the kitchen doors and cupboards, but Doreen asked Everton to hold it up against the existing dull grey paint while she took a few steps back and viewed it from a distance. The trouble was that the sample wasn't big enough. It was with relief when Doreen had agreed to that particular blue, with the provision that the decorator darkened it slightly. Everton saw trouble ahead and guessed that he'd have to repaint the doors himself at some future date.

Everton's prime delight was Doreen's reaction to the Shelbourne Hotel in Dublin. He had stayed there himself on many a business trip, and he'd become known to the staff who had pampered him, and now they were pampering both of them. Indeed such was Doreen's delight about The Shelbourne and the park opposite, they didn't go out to anywhere else other than one trip to Dun Laoghaire. Every time they'd discussed the Theatre, Trinity Library or The Art Gallery, she was unable to make up her mind which they should go to, so they had continued to sit in St. Stephen's Green, while the ducks and geese got fatter and fatter.

Doreen's indecision manifested itself best when they went to a restaurant, and they had to decide where to sit. Doreen would choose a table, but after sitting down, would look around her for one which she might think better. There was always something wrong, a draft or too near to the kitchen door which squeaked, a position where waiters moved too closely, or a bad view. Everton learnt to stand aside and wait for her to settle on the right table before joining her.

It had always worried Everton that Doreen would put pressure on him to give up some of his more time consuming hobbies, so as to have more time with her. He could understand that, but he didn't want to give up any golf or sailing. George had raised the matter with him and asked, "Should I be looking for a new crew?"

"Oh God no," Everton had replied. It was then that he'd thought up an imaginary occupation from which he could retreat, working on Saturday mornings. He didn't, but Doreen was not to know that, then when pressure was put on him to find more domestic time he simply said that he'd stay at home on Saturday mornings. He felt the need to square his Mum about this, just in case it 'should come out', so he said to her, "I've told Doreen that I work on Saturday mornings."

"But you don't," his Mum replied.

"I know, but I want her to think that I've given it up."

"How can you give up something that you don't do?"

"That's the point. I need to be seen to compromise, as I don't want to give up any of my hobbies and that's the alternative."

"So you want to deceive her?"

"I don't like the word 'deceive'."

"And what do you want me to do about it?"

"I don't want you to let slip that I don't work on Saturday mornings."

"I'm not going to lie about it."

"I don't want you to, but just be on your guard."

"Listen, Son, marriage is about trust. Doreen is a nice girl, much nicer than I ever gave her credit for. Be open with each other, and if you have to, cut back on your hobbies."

"I've asked Doreen to join George and I in the boat on Saturday afternoons."

"That's good, but there are other things."

"Other things?"

"I hope you're going to start a family."

"There's plenty of time for that, Mum."

"Do it while you're young."

The argument with Doreen about what time to come home from work had annoyed him. Girls couldn't expect to fully understand business, and the need to meet deadlines and get things finished. He saw trouble ahead, but he'd have to try to be more punctual. He hadn't been able to handle Doreen well, and when he tried to dig his heels in she just switched off completely and went into a sulk; when she did, Everton realised how badly he missed her chatter which he'd partly ignored. He didn't know how to bring her back to life again, so her sudden advances to him in bed surprised and delighted him, and their love act brought the sulk to a close. Doreen appeared more passionate than ever; he'd worried about not using a condom, but Doreen seemed to know what she was doing. In future he'd let her be in charge, and it was therefore up to her when to take precautions, and when not to.

When they returned to Helen's Bay and Everton went back to work, he managed to keep both work and hobbies in check, so as to give as much time as possible to their marriage. To begin with Doreen had joined Everton and George in sailing, but she complained about getting cold and wet, so only went when the weather was fine. The painters were working flat out at the Church Road house, and Everton found time to go round the auction houses with Doreen and his Mum, trying to find as much furniture as possible 'on the cheap'. Everton wondered if they'd ever get to an end of filling three reception rooms and four bedrooms. His Mum and Doreen went curtain and carpet hunting on their own; all he had to do was approve the purchases and sign the cheques.

Shortly after moving into their new home, Everton had to go off to Cork to try to buy the business there, and allow Meadows' to spread out to all the smaller towns in Munster. Doreen was so busy at the house that she appeared to easily accept Everton's absence and said that she'd stay with his Mum until he got back. Everything seemed to be working out so well, and their love making improved daily. Everton wondered whether he was just a lucky person, or if he'd had to work at all he'd achieved, and he decided that it was probably a bit of both.

Doreen also had to tolerate Everton's frequent trips to Liverpool for board meetings; for these he would fly over for the day so he'd be back that same night, not, of course, at the six thirty deadline!

With relief Everton had noticed after what he'd considered a re-bellious and argumentative period following their marriage, Doreen had become serene and caring, and did not suffer those times of bloody-mind-edness which his Mum had warned him were a girl's need before a period was due. In fact, he'd been unable to detect when she was having periods and wondered whether he should have noticed something; as far as sex was concerned he felt that he was still hopelessly inexperienced. He did notice that Doreen was using the condom less and less, and presumed that she was getting their love making down to a fine art.

After a successful acquisition of the Cork business, another possibility came up in Limerick, and he presumed that if he settled on a deal money would be readily made available from the Meadows' substantial reserves. He was, however, concerned about the new relationship between Colin and his new Financial Adviser, Neville Singer. Neville kept on popping up at board meetings, and then he suddenly became a Director, the only other Director, other than himself, to be non-family. Then it turned out that Neville was another of Colin's old school friends who was something grand 'in the City'.

Everton found himself to be continually opposing some of Neville's wild schemes, which didn't seem to relate to Meadows' more core activi-ties, of Outdoor Advertising. Everton's reputation for sniping at Neville was such that on one occasion Colin had insisted on him travelling over to Liverpool the day before, so that they could discuss one of Neville's proposals, without Neville being there.

"Neville has this fantastic scheme for us to join the Leisure Industry," Colin had said.

"We're Poster Contractors. What do we know about leisure?"

"Oh, you can buy into that knowledge."

"Has Neville something in mind?"

"He has indeed. There's a holiday village company in South Wales, called Sun Rise Holidays, and it's currently for sale."

"Why?"

"They've run out of money and it needs considerable investment which we could provide. Also, there's another holiday village within five miles, and we have a chance of buying that too. We could economise by running the two together. Who knows, in a year or two we could have the monopoly of the industry in Wales, just like Meadows' are doing in Posters in Ireland."

"We've done well in Ireland because we know our industry. We don't know anything about holidays."

"It only needs a first rate accountant and Neville is that."

"Have you got profit projections?"

"It's all here," Colin said and produced a glossy folder.

Everton took a quick look at the figures, and then said, "But we only start to make a profit in five years time!"

"We can wait; it's getting started that matters."

"Is this your idea or Neville's?"

"Neville's, but I back him, and we have the money."

"Hasn't Neville got the money himself?"

"It's all tied up."

"Colin, I'm sorry, but I think the whole idea stinks, and I'll vote against it, not that that would make any difference."

"I'd rather have a unanimous vote of confidence."

"Sorry, I'm not in favour. In fact I'm terrified of the whole project, but I'll take these figures away and study them."

"There's another thing."

"What?"

"Carol is divorcing me and Francis and I are now living together."

"I'm very sad about that, Colin. Is it too late to save the marriage?"

"Yes. Neither of us wants it to continue, and I can't bear Carol's moral superiority any longer. Anyway, I'm not discussing it, but it introduces another problem."

"Problem?"

"Yes, I have to pay Carol off. It's costing me two million."

"Wow," Everton gasped. "You're joking, aren't you?"

"No, I'm dead serious."

"Have you got two million, well, hanging around like?"

"No way."

"So what do you do now then?"

"Neville again to the rescue."

"What do you mean?"

"Neville is buying a chunk of my shares. We'll end up by him owning a third of the company. Now you see, it doesn't matter what I might think of holiday villages, it's all part of the same deal."

There was a long silence, and Colin looked out of the window at the passing traffic, as if he'd now removed himself from the discussion, like he'd done when his father was alive and in control. Everton saw no point in continuing the conversation because Colin was in a straight jacket, and he was putting his own company in jeopardy. "I don't need this information now," Everton said, and pushed the file back to Colin.

Doreen was pregnant, and the doctor had confirmed it. The next question was when and how was she going to tell Everton? She spoke to his Mum first, on one of their frequent trips together to the beach, and broke the news. As they were sitting on the edge of the water, watching small children rush in and out of the water, Doreen said, "I'd like a family like that, two or three maybe."

"Why don't you?" Everton's Mum asked.

"I'm making a start. I'm pregnant now, and the event is due in February."

Everton's Mum shrieked with delight, and threw her arms around her daughter-in-law. "You clever girl," she said. "What does John think?"

"He doesn't know yet. You're the first person I've told, and I need your advice."

"What about?"

"We had agreed to wait for two years, but I didn't want to wait that long, so I cheated."

"Cheated?"

"Yes, I told him that it was safe and I took no precautions."

"But he'll be over the moon, I'm sure he will."

"Yes, but do I say I cheated, or do I say it was an accident?"

"Which was it?"

"I cheated."

"Well, don't use the word cheat, just say you deliberately took no precautions, because you wanted a baby so badly."

"He might be mad at me?"

"No, he won't, not for long anyway. He would be mad if you tried to deceive him now, and eventually the truth would come out."

"Thanks Granny, I'll take your advice."

When Everton returned from Liverpool he said to Doreen, "I've got news and it's not good."

Doreen replied, "I've got news, and it's good, at least I think it is."

"All right, you first," Everton said.

She took a deep breath and said, "I'm pregnant and it's due in February."

Everton appeared stunned at first, then a smile started to form and he opened up his arms, "Come here, you clever girl," he said. "You clever, clever, lovely Mum, you," and he embraced her.

"You don't mind then?" Doreen said after she had caught her breath.

"Why should I?"

"You said two years."

"Why wait? I said two years because I was fearful."

"Fearful of what?"

"The extra responsibility, about you...Oh, I don't know," and he kissed her. "You do want a baby?" he asked.

"More than anything."

"Was it a mistake?"

"No, I wanted it."

"You were right."

Relieved that the news had been taken so well, Doreen said, "You said you had news too; what is it?"

"Oh, it's unimportant, or at least it is now anyway."

"What's unimportant?"

"Colin's wife wants a divorce, and to pay him off he's sold a third of the business to that rat, Neville; he'll probably ruin us."

"Who will still own the other two thirds?" Doreen asked.

"Colin Meadows and family."

"Then what are you worrying about?"

The baby was expected in February. Doreen carried it well, and as she put on weight she seemed to Everton to have become more mature, cool and serene, less like a young girl, and certainly not like the young schoolgirl who had offered herself for employment all those years back. Neither Doreen nor Everton knew anything about babies, so they relied heavily on Everton's Mum who said, "You should get a nurse for six weeks. She'll live in and get you started in good habits. I'm sure Everton can afford it."

Perhaps Everton could, but Doreen thought it very expensive, and didn't fancy having a stranger in the house, so then a thought came to her. "Pauleen!" she said.

"What about Pauleen?" Everton asked.

"Pauleen can come and stay and help us out."

"Does Pauleen not have a job to go to?"

"She's in and out of jobs, so there'll be no problem."

Doreen was right and Pauleen agreed to come when called for.

"What does Pauleen know about babies?" Everton's Mum asked.

"Probably little or nothing, but she'll be an extra pair of hands, and it'll be a good rehearsal for when she has a baby of her own."

Three weeks before the baby was due, Everton had to go to Liverpool for a board meeting. It was going to be a vital one because he hoped to have approval for the purchase of the Limerick business for twenty thousand pounds. Negotiations had been long and torturous, but patience was due to be rewarded. He told Doreen that it would be the last trip away before the baby was born. He would travel over by air and back by the night ferry, so he'd only be away for one night.

When Everton studied the board meeting agenda he was alarmed to see that the Limerick proposal was way down the list, and somewhere near the top was a further proposal for an extension in the leisure business, the purchase of a company called Wood End Holidays for two hundred thousand pounds. Around the Boardroom table were Colin and three members of the Meadows family, Neville Singer and John Stokes, the Company Secretary. The Meadows' family were counted on to rubber stamp everything Colin wanted, and likewise John Stokes would venture no opinion of his own and would also back Colin. If it came to a fight, Everton had no support.

"Item three, Wood End Holidays," said Colin, "Neville, would you talk us through this one please?"

In a passionate voice, Neville explained his proposal. Wood End was in a neglected state and had therefore lost customers. All it needed was a facelift and customers would return in their droves. It was five miles from their other leisure centre, and therefore there would be economy in maintenance and management. It could be the start of a chain of leisure centres across Wales. At present Wood End did not make a profit, but it probably would do in two years time. Colin called for questions.

"Have we got the money?" Everton ventured.

"We would have to borrow one hundred thousand," Colin said.

"Have we checked that we can?"

"No problem."

"So we would have to use up our reserves and then borrow heavily?"

"As long as it's borrowing for expansion, we have nothing to lose."

Neville cut in and said, "If you look at the analysis you'll see that the leisure group as a whole will be in profit in three years time, and by year five we should be making a twelve percent return on capital."

"What does our existing Poster business make?" Everton asked.

"About fifteen percent."

"And the Irish business on its own?"

"Twenty percent."

"Well?"

"I get your point, Everton," said Colin, "posters are doing well at present, but we need a 'hedge' for protection."

"And are not tourists flocking to Spain and giving up on English weather?"

"Over rated," Colin said. "Anyway I now need a vote on this. Neville has been doing a lot of work on this one and he has my full confidence."

He called for a vote and it was carried, with only Everton objecting. Everton knew that when the proposal for the Limerick business came up, suddenly there would be no money for it, and so it proved. "We are fully committed at present," Colin said.

"This is our core business," Everton said, "and the rate of return is twenty percent – a better buy than Wood End."

"It's not absolutely necessary," Neville said, "surely Meadows in Ireland can expand organically, like it always has."

"This would give it a push."

"I'm afraid that the time is not appropriate," Colin said. "You got the money for Cork because there were reserves at that time; there are no longer any reserves."

The matter wasn't even put to a vote.

At the end of the meeting Everton stormed out of the room and went to see the switchboard girl. As soon as she saw him she said, "Oh, Everton, your Mum has been on. Will you please ring her?"

"Not yet," Everton replied, "I need to speak to my Bank Manager and I have his number here. Can you give me a line please?"

After a few moments Everton was able to get hold of Jimmy Henderson, his friend at the bank. They exchanged notes about the weather, and then Everton went straight to the point. "I'm looking for a loan," he said.

"Surely not, the bank owes you money. You must have at least five thousand pounds on your deposit account."

"I will need to close that and borrow twenty thousand pounds."

"What on earth for?"

"To buy a Poster Company in Limerick for twenty thousand, and I'd need five thousand for working capital."

"Why isn't Meadows buying it?"

"They don't want to; they're starting to invest outside posters. It's called 'a hedge', I believe."

"Does Meadows know anything about your personal interest?"

"Not yet, but I shall not keep it a secret. The Limerick Company in my hands is better for Meadows than in a competitor's hands."

"I hope you know what you're doing?"

"I do, but what about the loan? Do I get it?"

"I see no problem, but I'll need precise information about what you are buying, and it will still have to go before the Board."

"I'll see you when I get back, Jimmy."

Everton started to rush out. As he went through the front door he was conscious of the switchboard girl calling out, but he didn't pause. If he was to get a meal before catching the boat he needed to get a move on.

Everton relaxed in the ferry bar, and began to go over the events of the day in his mind, then suddenly he remembered – he was to ring his Mum; of course, that's what the girl was calling out to remind him. Oh well, it could wait, he'd see his Mum in the morning. Then out of the corner of his eye he saw a familiar face, a young woman with a round face, big brown eyes and closely cropped brown hair. The woman recognised him and smiled, then quickly moved towards him. Why, it was Pauleen! What on earth could she be doing coming over so soon? The baby wasn't expected for three weeks. "Hello Everton," Pauleen said. "Congratulations, what does it feel like being a father?"

CHAPTER TWENTY THREE

"DID YOU GET HOLD of John?" asked Doreen.

Everton's Mum replied, "I rang Liverpool office and left a message for him to ring. They rang back later to say that he'd dashed off in a hurry."

"So he doesn't know?"

"No, but he will do in the morning, unless he's met Pauleen. He should have been there. Why on earth did he go away so close to the birth?"

"It was three weeks early – he wasn't to know. Anyway, I'm glad he wasn't here; I just wanted to get on with it on my own; it was hard work!"

"You were marvellous. If you had it that easily, maybe you'll have plenty more?"

"I'm not thinking about that at the moment. John is depressed about business; he'll need to see better into the future before thinking about babies."

"Depressed? How could he be? Look at what he's achieved here. He's in an unassailable position."

"They are not doing too well in England; television advertising has cut into the poster market, and Everton is worried about this new man who has come in. He badly misses old Mr Meadows' steady hand."

"John gets moods. I know because I'm his Mum. He'll be overjoyed to see little Richard. You're a family now, Doreen, a real family."

Everton had celebrated with Pauleen the night before. During the night it had got rough and he'd been sick. He was ashamed to discover that Pauleen had been all right. They'd had breakfast together on the boat, and then they went to the Clinic to see both Doreen and Richard. In his heart he wished for a girl, a duplicate of Doreen, but there wasn't any way he was going to say that to anyone. Looking at Richard's small pinched up face and tiny neat hands and feet, he saw his son as a bond between Doreen and himself which would bring them even closer together.

Nothing could wreck this marriage now; they were a family and that was the most important fact in his life. He felt that overnight he'd grown old and wise, and his work no longer seemed so urgent and important. The future was not Meadows, or his ego, it was here in his hands, cradling his son, his first child. Perhaps next time it might be a girl?

Everton closed his deal on the Limerick business and then sought to make his peace with Colin. The subject came up quicker than he had planned, chiefly due to a surprising phone call from Colin who sounded almost panic stricken. He said, "Everton, you have a thousand shares in the company, and as you know I've been disposing of some of my shares."

"I know, you had to raise cash to pay Carol off."

"That's only the start of it. There's now the question of death duties. When Father died he left all the shares in the company to me, and my mother got the house and everything else. If he'd left the shares to my mother there would have been another lot of death duties whenever she dies, so to compensate I'm obliged to pay her an allowance. I borrowed heavily to pay death duties, and expected to repay from the sale of my shares to Neville, but instead had to hand most of it over to Carol. So I've still got the loan to clear, and Neville has agreed to buy more shares from me, and that leaves me with a fifty-two percent stake. I would like you to buy up some of the shares before selling to Neville. Could you raise the cash?"

"How much?"

"Not less than ten thousand pounds."

Now it was Everton's turn to panic. He'd had to borrow to buy Limerick, and now he had a wife and child to care for; he couldn't afford to borrow again. "I'm sorry, Colin, I've just had to borrow twenty thousand pounds. I can't put myself further in debt."

"Why on earth did you need that sort of money?"

"I'm coming to that. When the board didn't agree to buy Limerick, I decided to buy it myself, so to avoid the business going into unfriendly hands."

There was a long silence and then Everton silently asked, "Are you still there?"

Colin then exploded and shouted, "You can't do that, Everton, read your bloody service agreement."

"I know, Colin, and I'm sorry about that, but I have proposals to help Meadows."

"What proposals?"

"Meadows can put the Limerick sites on their selling list, and I'm prepared to pay Meadows ten percent commission. For Meadows that's money for jam."

"You have all this worked out, haven't you?"

"Yes."

"And are you going to spend Meadows' time running your own business?"

"There's a good foreman down there called Liam. He has good potential, so I'm making him Manager and he'll run the business. Yes, I know, some of my time will be spent on the Limerick business, but remember I already work a fifty hour week for Meadows."

"I'm going to say this once, Everton, and only once, never do this again, and in future accept board decisions with good grace."

Everton drew a deep breath. He'd survived the crisis, and he knew that Colin needed him more than he needed Colin. But he had no money to buy Meadows' shares, and if Colin didn't watch it he'd lose control of his own company, then where would they all be?

Eight days later Everton took Doreen and Richard home. He'd decorated Richard's room, and all his gear was there, the cot and carrycot, the bath and piles of nappies; at least it was another unused bedroom now brought into use. Pauleen was already occupying another bedroom, and the big house was beginning to fill up.

Doreen came into the kitchen, still suffering from post natal blues, in spite of Everton having told her that he was taking a week off, so he could start to be a father. She stared at the blue doors and grimaced. "I can't stand that colour," she said, "it's too dark, too blue, get me another shade card."

Everton got several shade cards and Doreen made her choice, then he bought the paint and started to repaint them.

"You can't do it now, silly," Doreen said, "we've got a baby in the house."

"When can I finish it?" he asked.

"Give it another month."

So the kitchen doors remained in two shades of blue.

A month later the kitchen doors had not been painted; they still couldn't agree on the correct shade. Six weeks later, Pauleen left, promising to be back for the christening. Eight weeks later, another Meadows crisis arrived.

A massive amount of capital flowed out of the company into the leisure business in Wales and yet still potential customers stayed away.

They had discovered France and Spain and the Canary Islands, and thus the Meadows' dividend was cut. Everton urged Colin to 'cut and run, sell the bloody camps before they throttle us'. Neville urged Colin to stand firm, 'it would only be a matter of time before they turned the corner'. They decided to give it another three months by which time the season was over. Meadows were prevented from paying any more dividends, and Neville didn't try to defend his position any more, and he found a conglomerate business in the city, Baker Securities, to take the camps off their hands, and the company had to accept a whopping great big loss. There remained the tricky situation of what to do with Neville, and a board meeting was called to deal with the matter. Once again Everton was called to Liverpool the night before so that he and Colin could have a private conversation about the crisis.

"I told Neville he'd have to go," Colin said.

"Did he agree?"

"He still says that we didn't give the Leisure Group a chance, and he'd always said that it would take a few years before making a profit."

"So is he going?"

"I've accepted his resignation and he's sold the holding."

"To whom?"

"The same conglomerate company who've bought the Holiday Camps, Baker Securities."

"Just what do they do?"

"They're in bricks, Estate Agents, printing and God knows what else. They now own a chunk of Meadows and we'll have to put up with them. They insist upon a representative on the board."

"Well, they'll be a minority shareholder, so what does it matter?"

"The only thing that matters is that their representative is Jack Purvis."

Everton was flabbergasted. "Not *THE* Jack Purvis, the one who worked here and messed everything up?"

"The very same one."

Then in a mood of rage and impetuosity Everton said, "If he gets voted onto the board, I go."

"Steady on," Colin reacted, "go where? From the board or the company? Remember, you have a service agreement."

"If the service agreement permits it I'll go from the board. You don't listen to me, anyway."

"I do listen, though I don't always agree. And yes, you're right over nearly everything, so I can't afford to lose you. But why do you object to Jack so much?"

"Can't you remember, Colin? He fluffed everything, he had no touch and rubbed everybody up the wrong way; he was too rigid, and his judgment was flawed. Worse still, he thought Poster Advertising was crap and not good enough for him."

"Perhaps he was at the wrong end of the business, at the coal face, so to speak. Perhaps he'd be better at the top level. Bakers must think something of him."

"Colin," Everton pleaded, "couldn't you ask for someone else?"

"If you feel that strongly about it, I will."

For once, Everton was heeded. Bakers sent an elderly man, a Tim Crowe, polite and humble, cultured and keen to get on with his fellow Directors. Neither Colin nor Everton saw him as a threat.

Autumn came and went, then Christmas, the first Christmas as a family. They bought a Christmas tree and lights and placed it in one of the big bay windows. On Christmas afternoon they put Richard in his high chair and unwrapped his presents in front of him, all of them disappearing into his mouth. Next year perhaps he would understand it all a bit more, then the year after he'd know about the magic of Father Christmas. There was so much more of life to enjoy.

As the cold winds of February and March blew themselves out, crocus' and daffodils popped their heads up again. Everton and Doreen talked more about a new baby, and Richard gave up crawling and tried to walk, often falling over and crying. Everton put fatherhood first and work a close second. He had time to consolidate Meadows' grip on Ireland, and his business in Limerick, under Liam's care, grew and was profitable; slowly his loan to the bank was repaid. For once Colin was being sensible and the ever smiling Tim Crowe appeared more than happy with his employer's investment and did not interfere. What could go wrong?

Then it happened! It only took one phone call from a subdued Colin asking Everton to come to an emergency board meeting. There was the usual arrangement where Colin and Everton met the night before, this time in his office. As with old habits, Colin produced the gin and tonic from the drinks cupboard. "Cheers," he said.

"What's all this about, Colin?" asked Everton.

"I'm fed up, Everton. I'm left with fifty two percent of the business, and none of my family is the least bit interested in it. So why should I keep it going for them? I'm getting bored with the day by day running routine, and I'd like an early retirement, to enjoy the rest of my life with Francis, well away from Carol, in some warm spot, Australia perhaps? With these thoughts in mind I get a sudden and unexpected offer of three pounds a share for all my shares. I'm getting out."

Eventually a shocked Everton said, "To whom?"

"This is the bit you won't like."

"I don't like the bit you've told me."

"Tim Crowe has arranged it."

Tim Crowe, thought Everton, the dark horse. "What has Tim Crowe got to do with it?"

"Baker Securities are buying me out."

As if he didn't know what was coming, Everton thought, then said, "And what do they know about posters? It's not bricks and printing, for God's sake. They're a conglomerate; they are financial wizards; they'll strip Meadows' and sell the rest off in bits, then move on to do their worst with some other poor unsuspecting soul. That's what conglomerates do. Who do they have in mind to take charge? It won't be me because I couldn't stomach their policies."

"You won't like this bit either - it's Jack Purvis; I'm sure that if the two of you put your mind to it, you'll get on famously. I've spoken to him and he has no problems as far as you're concerned; in fact he looks forward to working with you again."

There was a dead silence. Colin lifted his glass and had another sip of his gin and tonic. Everton boiled over, and thought of all the things he could say to Colin, and then dismissed it all – it would be an entire waste of time. He looked at his watch and saw that if he hurried he could catch the night ferry to Belfast, so he got up, and tucking his brief case under his arm he left, without a word.

The next morning Everton did not return to the office, and he knew that they were not expecting him. He went home to his family, where Doreen was surprised to see him. "Why do you look so glum?" she asked.

"Colin has sold out, to Jack Purvis of all people. I couldn't stand him before, so how can I stand him now?"

"It may not be all that bad, perhaps he might have matured?"

"I think I may have to go it alone," Everton said, "and I've already got a business in Limerick, so thank goodness for that."

"Don't be too much in a hurry," Doreen said, "and I've got news for you."

"News?"

"Yes, I'm pregnant!"

CHAPTER TWENTY FOUR

EVERTON'S TEMPORARY DESPAIR WAS lifted by Doreen's news. What did his work matter any longer? He would do his best for his employers, but not put himself out like he'd done before. His priorities had changed, and soon he'd have a real family, perhaps even a girl this time?

The next day he went back to the office and told the staff about their changed circumstances. He then carried on as usual and waited for news from Liverpool. On Friday, just as he was about to go home, a call came from Liverpool; it was Jack Purvis.

"We meet again," Jack said cheerily.

"I hope you don't want me to call you 'Sir' any longer?" Everton said coldly.

"Those days are over, and also the demon you used to know. Call me Jack, please."

"Jack it is then, Jack."

"I want to come over and talk things over. Will Tuesday suit?"

"I have an appointment which is not urgent, and I can easily re-schedule it, willingly in fact."

"Willingly? What sort of appointment?"

"The Dentist," Everton replied, and they both laughed. The ice had been broken.

Jack flew over on the early morning plane, and Everton met him at the airport. He had changed little and still had that confident strut. He was, however, less grumpy and insulting, and appeared to accept the good work which Everton had done. He requested that they spend the morning going around Belfast to see some of the Meadows' sites and Everton's triumphs. At lunch time they called at the office, and Jack bustled through from room to room, deep in thought. "Right," he said, "take me to lunch."

"Is it a quick snack or a three course meal and a bottle of wine?" Everton asked.

"A long lunch, though I won't be eating much. We need to talk and away from the office."

Everton took him to an upmarket restaurant where he was well known, where they were given a very private table in an alcove.

"We need to put the past behind us," Jack said.

"I agree," Everton replied.

"We must accept disciplines that sometimes a private company does not demand."

"Such as?"

"We have to make sure that all our assets are employed to the full, and if any of them don't provide a satisfactory rate of return, they'll go."

"There are none of those here."

"You may think so, but it is a requirement that all sites are individually computerised so that we know where non profitable ones are."

"As I say," Everton cut in, warming to the subject, "I inspect every site in Ireland three or four times a year. I already know the poor sellers, and if any bad seller can not be improved in some way, then it goes."

"Knowing you," Jack said, "I fully believe you, but it's not the case in many other areas and we can't make an exception of Ireland. By all means carry on with your inspections, but all your sites will have to be computerised like everybody else's."

"It seems such a waste of time and a waste of resources."

"In your case you could do it yourself as you go round."

Everton could see no serious problem with this chore, other than that it was not necessary. It was because he had no unprofitable sites that the Irish figures were always the best. You couldn't blame Jack trying to bring everybody else up to Irish standards. "I will be glad to do it, if only to prove to you that we know what we're about here."

"That's the spirit," Jack said, in a rather patronising way. Then he added, "Now there are two specific problems which we need to deal with at once, Limerick, and the office. I'll deal with the office first."

"You've seen it, so what's wrong with it?" asked Everton.

"Absolutely nothing, but it's a city centre site and it's worth a lot of money."

"We've got to have an office."

"Yes, but not there. There are Industrial Estates in every city where developers are crying out for tenants, and deals can be struck. We can take a warehouse type of building and convert to our needs."

To Everton this thought was hideous. To leave a prestige city centre building which was convenient for clients, and move out to a tatty estate, would be a down move and cause disruption. "The industrial estates are horrible," he said.

"That may be your opinion, but they are functional. The money which the sale of the office will release can be re-invested in the company, where returns are good."

"Such as?"

"The purchase of another company, perhaps?"

"Another billposting company or something outside billposting?"

"That depends. Yes, I know, you're thinking about the holiday camps. Neville was wrong to try to build them up. We've now sold them off for housing, at a huge profit."

Perhaps they weren't that stupid after all, Everton thought, but before he had time to make further comment Jack had moved on. "This brings me to Limerick," he said.

"Limerick?"

"Yes, your company. I can't allow you to run your own private company while you work for Bakers."

Everton felt alarmed. Limerick was his life line in case anything went wrong. Jack had no right to interfere. "Colin accepted the position," he said.

"And you don't work for a private company any longer. If you want to continue to work for Bakers you'll have to sell Limerick."

"To whom?"

"To Bakers. We'll pay you the twenty grand you paid for it."

Everton could see the logic of the proposal. After all, he had only bought the company in the first place to save it for Meadows, and Meadows was now Bakers. He would get back the twenty grand, and with the three grand for his Meadows shares he'd be better off now than he'd ever dreamt he could be.

"Agreed," Everton said simply. "Are there any other matters?" he asked.

"Not on this trip." Everton did not know if that remark was said lightly, a joke maybe, or if it disguised a hidden agenda, a warning shot that there would be further tightening of the belt, month by month, until the old Meadows business had become weak and unrecognisable?

"Well," asked Doreen that evening.

"It's not a bad start. I have to sell Limerick to Bakers, but I'll get all my money back. We have to move to a bloody industrial estate some-where, and I'm getting involved in a computer evaluation exercise so that I conform with company policy."

"But you keep your job?"

"Yes, of course I do."

"What about your salary?"

"What about it?"

"When do you get a rise?"

"For crying out loud, I'm bloody lucky to still have a job, so salary is the least of my worries."

"Then remember to ask him," Doreen persisted.

"I will not, at least not yet," Everton concluded.

Everton did not know it at the time, but this was the last time he'd see Jack Purvis. Further communication was by correspondence which became increasingly acrimonious.

Much of Everton's time was spent in trying to find an alternative site for the office, and he got progressively depressed as he visited one estate after another. The common feature was that they were all isolated, introducing all sorts of complications for his staff getting to work. Those with company cars and owners of private cars would not be penalised, but the junior staff would probably give notice, and he'd have to rebuild a new staff base from local talent.

There then followed a rapid series of Jack Purvis' directives. The first read, 'Our rent levels are too high, so you must take action to reduce the total rent bill by twenty percent. If this means giving up the less profitable sites we must accept that, but we rely upon managerial skills in re-negotiating with landlords more realistic values'.

Everton had no idea what he was going to do about it. It was madness, and anybody could see that. Landlords would not agree to reductions because rents went up, not down. He would have to give up sites, but which? If he gave up the less profitable ones they would already be at low rentals and it would therefore take a lot of them to make up the figures. If he gave up fewer sites at the upper value end, then he would lose his best sites, so he did nothing.

Then he received another one saying, 'The cost of site maintenance has become extravagant. Sites do not need to be painted each year; a routine of five years is sufficient, and more urgent ones can be done once every three years. The painting budget must be cut by seventy five percent'.

Everton stopped all painting. When he next saw Jack he would have to tell him a thing or two, then he could re-start. Jack obviously didn't understand the need to paint hoardings and panels on a yearly basis. Billposting was a mucky business with paste often being thrown around lifting painted surfaces. You had to repaint to keep the sites looking fresh, the way clients expected it, and they were the ones who mattered. Jack Purvis didn't.

Then Jack Purvis wrote, 'We have a lot of company properties to safeguard our advertising sites, but some of these properties could be sold off for general redevelopment at market values. We can afford to lose some sheetage, but we can not afford to lose the capital values these properties would release, thereby giving us the opportunity to re-invest in other ways'.

What other ways did he have in mind, wondered Everton, Holiday Villages perhaps? It was then that Everton became rebellious. The thought entered his head to buy some of these properties himself and rent back to Bakers, not revealing that he was the new owner.

Everything had changed. Everton was used to setting his own agenda, of storming ahead with his own initiatives, one after another. There was no time for that now; he was running trying to keep up with Jack Purvis' demands. The next directive was the last he was to receive and it read, 'Your office staff levels are over weight. In some cases two jobs could be run into one. I have measured the Irish staff weighting with the rest of the company and you are at least twenty percent over. Please make the required reductions, which can not, on their own, be taken up by natural wastage'.

Everton sat at his desk holding this latest letter, seething with rage. He would not let anybody else see him like this so he shut the 'forever open door'. It wasn't that what was being demanded was unachievable, it was the straw that would break the camel's back, so Everton wrote and asked Jack Purvis to come over again, before agreeing to any more economies.

The reply was not what he expected – 'I am not satisfied with the progress you are making on the new company policy in Ireland. I have therefore asked Robert Hardy, our Manager in Newcastle-Upon-Tyne, to come over to Ireland and take control of the day by day management of the area. He will arrive on Friday. I want you to take leave of absence on full pay until Robert reports to me about the general situation in the Irish area'.

Everton couldn't believe this rubbish at first. He re-read the letter over and over again. Was he being sacked? What should he do? He rang his solicitor friend, David, and sought an immediate appointment.

David read the letter along with a copy of Everton's service agreement slowly and carefully. He was on a salary of five thousand a year, with one year already gone of the five year contract.

"It's bad," David said.

"Can they sack me?"

"They can get rid of you, but they'd have to pay compensation."

"What, four years at five thousand a year?"

"No, they'll probably offer six months salary, and finally agree to a year."

"But I've got four years to go."

"They'll say that you're capable of finding another job within six months, in which case you don't need a four year pay off. And if you don't find another job, you've obviously been overpaid for what you've been doing."

"For God's sake, is this justice?"

"Not at present. The government is currently looking at new legislation, but in the meantime you're not covered."

Sweat began to pour down Everton's back, as the realisation of what was happening to him sank in. It was not only that he would be facing poverty and an uncertain future, it was also all that he'd achieved for Meadows' by cunning and hard work now counted for nothing. He had wasted his time.

What was uppermost in his mind when he drove home was what Doreen's reaction would be? In seven months he would have another child. At least he had a reasonable financial cushion, and they could manage for a year or two. He would pay off the mortgage on the house from the sale of the Limerick business, and that would ensure that they would always have a roof above their heads. Would they have to go to England to look for alternative employment? He had no qualifications other than in billposting, and that was a very restricted area of employment. The more he thought about it the more he realised that if they were going to stay where they were, he'd have to start a business of his own, so he began to count his pennies. He had three thousand pounds from the sale of his Meadows' shares, and after paying for the house in full, and paying back some long term loans taken out to cover the Limerick purchase, he would have about twelve thousand pounds worth of capital; anything more he could drag out of Jack Purvis for compensation could be added to this amount. He would not risk all his capital on a business venture, so he'd put in ten thousand pounds, a nice round sum.

Robert Hardy was to take over and file a report on what he was doing! What a cheek! The only thing Robert could ever do was to do what he was told, precisely, so he would fit in very well with the new company.

When he got home Doreen noticed his long face at once. "For goodness sake," she said, "what's the matter? Have you seen a ghost?"

"Worse," Everton replied, and showed Doreen the letter.

"What does it mean, apart from it being very rude?"

"I think I'm being sacked."

"You can't be."

"The Solicitor thinks I am."

"Oh God, what are we going to do? I'm not going back to England;
I fit in here now."

"Well, that's decided," Everton said, "I don't want to either. The only
alternative is to start a business of my own."

Doreen thought very carefully about that, and then said, "You'd be
starting from scratch again, working your way up like you've always done.
I've got used to the pressure being off you for a bit, so I suppose it will all
be work, work and work again?"

"What's the alternative?"

"I don't know."

David told Everton not to take any steps of starting his own business until
he'd received the pay off. He did not have long to wait and after a month
of inactivity, apart from having another go at painting his kitchen doors
blue, he got his final letter from Jack Purvis. It concluded, 'we are therefore of the opinion that you either do not understand company policy or
have decided to ignore it. We now need a vibrant new Manager to look
after Ireland and one who will achieve our targets. We appreciate the hard
work you have put into the business over the years, and feel sure that your
experience and track record will equip you to find excellent alternative
employment. We can not imagine that you will be out of employment for
long, therefore consequently we have decided to pay you six months salary as compensation. Please confirm your acceptance. We will, of course,
provide you with a first class open reference'.

The hard part now was to tell Doreen, although by now they'd got
used to the idea that Everton's days with Meadows' were over. "You go
on your own, love," she said, "I have complete faith in you."

Everton went to see David to obtain advice about his compensation.
He was told, "You can hang around and make submissions and threaten
unfair dismissal, and after twelve months you might get a year's pay, but a
full year will have gone by. If you're going to start a business of your own,
go for a quick acceptance, and be careful what you sign."

"So what do I do?" Everton asked.

"Tell them to make a formal offer. Keep everything in writing. Sign nothing that you've not cleared with me."

A post dated cheque plus a letter of resignation for him to sign was quickly sent. David said, "I thought they'd try this one. If you resign you'll not be able to start up in opposition. Tell them that you require a formal dismissal letter, and if you don't get it you'll go back to the office next week to take up your duties again."

"I can't do that, Robert Hardy is sitting in my office doing my work."

"Sack him then."

They both roared with laughter, and for the first time since he'd had Jack's horrid letter, Everton felt more relaxed and more confident about the future. For the past few weeks Jack Purvis had been in charge, the way he liked it, now he, Everton, would take charge and mould events his way against a weak and withering Meadows company in Ireland.

He got the letter of dismissal he'd sought and a request that he now lodges the post dated cheque. He was also asked to return the company car. He rang his ex-secretary to say that the Humber Hawk was ready for collection. Three days later Peter arrived at the door. He looked ill at ease and very unhappy as he explained that he'd come to collect the car. "What are you going to do with yourself?" he asked.

"I can't tell you Peter, you're the enemy."

"So you're starting up on your own?"

"What if I am?"

"Can I join you?"

CHAPTER TWENTY FIVE

HOLDING OUT HIS CAR keys with one hand, Everton held out his other hand towards Pete and said, "Welcome aboard. We'll form a company together, Smyth & Turner. I was wondering what to call it, now I know."

"I'll not be able to put any money into it, well, not much anyway," Pete replied.

"Doesn't matter, it's you I want, you're the brightest star in what is left of Meadows."

"I'll have to give a months notice; that'll suit them, they say there are too many staff. Don Wells is leaving; couldn't stand the uncertainty. He's joined an Insurance Company – knows as much about that as he ever did about billposting."

"What about Alec Hamilton?"

"Alec has been going crazy, working out what he's going to say to over a hundred landlords from whom Meadows are demanding rent reductions; of course he continues to worry about his age, so he would join us, I'm sure. Shall I have a word?"

"Yes please, and then the three of us can meet up here." Then, as Everton looked longingly at the Humber Hawk, he said, ""All of us will need transport, so I intend to buy three Renault Fours. We can't afford anything fancy at this stage; we just need a work horse each."

"I don't mind what I drive," Pete said, "so long as I'm out of that bloody place."

Alec Hamilton came to see Everton three days later. "Are you joining us?" Everton asked.

"If you'll have me. Do I put in my notice?"

"No, I'd prefer it if you could arrange to get sacked."

"What?"

"If you're sacked they can't object to you working for me. If you just join us and go into opposition, they could sue us for unfair competition and using an ex-employer's secrets."

"How do I get sacked?" Alec asked.

"That shouldn't be difficult. You could argue about the rent reductions – one thing which drives them mad is letting them know that you have an opinion as well! Have you got a full list of Meadows' sites and rentals?"

"No, but I can put my hands on it, stay late and copy it all out one night."

"You mustn't let anyone know."

"I'll cover my tracks; leave it to me, Everton."

"Then, when you're sacked you can come and join me. I can't hire you 'til you are dismissed."

"And until I've got the list!"

"Exactly."

"Everton, I'm really looking forward to this. There was no challenge for me any longer – it was like closing up an old home and covering the furniture with dust sheets. Are they all mad?"

"No, just greedy."

It took Alec two days to get the list and three more days to get the sack, his employment was to cease at the end of the month, but he was put out of the building and told to go home that same day. He told Everton that Robert Hardy had appeared terrified at the prospect of him leaking secrets to a competitor. He brought the list down to Everton and together they decided what he would do the day after his employment had ended.

Everton kept Doreen advised of what was going on. He expected her to be excited and joyful, but she was worried. "Do you have to poach their sites?" she asked.

"No, but it's the icing on the cake."

"Can you not build up your sites from unoccupied prospects, like you've always done? It may take longer but you're good at that."

"I could, but I want to give them a bloody nose."

"That's what I thought, and there'll be trouble, I know there will. I'm pregnant and I don't need worries."

"You've nothing to worry about," Everton concluded.

There was plenty of room in the Church Road house, so Everton converted one of the downstairs rooms into an office. He bought a second hand typewriter, but didn't ask Doreen to use it; however, she readily agreed to answer the phone, saying "Smyth & Turner, can I help you?" He went to a local printer and ordered printed notepaper, and consulted David to have the company registered as a limited one, the capital being limited to the ten thousand pounds he was prepared to risk. Although he told Doreen that he was employing two ex–Meadows' employees, one of whom had been sacked, he did not mention 'the list'. He did not want to be told what he could and could not do, but would do come what may. That was negative thinking, and if there was trouble, as Doreen forecasted, there would be trouble for Jack Purvis as well, and that was what he wanted more than anything else.

On day one, Alec went out to call on landlords who were on the 'Rent Reduction' list. He found that they'd all been written to by Robert Hardy, saying that due to competition from television advertising and diminishing returns, they had been forced to make cost reductions all round, including site rentals. It continued, 'It is with a great deal of regret that we must either give the site up, or as we would prefer, retain it at a reduced rental. In a few years time, if the situation improves, the rent can be revised'. It was, of course, a lot of rubbish, and Everton knew that soon landlords would tell Meadows to get lost, and whereas some of them would agree to the reductions, others would not. It needed a fair balance between the two alternatives for Meadows to achieve their target savings.

Alec made it very clear to these same landlords that there was a third option. They could tell Meadows to remove their boards and sign up with Smyth & Turner, either at the old rental or even an increased one. "I don't mind only achieving a small profit margin," Everton said, "I just want to get in there, get started and get known. I'm in a hurry."

At the end of the week Alec had signed up about a dozen sites, most of them ex–Meadows'. At the end of the month it had become a rout, that is to say until the injunction arrived.

Robert Hardy was pleased with himself. He had impressed Jack Purvis by his swift action in Newcastle in finding a new office and depot, in an Industrial Estate on a converted old airfield. Although one client had described it as 'a hovel', it was what Jack Purvis thought that mattered. Robert had been absolutely ruthless about site rentals, and had managed to bully scared landlords into accepting rent reductions. It was all a matter of attitude, and if they thought you meant it, they gave in – and he *DID* mean it. Jack Purvis had wanted it, so thus it would be.

He had never been to Ireland before and was excited by both the promotion and the increase in his salary, and the opportunity for him to work his magic touch in another area. Keep this up for a few years more, he thought, and then he might become a Director? He had no regrets about Everton having to go. He had made his way by licking Father's boots when he was alive, and for too many years he had been allowed to do what he wanted in Ireland. He was sick to death of being told by Mr Colin that everyone else should copy Everton's example, his initiative and boldness. On rare meetings with Everton, Robert regarded him as patronising and full of his own self-esteem. Well, time moves on, and it had taken Everton with it this time.

There was a lot of talk in the office about what Everton would do now. Perhaps he might go back to Liverpool; both he and his mother came from there. Robert would be happier if he did because otherwise he could be troublesome in Ireland. He had voiced these concerns to Jack Purvis who was pretty scathing and said, "He's all wind and bluster and has been propped up by the company for years. On his own he would be nothing. He's history."

Pete was instructed to collect the Humber Hawk from Everton's home. He thought Pete a surly creature who always replied to every order with, "Are you sure?" But he was bright and with a bit of discipline could prove to be useful. When he came back with the car he left it at the door, and sent someone else up with the keys. Robert was annoyed; he had intended to have a gossip with Pete about Everton – what was the house like? Did you see his wife? Did he indicate that he was going to stay in Ireland? Now he would have to wait until morning, so in the meantime he went to see the car, now *HIS* car. He was disgusted – it was filthy, both inside and out, and he noticed that the mileage exceeded seventy thousand, and he did not expect that Jack Purvis would be replacing it just yet, not with all the other economies going on anyway.

Next morning Robert sent for Pete. "How did you get on yesterday?" he asked.

"Meaning?"

What was the matter with the lad, thought Robert, why couldn't he give a proper answer to a proper question? "Meaning, did you see Everton and how is he?"

"What do *you* care?"

Robert was furious, but he wasn't going to play games. Pete was not going to be communicative, so he tried another line, "Would you get the Hawk cleaned up, please, it's filthy?"

"Who's going to do it?"

"Jimmy, the Yard Man, of course."

"Have you forgotten, Jimmy was made redundant last week? Clean it yourself."

Robert had forgotten about Jimmy, but this sort of cheek could not be tolerated. "Remember whom you're talking to," Robert shouted, and continued, "I won't have staff talking to me like that. You're lucky to be still employed here – and why did you skive off so early last night?"

"Because I'm fed up. Without any consultation you fire half my staff and halve my hoarding maintenance. I can't operate like that."

"You're a bright lad, so you can accept the challenge and work it out for yourself; all of us are having to make changes and be flexible."

"Well, you can get someone else to do it. I'm leaving at the end of the month."

"Hang on, Pete, did you get out of the wrong side of the bed this morning? Think about what you're saying, you'll wreck your whole career."

"I'm leaving, and as I'm due holiday time I'll take it now and that means I'll only be coming in again to collect back pay. I don't need a reference."

The man is being impossible, thought Robert, but he was determined to have the last word. "You're fired," he said.

"Will you please put that in writing?" Pete said.

It was the day for trouble with staff and he'd been looking for Alec Hamilton who was to report on the rent reductions exercise. Unlike his predecessor he kept his office door firmly shut, so he missed out on the movement of his staff up and down the corridor. He rang the extension for the top floor and for about the fifth time asked for Mr Hamilton. On this occasion he was lucky and Alec was able to report downstairs at once.

"It's about time I had an interim report," Robert said.

"About what?"

"Your rent reduction exercise, of course. What else?"

"Oh that."

"Yes, that."

"I've been busy negotiating with Newton Estate Agents over their request for across the board rent increases."

"Increases!"

"That's it."

"We don't do rent increases."

"Yes, and they don't do rent decreases."

"I'll talk about Newton later; what about the list?"

"What about it?"

Was the man stupid or was he deliberately being unhelpful Robert wondered? He was getting too old and he'd have to go, and the sooner the better. "I'll spell it out," he said, "how many rent reductions have you agreed?"

"None," Alec replied.

"None?"

"That's what I said."

"Then what the blazes have you been doing?"

"The Newton business has taken a lot of time."

Robert's patience was exhausted. He would have to take over the task himself, in which case Alec would be made redundant. "You're fired," he said.

"Would you put that in writing?" Alec answered.

God, another one wanting his sacking put in writing and appearing totally unconcerned. They'd all been allowed to become slack under Everton's management, so perhaps a clean out was the best thing which could happen?

Both Alec and Pete were happy to go immediately and the feeling was mutual. Robert decided not to replace them, so at one stroke he was well on his way to achieving his salary savings. Pete's work could be taken up by the Foreman, and he, Robert, would take over the rent negotiations. First he would attend to the Newton matter, and he looked forward to being strong with them. Little did they know that they would end up with a rent reduction instead of an increase. These Estate Agents need to be stood up to once in a while, and the time had now come, he thought.

Robert made an appointment with James Newton in his plush new offices in the city centre. No wonder he wanted rent increases, so that commission earned would pay for the décor. Robert brought a full list of the twenty sites rented with him, having made notes against them of what sites to keep, perhaps with slight increases, and what sites to give up or agree vastly reduced rents. He handed the list to James Newton who studied Robert's pencilled notes, in stony silence, but his eyebrows were rising, then fiddled about on his desk looking for a rubber. When he'd found it he ceremoniously rubbed the pencil notes out. "What have you done that for?" Robert asked.

"Because I don't agree to any of it."

"But that's my final offer. These are hard times and with television advertising bursting in on the scene we can't afford to pay high rentals any more; in fact we have too many sites right now."

"Times are hard for my clients as well," James replied, "and we need more money."

"If we give up these sites, how is that going to help your clients?" Robert asked.

"Simple, we put them out to tender."

"I think you'll find that nobody will take them."

"I agree that no poster contractor in your cartel will take them – self preservation and all that – but there are other players in the field. There is a new contractor in Northern Ireland for instance. They'll not be inhibited by the fact that you currently hold these sites at present. Robert, I'm so confident that I can move the business elsewhere, I've already had letters written out giving you notice for all twenty sites."

Robert returned to the office totally dumbfounded. Who was this mystery player? Perhaps Head Office would know? Head Office did not know and simply asked to be kept informed of any developments. They assured him that there was nothing to worry about, and he'd handled the matter perfectly correctly. If any inexperienced newcomer had entered the field they would be dealt with, firmly and decisively.

In the meantime Pete and Alec swiftly changed employers and reported to Everton at the Church Road house. The Newton portfolio became his first success, and then he moved on. Two weeks later a large registered packet was delivered to Everton's door. In amazement he looked at its contents. It appeared to be an injunction against Smyth & Turner forbidding them to compete with Meadows, in fact not only preventing them from making firm offers for sites which they currently held, but also to prevent them from operating as a competitive company in Ireland. He needed to see David quickly.

David studied the documentation carefully and then asked, "Have you been a naughty boy, then?"

"I've been competing against Meadows if that's what you mean?"

"Yes, but have you been making offers for sites currently contracted to Meadows?"

"Yes, and why not?"

"Because it could be construed that you are persuading landlords to break their contracts with them and that is an offence."

"Suppose the landlords come to us?"

"Too late now. You must have stirred something up, in an aggressive way, and now they have the right to clamp down on all your activities. You'll have to stop business altogether, 'til the matter is sorted. They've stolen the initiative now."

The thought that Jack Purvis was winning infuriated Everton. In a depressed tone, almost weeping, he said, "It's not fair. I had a right to start up my own business, Jack Purvis put me out of a job, and he has no right to keep me permanently unemployed."

"Hold on," David said, "you have been very foolish in the way you have chosen to compete. They will argue that you are using secrets gained when you worked for them and are therefore competing unfairly against them, but all is not lost. You can challenge the injunction, and at the same time enter into negotiations for an out of court settlement."

"What sort of settlement?"

"Am I right in saying that in your Trade Association contractors do not try to pinch each others sites?"

"Yes."

"Well, then you can enter into an agreement to stand by those rules, neither of you moving against each other, and they'd probably want you to withdraw any offers you've already made for their established sites. You'll end up like any other competitor, making offers for virgin sites in the market place. The exception would be that if a landlord, of his own choice, without any approach or prompting from you, should terminate a site, then that site becomes available to you as soon as it has been terminated and removed. That is the sort of decision the courts would make, so you might as well try to achieve it out of court and avoid legal costs which could eat up your capital. The courts could not possibly disallow you to fairly earn your living in the only way you are qualified to do so. Let me talk to Meadows' solicitors, and see if I can set up a meeting."

"A meeting with whom?"

"You, and this Jack Purvis and his solicitors."

"Do I have to be there?"

"Why not?"

"I don't want to be humiliated by Mr Purvis."

"Now you're being childish, but at the least I'd need you in the next room."

Everton related everything to Doreen who had strong views of her own. She said, "You've got to learn to live with Jack Purvis, so go to the meeting and be firm but polite, but not begging. You can beat him by being patient. You'll get his sites in the end, even if it isn't tomorrow, and in the meantime you can start to build up a holding without the need to take from others. Let it be a lesson to you."

Reluctantly, Everton struck a deal and business was resumed. He reckoned he would put Meadows out of business in ten years, instead of the three he had planned.

BOOK FOUR
DECEMBER 1983

CHAPTER TWENTY SIX
December 1983

NOW FORTY FIVE AND with her children at university in England, Doreen felt a little inadequate. Like an old fashioned Mum she'd refused to take a job while the children were growing up, and now she fussed over Everton, when he was there, and kept an eye on Everton's Mum who was healthy enough, but at times forgetful. Doreen ran her around in her car, to the doctor, the dentist and the shops. In between such chores she played golf and got her handicap down to twenty.

It was as well that Doreen was kept fully occupied, because she seldom saw Everton. Five years ago he'd triumphed and finally bought out Meadows' rump. Jack Purvis had long since left the scene, 'to make a mess of another company' Everton had said. Smyth & Turner had inherited Meadows' office and depot in a run down Industrial Estate in North Belfast. Everton vowed that they would get out of there just as soon as he'd finished paying off massive loans he'd taken to grow the business, so he worked all day and sometimes all evening. He was frequently away, in Dublin or London. Sometimes he took Doreen with him, but she felt out of place shopping in Grafton Street in Dublin and Oxford Street in London. Besides she resented paying for expensive things while the business carried those loans.

Doreen would have liked to have gone to the company Christmas parties, but Everton had refused to take her; he said that nobody else took wives or girlfriends so why should he set a precedent. "For God's sake, John, you own the company and you can do what you like." Everton carried through his socialistic ideas to company cars – any employee with one had the same, old Renaults bought second hand, but for Doreen, he'd bought a smart Vauxhall Viva which she washed and polished each day.

In Meadows' old office Everton had kept his door open so he could keep an eye on his staff. Not that there was any need any longer because there was no door. The main office was open plan, Everton sitting at his desk at one end, surveying all his staff before him. If he wanted somebody he shouted over their heads. With the clatter of typewriters and staff on the telephone, the noise level was unacceptable. Doreen had said, 'You should partition yourself off with glass panels and a door. You would still see the staff but there'd be a little less noise, besides it would mark you out as the boss'. Everton had replied that they wouldn't be there much longer, but there they still remained.

It was ten months ago that Everton had employed Valerie, a new Rents Ledger Manager. She was single, about forty and extremely glamorous with long straight blonde hair, a perfect oval face and a model's figure to match. Everton had to admit that he'd employed her because of her looks. He thought that she would look good in the office, cheer them all up, and besides she was bright and quick witted. It was not surprising, therefore, that she took the job of organising the Christmas parties.

But Everton felt threatened by Valerie. She was particularly keen on married men and in six months had had separate affairs with three married members of staff. The last affair was with Pete, and when his wife found out she begged Everton to sack her. But Everton could not because she was too good at her job.

For a time, all was peaceful again, and everybody was looking forward to the Christmas party. Also, the company had had a good year and staff bonuses were bigger than usual. They were to go to the Star Hotel in Bangor for a dinner dance. Because it was quite some distance away from most people's homes, a bus had been laid on, to take them there and back home again afterwards. Some of the staff, including Everton, went in their private cars. Everton could decide what time to leave the party that way and return home to Doreen.

Valerie threw herself into the party organisation with her customary enthusiasm. She'd arranged for little printed invitations to each member of staff, and organised the table arrangement so that everybody would be able to sit next to or near their buddies. She put Everton at the head of the table, and put herself at the opposite end, almost as if each of them were 'in charge' of their ends.

Like all events of this kind, it ran late. The staff had far too much to drink, so they were late starting their meal and the food was not as hot as it should have been. Most of them dealt with this by drinking even more, including Everton, who now wished that he'd taken Doreen; the party was getting out of hand and she might have been able to have helped Valerie to handle it.

Everton noticed that Valerie had wisely had little to drink, and she was the only one sober enough to organise everybody, not only the office employees but also the hotel staff. Everton was grateful for that because it meant that he could relax and leave everything to her.

The meal part of the evening was brought rapidly to a close by Valerie rapping on the table with her spoon, and demanding silence. "Before we go next door to the dance floor," she said, "I'm sure that Mr Smyth would like to say a few words."

Everton had already considered what he was going to say, and had written little notes on the back of an envelope. While everyone waited patiently for him to find the envelope by feeling in every pocket, he then realised he'd lost it, and had also forgotten most of what he was going to say. Silently and unobtrusively Valerie edged up next to him and quietly slipped into his hands a Photostat copy of his own notes which he'd no idea she'd copied in the first place.

For the rest of the evening Everton dutifully danced with all the ladies, some of them more than once. The only person he did not dance with was Valerie who appeared to be in such great demand and mostly tantalisingly unavailable. However, when the last waltz was called, she appeared from nowhere, her bosom practically falling out of her low cut golden dress. "This is ours, I believe?" she said.

They clung together on the dance floor, and Everton tried to think what he could say to her, something to indicate that he was grateful for all her organisation, without going over the top and giving her all the wrong signals. Almost as if she was reading his mind she put two fingers on her lips to silence him, and said, "Say nothing now, I know how you feel, just hold me tightly." How could she know what he felt? He felt like he had done all those years ago when he'd interviewed Doreen and knew that he'd wanted her but could not have her. Everton did as asked and held her more firmly, and Valerie rested her head on his shoulder. Other members of staff looked on knowingly.

All of a sudden the evening was over, and staff were collecting their coats and making their way towards the bus. Everton was aware of Valerie talking to the girl on all night duty in 'Reception'. She'd only been gone a couple of minutes and already he was missing her. He looked at his watch and saw that it was one o'clock in the morning. He'd had far too much to drink and wondered whether he should attempt to drive home. Police were about at this time of year, catching people out. If he lost his licence it would wound him severely, clip his wings and impede him from doing his job. He spent more than half his working time on the road; it was the way he ran his business, out and about. There was nothing for it, he'd have to try to book a room and if they didn't have one he'd sleep in a chair and sober up. He'd also have to ring Doreen and explain that he was staying the night, but it was so late he'd wake her and worry her. A taxi was an alternative, but then he'd be left with his car in the wrong place, and he knew by experience that taxis were hard to locate at this late hour. Life was full of problems. On his way to 'Reception' he bumped into Valerie. "I'm going to try to book a room," he said, "I'm too drunk to drive home."

"It's all right; I've done it for you."

Everton was surprised. This girl always appeared to be two steps ahead of everybody else. "You've booked me a room?" he repeated.

"Yes, I knew you'd need one."

"But I don't know if I should stay. I can't ring my wife at this late hour."

"You don't have to ring her, I've done that too."

Again, totally surprised, Everton asked, "When?"

"About an hour ago."

"Why?"

"Why what?"

"Why did you book a room without consulting me first?"

Valerie was taking charge, and he didn't like it.

"Because I knew that you'd eventually need a room. I knew that an hour and a half ago you wouldn't have seen it that way."

Everton pondered. What on earth would Doreen have thought? A strange woman ringing her and saying that her husband was staying the night?

"What did you say?" Everton asked nervously.

"I said that you were busy organising the party but you knew that you wouldn't be able to drive home whenever the party broke up, and you'd asked her to ring her and say that you'd decided to stay the night, and not to stay up for him, and you sent your love."

Everton was amazed. "What did *she* say?"

"She said how very sensible of you as she was worried about that, and she'd see you in the morning."

"Good God!" Everton said, and then added, "What about you? Are you driving home; I see that you haven't gone in the bus and you haven't had all that much to drink, have you?"

"Oh, I'm staying too," then added, "They only had one double room, so I booked it for both of us."

Everton felt shell shocked, as Valerie's plan of action unfolded, one bit at a time. Would he now stand up to her and scold her for being presumptuous, then try to get a taxi? On the other hand, an adventure was opening up to him; other members of staff had had affairs with this bombshell, but she'd been totally discreet; it was just bad luck that Pete's affair had got out, mainly because of Pete's carelessness rather than Valerie's fault. If he was sober he probably wouldn't have gone along with this, but in truth he was exhausted and even felt a bit sick. It was ironic that because he was in this condition he would not be able to take advantage of it, and that was where his safety lay. "Is there anything else I should know?" he asked, "Have you sold the business, bought the hotel or are you having twins? I don't know what to expect next."

"One final point," Valerie continued, "the room has a double bed, but they're made by two singles put together, so they can be separated and made into two. They've got no staff at this time of night, but they've left sheets and blankets for us to make up the beds ourselves."

Everton didn't know whether to laugh or cry. He'd allowed this girl to take complete charge, and she could spell trouble, but the feeling of adventure and the unknown excited him. He'd allow himself to be taken over, and he'd try to forget about Doreen for one night.

At Valerie's insistence they ordered one more drink, a double whiskey each, before they staggered up to their room. Everton felt exhausted and slightly dizzy, the room starting to revolve. He only got as drunk as this about three times a year and he knew that he'd have to lie down at once and allow himself to conk out. He had time to kick his shoes off and throw himself onto the double bed, before he blanked out.

A few hours later Everton came to, because he was aware of someone on top of him, and he was completely naked and so was Valerie. He realised that he was being raped, except that he was enjoying it and it had been part of his dream, but now it was for real. They completed their love making and then Valerie fell on top of him. He hugged and kissed her, and then he went to sleep again.

When he woke next it was morning, and the light was coming through the windows, and he heard someone move about. He looked around and saw Valerie, fully dressed and in her day clothes, come towards him. He would have to ask her all sorts, but before he could speak she had put two fingers on his lips, like she'd done before, then she said, "It was an experience of a lifetime but never to be repeated. I'm not a family breaker and I want nothing from you – our secret is safe. I shall never refer to last night ever again, either to you or anybody else. And thank you."

"What for?" Everton asked.

Valerie looked puzzled, and then smiled. "For the Christmas bonus, silly," then she left him, taking her suitcase with her.

CHAPTER TWENTY SEVEN

DOREEN HAD BECOME UNEASY. It had all begun just before Christmas when that girl had rung her up to say that Everton was staying the night. She was very sweet and sensible about it, and she hadn't wanted Everton to drive home half pissed with the police everywhere, but surely he could have foreseen that and made other arrangements, and why couldn't he have rung her himself? It had been uncharacteristic of him. Next year she would insist upon going with Everton, and she wouldn't care less whether or not it set a precedent.

Since the party Everton had seemed quiet and reflective, but on the other hand most loving. It was as if he was trying to prove something to himself, and she welcomed the care and attention which had been sadly lacking at this stage of their marriage.

After the children had gone back to university in January she decided to pay a short and unexpected visit to the office. She was worried that perhaps Everton's change of mood was due to some new business crisis – they had the habit of popping up once every five years, and one was now overdue.

Doreen was amazed at what she found. That dreadful office in the run down estate had been improved. They had dug a couple of flower beds outside the front door where all the mud had been, and inside Everton had done what she'd frequently suggested – to partition off an area for Everton's desk, with glass panels so he could still see what was going on, but could work in a quieter space. He was there with his secretary, a rather frumpy middle aged woman with large horn rimmed glasses. She was a pleasant soul and told Doreen how sad it was going to be to have to leave at the end of the month, but she had to look after her sick mother. She suggested tea and called out to a stunning blonde and asked for tea for Mr and Mrs Smyth. The blonde came back five minutes later with a pot of tea and a jug of milk, two chocolate biscuits and two fancy cups. When she had made sure that they had everything they wanted, she turned to Doreen and said, "I haven't seen you before, Mrs Smyth. I do so hope that you will come to our next Christmas party."

Doreen left in a happy mood. There was no crisis at the office and she would have sensed it had there been. The office itself was smarter, and she was glad that Everton had taken up her suggestion of building a partition, enabling them to have their tea in calm surroundings. Perhaps Everton had reached a mid life stage of less arrogance and assertiveness, and had taken on a more caring and attentive attitude. Life had indeed been kind to them.

It was a long time after the Christmas party that Everton was able to look Valerie in the face. He went about his business, aware of a heavy weight bearing down on his shoulders, and he continued to feel guilty. He reacted by trying to turn over a new leaf on the domestic front. He gave up crewing for George on Saturdays, and restricted his golf to having an early morning game with Doreen on Sunday mornings, before the course got busy. Doreen appeared to be pleasantly surprised but suspicious. He even had another go at painting the blue doors in the kitchen, but before the job was half done Doreen stopped him again. "Yes, I'm sorry Everton, it's not your fault," she said, "It's me, and these shade cards turn out to be nothing like what they pretend to be. Just leave it. Come to think about it, next time you're in Katie's house have a look at her kitchen – that is the blue I want."

In the office Everton decided to follow Doreen's advice about a glass partition for his own end. It would be some years before they could afford to move out of the premises, so he thought that they might as well make the most of what they had. He made the partitioned part large enough to include his secretary, Miss Pringle, even though she'd said that she was leaving. Outside the front door she got the Yard Man to dig over the two muddy patches and create flower beds into which he put some shrubs and tulip bulbs.

He was sorry about Miss Pringle going, and he'd begun to fully rely on her. Now he'd have to try to find someone else, to learn the job and his way of doing things, to put up with his short temper, and to be able to quickly find things in the filing system. One lunch hour while he was quietly composing advertisements for Miss Pringle's replacement, Valerie knocked on the glass door. "What is it Valerie?" he asked.

"Your Secretary's job; is it still vacant?"

"Yes, why?"

"I could do it."

"Can you type and do shorthand?"

"Oh yes, no trouble."

"Why do you want the job? It wouldn't be promotion, you know; I couldn't pay you more."

Everton's heart was beating fast. He didn't want to get involved again, to risk everything, but the idea was attractive. Valerie would learn quickly and be efficient. She'd be a godsend, but could he trust himself? What were Valerie's motives? She seemed to read his mind and said, "I meant what I said before, you know. The incident has been closed and erased from my mind. You'll be quite safe with me..." then she hesitated before continuing, "unless..." then said nothing.

"Unless what?"

"Unless you wanted to, you know – have an affair, not just a one night stand. Something like that, I'd be discreet."

Everton's heart was still racing when he said, "Quite definitely not, never again; you do understand, don't you?"

"Perfectly."

"The job's yours then."

Valerie took the job and behaved herself, not even showing as much as a knee when she took dictation. She quickly picked up the work and found her way around. Each morning she came in dressed smartly and decently, but looking and smelling like heaven. Everton did not know where she got her money from to afford such a wide ranging wardrobe, well in excess of Doreen's own substantial wardrobe. She made no evocative move, and Everton kept himself in check. He thought that the past had been decisively buried – he was safe, and he also had a perfect secretary!

The first breakdown of the strict protocol came when Valerie was making arrangements for the Poster Advertising Conference in Harrogate. "Will you be going on your own or taking your wife?" she asked.

"I don't know," Everton replied, "I'll check."

That evening he asked Doreen, "Will you be going with me to the conference this year; it's in Harrogate?"

"Is Harrogate by the sea?"

"No."

"When is it?"

"Third to the fifth of June."

"Well I don't like being inland and Lady Captain's Day is on the third of June, and I've agreed to partner Katie."

"So you're not going?" asked Everton, wishing the matter to be confirmed and mindful of Doreen's frequent changes of mind.

"Probably not."

"Yes or no?"

"Do I have to make up my mind now?"

"Yes. Valerie is doing the bookings and they have to be in by tomorrow."

"I'll say 'no' then."

"Definitely?"

"Probably."

"Probably what?"

"Probably definitely."

"Knowing you I better book a double room just in case you change your mind!"

There were several changes of mind before the event, but the double room was kept booked. Then a week before the conference Doreen finally gave her decision. "I'm not going," she said, "I can't let Katie down."

Everton told Valerie who said that it was too late to change the room to a single and said nothing more – or at least until forty eight hours later, then she struck, "Shame about the room" she said.

"Yes."

"Why don't you take someone else?"

"What? To share the room?" Everton's heart started to race again. Did she mean what he thought she meant?

"Yes," then looking at him straight in his eyes she said, "Do the delegates know Doreen?"

"Yes."

"Tell you what, I could come the first night only, and slip into the room in the evening and stay the night. We could have breakfast in the room, and then I'd be off."

There, she'd said it and he knew she would. He also knew how he was going to respond, because he'd been thinking about it for days, and it need only be for this once. He desired her more than anything else, and it was unfinished business. Before he'd been drunk and half asleep; this time it would be different. Without hesitation Everton said, "Yes, I would like that very much."

Valerie smiled a kind of victory smile.

Everton flew to Leeds and took a train connection to Harrogate. In Meadows' day he would have hired a car, but now he was counting his pennies. Valerie was already in England staying with friends in York. She would slip into the double bedroom late on Sunday evening, and book in as Mrs Smyth.

Familiar faces appeared at the conference hotel and Everton began three days of socialising, and being polite and courteous to colleagues in the trade. He always regarded this annual event as a waste of time, but of course, you never knew.

After dinner with a few of his friends he went to check if his room key had been taken – it had; so Valerie must have arrived. With breathless excitement he took the lift to room 303 and let himself in. There were shower noises coming from the bathroom so he cheerfully called out, "I'm here, the evening's ours."

"I'm glad it wasn't anyone else," Valerie called back. "Come and join me." Everton didn't hesitate and started to undress, and then the phone went. It was Sam Eccleston, one of the big players. He owned twenty percent of the poster stock in England and Wales. "Got a moment?" Sam asked.

"Not really, I've decided on an early night."

"Pull the other one; you've got a bird in there."

God, how the hell did he know thought Everton, and for a moment he was speechless.

"Only joking," Sam continued, "but seriously I need to talk to you urgently; it need only be for a few minutes."

"Does it have to be now?"

"Very definitely, there's something I want to discuss with you before tomorrow, it's vital."

"Will it take long?" Everton asked anxiously.

"No, no, I won't keep you."

"See you in a minute then."

A puzzled Everton put on his jacket again and went back to the bathroom. "That was an urgent call," Everton called out, "and I have to see someone for a few minutes. I won't be long."

"I'll be waiting for you in the shower," Valerie replied, apparently unconcerned.

Everton entered Sam's posh and spacious suite. He refused a whisky offered to him and he had visions of sipping it while Valerie drowned in the shower. They sat in easy chairs in the bay window, overlooking the colourful gardens which were such a feature of the town.

"It's the Americans," Sam said.

"What about the Yanks?"

"They want to buy a chunk of a Poster holding in the British Isles. I happen to know you'll be approached tomorrow. They've invaded our conference."

"How does that involve me?"

"They want to buy your business in Ireland. You own your company outright, so they have only one person to persuade."

"It's not for sale," Everton quickly replied.

"Anything can be bought for a price."

"What sort of a price?"

"Well, I'd pay you three million."

Everton was still thinking of Valerie in the shower, but suddenly he realised that this was a serious conversation to which he would have to apply his mind. "Three million what?" he asked, to give himself time for his mind to switch.

"No, not dollars, pounds."

Everton paused, his mind racing, and then he asked, "Are you sure?"

"Quite sure."

He was not going to turn it down outright. He really would have to think about this one. "How long can I think about this?" he asked defensively.

"Take your time, but I want you to know, whether or not the Americans make a bite, I will still keep my offer open."

Everton stood up and said, "This is unexpected and I've got to turn it over in my mind, on my own, so if you'll excuse me I'll go now and start the process."

"You really have got a bird down there," Sam joked.

Doreen was looking forward to her game with Katie, so she was bitterly disappointed when she rang and said, "Guess what?"

"What?"

"I've twisted my ankle, I can't play."

"You're joking!"

"Dead serious. Honestly, I'm so sorry Doreen. Do you think there's time for you to find another partner; I know Pam is available and looking for a slot?"

Doreen hated Pam. No, she'd scratch, and go to Harrogate instead and surprise Everton. He'd said that he would keep the double room, just in case.

Doreen arrived late on the Sunday evening and went to reception to ask for Mr Smyth's key. The girl looked oddly at her and said that there must be someone else in the room, so she went up. She knew that there was someone there because there was the noise of running water. Everton was probably having a shower, so she knocked louder than she would otherwise have done, then she heard someone lightly approach the door from the other side. The door swung open to reveal a young woman wrapped in a bath robe and she said, "I thought you were never – Oh, my God," then as quickly as the door had been pulled open it was shut firmly in Doreen's face. She looked at the number on the door in case she'd come to the wrong room. Just at this point Everton appeared out of the lift, his head lowered, apparently deep in thought.

Everton left Sam's suite and rang for the lift. He had been disorientated by the earth shattering approach. Was the company really worth three million pounds? What was he to do? The temptation was powerful; he could pay off his massive debts and never have to work again, but what would he do? As he went down in the lift he tried to wrestle with the options. Why had this come up now, just as he was going to spend the night with the most beautiful woman he'd ever met? How on earth was he going to be able to put his mind to that, when lurking at the back of his head would be the three million offer? Impossible! He got out of the lift still pondering everything, then became aware of a woman standing outside his door – My God, it's Doreen!

"Good heavens, Doreen, what are you doing here? How wonderful to see you," he lied.

"Who's in your room?" Doreen asked coldly.

So she knew, but how much did she know? Quickly thinking he said, "I think its Valerie, my Secretary; I said she could use my shower."

"Why can't she use her own shower?"

Good point that, but again rapidly thinking he said, "She's staying in another hotel and hasn't got a shower."

"Let me in," Doreen shouted, obviously not believing a word of it.

"Perhaps I better find out if she's finished?"

Doreen appeared angry and impatient, and most importantly, unbelieving. She knocked at the door again and called out, "Let us in." There was the sound of movement from behind the door and then Valerie opened it, now fully dressed and decent.

"Why, hello, Mrs Smyth," she said confidently.

They went in and Doreen said, "What are you doing here?"

"I was having a shower. I'm afraid I wasn't decent when you first knocked."

"So why have you brought two suitcases with you?" Doreen asked as she pointed to the cases, one of which had been partly unpacked.

"Ah!"

Everton had said nothing, but now he said, "Shall we all sit down?" He knew that Doreen knew everything and that there was no point in trying to deceive her any longer. He gently nodded to Valerie, as if inviting her to come clean. Everton had invited them to sit down but they had remained standing. He detected tears in Doreen's eyes – this was the worst moment of his life. Valerie spoke, "We booked a double room for Everton and yourself," she began, "but you cancelled. We left the room as it was in case you changed your mind. It was decided that I should stay one night in the room, but we haven't done anything, and I've just had a shower."

"I know what you were both up to," Doreen said, "and our marriage is over."

"I'm not a marriage breaker," Valerie snapped back. "I'll go now," she continued, "and I'll leave the company, and neither of you will ever hear of me again."

"Good," said Doreen, stuttering now, and openly crying, "and I'm going too…going home as fast as I can…," then more confidently, "You'll not find me at home after the conference, Everton, then I give you a week to make other arrangements and get out of my house. We're finished and I'm suing for divorce, and boy, is this going to cost you!"

CHAPTER TWENTY EIGHT

EVERTON WAS SUDDENLY DESERTED by both Doreen and Valerie, almost as if he was too hot to handle, and nobody wanted to take him on. What a bloody fool he'd been! The world had lain at his feet. He had his own company, and now he knew that it was worth three million pounds; he had a loving wife and two grown up children, both doing well, and a lovely home with a luxurious life style. But without Doreen, none of these advantages were worth having. Only minutes earlier, he'd come down from Sam Eccleston pondering his latest good fortune, and unable to relate to a night of passion which he now knew he hadn't wanted. Valerie was evil, and why did she do it? She said that she wasn't a family breaker, but that was just what she was. Then he remembered Doreen's last remark about, 'boy, is this going to cost you!' It could cost him half of three million for starters, so at least that was a decision he could make at once – he was not going to sell, either to Sam or the Americans, or anybody else.

The next day Everton would have liked to have returned home and give the conference a miss, but Doreen could still be there and her instructions had been clear – she didn't want to see him.

The Americans did eventually make an approach and he asked 'How much?' They suggested a figure of around two million. Everton rather rudely told them to get lost, and he also told Sam that he wasn't selling at any price, and then he slept walked his way through the rest of the conference. He wondered if his firm stand against selling would have been the same without his bust up with Doreen, and he now remembered that Doreen had manipulated him into Ireland and the fortune that followed. Would he ever be able to be without her?

There was no sign of Doreen when he got home. Her request had been clear and he was to get out within the week. He had no idea where he was going to go; he couldn't go to his Mum yet because he didn't want her to know about any of this, so he'd have to find a small hotel as a temporary arrangement. He was reluctant to make any long term commitment, because Doreen was likely to have several changes of mind, and that for the moment was the only straw he could clutch.

He sat in his kitchen finishing his modest meal and looked around the room which had been part of his home for most of his married life. A lot had gone on here, arguments with Doreen and the children, but much happiness as well and memories flooded back, then for the first time since Harrogate he laughed – just look at those blue doors, in several shades of blue, all done over the years. What a mess! How could Doreen have stood it?! It reminded him of all the good intentions over half a life time when he'd tried to please Doreen and get it right. He didn't know whether it had been her fault or his, but he did remember that he'd always given up too easily and too early, with no patience to understand what Doreen was trying to achieve. 'I want them like Katie's,' she had once said, and so they would be. Katie lived just a few doors down so he would go there now, and he'd ring the office and tell them that he was busy at home and wouldn't be back for a week; in the meantime would someone please try to find him a new secretary, middle aged and experienced.

Katie was surprised to see him, her ankle now almost better. "I haven't seen Doreen since she left for Harrogate," she said. "She's usually in here every other day. Is she all right?"

"Just gone on a little holiday," Everton said. He wasn't going to be drawn in. "I've come to look at your kitchen," Everton continued, "and see the shade of your blue paint; Doreen wants exactly the same."

"Yes, she's always said that," and she led Everton into a beautiful kitchen, with shiny Royal Blue paint everywhere. Everton had to admire it, and it looked very well. "Who painted it?" Everton asked.

"My husband, and he bought masses of paint and he doesn't know what to do with it."

"How much?"

"Oh, it would cover half a dozen doors, probably more. We have no use for it, would you like it?"

"I'd be happy to pay for it."

"Stuff and nonsense, I'll give it to you; I'll just keep a small tin for repairs and patching."

Everton left with a full cardboard box of Royal Blue paint, and then he went to Homebase for matching undercoat.

He slipped into his overalls and using a sander, smoothed off all the surfaces. He took all day and he was pleased with the result. He ran his hand over the doors and they felt good, so he congratulated himself.

Everton knew that his marriage was over, but realised that there was one more thing that he could do before he went, and if Doreen was still unhappy about the result...well then, she could do it herself.

The second day saw an undercoat applied. He took his time, and everything in the kitchen that was not to be painted was well covered with old posters and sheets, protecting the surfaces from paint droppings. It was then that Katie called and Everton met her at the front door and so he invited her into the kitchen so he could show off. "Oh you have done well," she said, then added, "You must have done some sanding?"

"Yes, before I started."

"I can tell," Katie said, and ran her hand over unprotected plates and kitchen equipment. Everton hadn't noticed that, and after all he was a man, why should he have?

"I'll take a wet cloth and run over it all; it will be my small contribution." And so it was that both of them worked away together, almost as if they'd always done it, and when it was time for a break Katie made the tea. "Does Doreen know you're doing this?" she asked.

"No."

"My, she will be pleased."

On the third day he was half way through a second coat of undercoat when his Mum called. "What on earth are you doing?" she asked.

"Repainting these doors and cupboards – they've been a mess for so long."

"You're certainly making a good job of it. Is Doreen about? I haven't seen her for a few days."

"She's gone on holiday," Everton said. He couldn't bring himself to tell the truth, at least not yet.

"On holiday! On her own? Why haven't you gone too?"

"I said I would do these doors."

"You're a Saint, but separate holidays are a bad sign. When is she coming back?"

"Oh, in a few days."

"She never told me anything. Are you sure that everything's all right between the two of you?"

"Couldn't be better," Everton lied, in an unconvincing tone. He wished that his Mum would leave it alone. He was not ready for this yet, and all he wanted was for his Mum, and everyone else, to leave him alone and let him finish the painting, then he'd return to the office and bury himself in his work which was what he did best.

"Where's she gone to then?" his Mum persisted.

"I don't know, really."

"Don't know! Have you two given up talking to each other?"

"Mum, she didn't know either, she just wanted a break and to take off and go somewhere, anywhere."

"I don't like it. Have you heard from her?"

"Not yet."

"Well ask her to call in when she gets back, but I expect she'll do that anyway."

"Of course she will."

"What are you doing for lunch?"

"Lunch?"

"What are you going to eat?"

"Oh, I'll work right through; I want to get this finished."

"That's men for you, quite incapable of looking after themselves. You've got to eat. I'll go home and get some nice egg and salad sandwiches, and maybe we could have some wine – it might cheer you up a bit?"

"Mum, there's no need."

"And a fat lot of thanks I get," she said.

Everton said no more because the banter was getting nowhere. He'd have to have a picnic lunch with her, and he hoped that she would keep off the subject of Doreen.

On day four, Everton applied the top coat, and then went to bed exhausted. He wasn't quite sure when Doreen would be back, but he'd check out all the paintwork in the morning, and make sure that everything was all right, then remove all the working gear, paint brushes and unused paint, and tidy it all away in the shed. Then he'd pack and go. At least he'd made an effort, and he hoped that Doreen would be satisfied with this latest shade of blue, so that he could leave with a good deed done. She would hardly fail to notice the new kitchen because she'd smell the paintwork. Then there was the ugly prospect that she'd still not be satisfied with the colour.

The fifth day broke in strong sunshine, lifting Everton's mood a bit while he went through the last tasks he'd set himself in this house. Then he went upstairs and packed two big suitcases and stumbled down to the hall with them. He left them there so that he could have one last look at the kitchen; the smell of paint was still strong so he opened all the windows to let the smell out, and the fresh air in. He'd make himself a cup of coffee and when he'd finished that he'd close the windows again and go, but first he noticed the floor was dirty, so he got some hot water and soap and gave it a good cleaning with the mop; he was ready for his coffee after he'd done that.

He made his drink and sat in the kitchen, lonely and sad, sipping it as he looked around. He was pleased with what he'd achieved, and when he'd finished his coffee he really would have to go, because he could not think of anything more which would delay the evil hour.

He was still slowly sipping his coffee and having a bad moment when there was a noise at the door of a key in the lock, and then Doreen was there. The smell of paint attracted her to the kitchen and she came in.

"I see you're still here," Doreen said.

"My bags are packed," Everton replied.

"What's that smell?"

"It's the doors, I've repainted them."

She stood back to admire his work.

"I'll tell you something," she said, "it's *EXACTLY* what I wanted."

"Sure?"

"Sure, how did you do it?"

"I went round to Katie's and she gave her unused tins of blue paint."

"You went to see Katie? I hope you didn't tell her about us?"

"No."

"You went to all that trouble?"

"It was the least I could do, but you're home early and I should have gone by now."

"Well, wash your mug before you do."

A slow smile came across Doreen's face and she asked, "Did you see Katie's bathroom?"

"No."

"Well, I want *our* bathroom done like that."

"*OUR* bathroom?" Everton repeated, clutching at straws.

"I don't want you to go away, you might as well stay...on the other hand - ."

"I'll stay," Everton said, before she changed her mind.

ISBN 141209337-6